AN IMPERFECT CRIME

An Imperfect Crime

A Father Montero/Detective Sanchez Mystery

Fred G. Baker

Other Voices Press
Golden, Colorado

Published by Other Voices Press, Golden, Colorado.

ISBN 978-0-9996684-0-5

Book design by Gail Nelson, www.e-book-design.com
Cover design by Nick Zelinger, www.nzgraphics.com
All rights reserved by Fred G. Baker.

Printed in the United States

Acknowledgments

I would like to thank the following people for their aid and support in the writing and production of this book: my wife, adviser, and primary editor, Dr. Hannah Pavlik, for her support and encouragement; my beta readers, who provided helpful comments and ideas; Faye Quam for editing support; Averlie Ingram for proofreading; Donna Zimmerman for word processing; Gail Nelson for the interior design; and Nick Zelinger for the cover design.

Chapter 1

March 2, 2013—Phoenix, Arizona

Peter Simpson was drinking beer and eating pizza at his apartment with his best friend, fellow unpublished writer Allister Brown, and Allister's girlfriend, Sarah Parker. The men were pleasantly drunk and had been commiserating about who'd gotten the most rejection letters from publishers. Both struggling young novelists felt they would never get published in the strange and competitive world of modern fiction.

"Let's face it," Simpson said. "We'll never get our books out there. If you expect to be noticed, you've got to know someone in the business or already be famous. I must've sent my manuscript to at least three dozen agents and editors."

"Funny," Parker said dryly. "It was *two* dozen a week ago."

"But not a one was interested!" Simpson blurted out, ignoring her. "They all told me it didn't meet their current needs or some such bullshit." He got up from his worn overstuffed chair and staggered to the kitchen.

"Yeah, I know," Brown said, chewing a mouthful of pizza. "You have to be a celebrity to get a deal. Or infamous. A maniac. A Charles Manson."

"Hear, hear!" Simpson yelled from the kitchen.

"Yeah, after you kill someone, you're a somebody," Brown said. "People would swarm all over you. Maybe then an agent would at least skim your novel," he said angrily as he guzzled the last half of his beer.

Parker gave him an annoyed look. "You can always self-publish your book, you know."

"Yeah," Simpson added, "but then you wouldn't get the attention or backing of a publishing house. It's all about getting the book into stores, and the big five have a lock on that."

Brown jumped up on the couch. "Let's do something *craaazy!*" He waved his arms around like he was demented. "You know, rob a dozen liquor stores. Or, better yet, go on a killing spree! I can think of two or three people I wouldn't miss."

Brown, Simpson, and Parker had been friends ever since their days as English majors at the University of California, Berkeley, back when they were confident they would write the Great American Novel and make the world take notice. Parker had eventually settled for a teaching career. The guys, however, survived on a life of dull jobs so they could feverishly write into the wee hours of the night.

Brown grimaced as Parker injected her voice of reason into the conversation. "Baby, you're always like this when you're drunk. You know your idea's insane."

"What do you care, babe?" Brown asked her as he crouched on the carpet in front of her. "You don't know what it's like to be desperate. You've already published a few stories in real literary journals. You can't understand the abysmal pain of obscurity."

Simpson returned to the living room, carrying three chilled PBRs in one hand, a mischievous smile on his face. He pushed back his blond hair with his free hand, a few strands of a cowlick defying his effort. "You know the idea of executing my perfect crime could work. But with today's technology, you'd get caught for sure, and most likely convicted."

"Caught, yes," Brown said, "but *not* convicted. You'd have to execute it right." He twisted the cap off his beer bottle. "Everything would have to be foolproof. If it was all circumstantial, you'd probably get off on a technicality or maybe a hung jury." He downed a swig of beer.

"But who'd want to risk it? It would have to be bombproof," Brown said.

Parker twisted her long brown hair into a ponytail and again tried to bring them back to reality. "And . . . if you were convicted, no agent would touch your book. Or, if by some miracle, you did sell a book, you wouldn't see a penny of the sales. In case you've forgotten, it's considered illegal to profit from a crime."

Tiring of Brown's obsession with the idea, Simpson sighed and said, "So you're saying you'd commit a crime, intentionally get caught, and then trust that you wouldn't be convicted?"

"Exactly!" Brown replied. "I thought of a new angle last week. It could work." He was excited now, an indication that it would be a long night. "Listen."

Simpson shrugged, knowing that Brown would go on, no matter what.

"Suppose you set up a crime—say, a murder—with all the circumstantial evidence against you, but there's no body. You set up what, without a doubt, looks like a murder, but you don't really kill anyone."

"There'd be no murder victim?" Simpson asked, his interest rising. "No body?"

"No, of course not. The victim just disappears. There'd be a trial. You *claim* you're innocent, but let the evidence prove you're guilty."

Simpson rolled his eyes. "Great."

"And—this is the part I really like—at the last minute, just before the verdict comes in, the supposed victim walks into the courtroom and announces that he's alive."

"OK, sure," Simpson said. "I get it. No body. No crime. No conviction."

"Right! Imagine the sensation this would create. You'd have more publicity than you could handle!" Brown looked expectantly at Simpson.

"Dude," Simpson said, "I gotta tell you, this has always been one of your stupider ideas."

"I thought he was nuts when he told me about the new angle last week," Parker said. "But I have to admit it would be something different. And with no crime, you could do a book. In fact, you could write up how you did it and probably sell a million copies." She began rubbing Brown's back. "You would have publishers crawling all over you then."

"Would you still be crawling all over me too?" Brown asked.

Parker squeezed the back of Brown's neck and purred, "You *do* know you're crazy, don't you, baby?"

Brown kissed her, and things suddenly got too hot to continue the conversation. Simpson suggested they move the passion out of his house to their own sofa.

That was the end of the evening, but they all agreed to plan a fake murder and see if it would work. They would follow the plot of Simpson's novel, *The Perfect Crime*, which described a complex murder scenario. The guys were convinced they could actually pull it off.

Simpson's famous last words were, "Let's do this!"

***

April 2, 2014—Florence, Arizona

Father Guillermo Montero paced the floor of the pre-execution cell at the Arizona State Prison Complex at Florence while he talked to

Peter Simpson, the young man who had been convicted of murdering Allister Brown and was about to die. "Do you want me to stay?" Montero asked.

Simpson said nothing.

"I want to," Montero said, "even if you think you won't need me." For weeks, he had listened to him tell his story and express his fears.

"Yeah, you can stay, Father." Simpson, dressed in an orange jumpsuit, constrained by handcuffs and shackles, was sitting on the cell's metal bench. His usual upbeat personality and clear blue eyes were cloaked in misery. "I'd like the company, even if there's nothing more to talk about."

"All right, then." Montero sat down next to him. "Now . . . are you sure you don't want me to pray for you or take your confession?"

"I appreciate the offer," Simpson said, "but, as I said before, I'm not religious. You're a good listener, though, so I guess I could tell you my story again." He started to laugh, but the sound came out as a gasp.

Montero put a hand on Simpson's shoulder. He must have told his story a thousand times. No one believed him. At least, no one who could do anything to help him in the next few minutes. He looked at Simpson's face, as he had looked at many a man's face during his last few minutes in this world. He knew most of them were guilty and probably deserved to pay for their sins, at least in God's eyes, but not Simpson. He was no killer.

Montero stood up and wrung his hands. "I still don't understand why you did this in the first place. It makes no sense."

"It's like I told you. It's nearly impossible to get published these days. So we came up with the idea to create a fake murder showing that one of us killed the other. We flipped a coin. I was to play the murderer, and Allister would be the victim."

"I think what you guys did was completely irresponsible."

"I didn't contest much during the trial because I thought it would all get straightened out in the end. I thought Allister would come forward, and that would be that. No murder, so no crime." He looked down as he opened his hands. "I told my public defender not to object to any of the factual evidence. I expected the cops to put it all together."

Given all the details of the trial, Montero couldn't help but think it was a shame Simpson hadn't put up more of a defense.

"At least now I know never to put too much faith in the justice system *or* my friends," Simpson said. "I guess I was stupid to think our plan would work." He looked wistful, but then suddenly bolted upright, took three steps toward the cell door, raised his arms in front of him with his palms upward in a pleading gesture, and shouted at the cell door, "Where the hell are Allister and Sarah? Why'd they let me down?" Then he lowered his head, covered his face with his hands, and leaned against the concrete wall.

Montero thought that the four plain gray walls of the pre-execution cell, reeking of pine-scented disinfectant, were closing in. He ran his fingers through his longish brown hair and considered Simpson's fate. Given the circumstances, he couldn't believe how calm Simpson was, at least on the outside. The sedative the prison doctor had given him had overridden his emotions, kept him from losing it and embarrassing himself.

Simpson was silent for a few minutes. Then he loudly exhaled and said, "It really did seem like a good idea at the time." He walked back to the bench and sat down.

"The cops looked for a body and for Sarah," Montero said. "It disturbs me that they didn't find her."

"Tell me about it," Simpson said, his voice drenched in desperation. "Something must have happened to them. They must've had an accident or been waylaid somehow. I know they would show up if they could."

Montero shook his head and shrugged his shoulders.

"Father, promise me you'll try to find them," Simpson continued. "I just don't know what to do." He hesitated. "All I ever wanted to do was get my book published."

"I know, Peter."

"Will you try?"

Montero reluctantly agreed to do what he could, even though he knew he shouldn't promise to do anything. But he felt sorry for Simpson and, more than anything, he wanted to give him some relief.

The cell door opened. The warden and three prison guards entered and surrounded Simpson.

"It's time, Mr. Simpson," the warden said. "Have you made peace with your maker?" He looked at Montero for an answer, but he didn't respond.

They eased him to his feet. Montero hugged Simpson one last time.

"Goodbye, Father. You're a good man," Simpson said. Then he began to weep openly as the guards led him to the door and toward the execution chamber. The heavy thunk of the door matched the hollow pounding of Montero's heart.

As Montero turned to leave, he noticed Simpson had left his manuscript on the bench. One of the guards retrieved it and handed it to Montero.

"You might as well take it, Father. He was real proud of that thing." He motioned Montero toward the door. "I like the kid. I don't know why he killed his best friend, but he didn't seem as evil as some of the men in here."

Montero stayed and watched the execution as Simpson had begged him to do earlier in the day. The whole thing unsettled him, ate at him. He had to make this right. But how could he possibly disprove something that didn't happen?

Chapter 2

April 3, 2014, Phoenix

Montero sat in the worn but cozy booth at the Denny's restaurant
on Main Street in Mesa, a suburb of Phoenix. He had just
finished looking over his notes on Simpson's book and was
scanning for the waitress to request a refill of his coffee. When
he looked up, he saw a tall, thin, shabbily dressed man in a
threadbare black suit enter the restaurant. He waved his hand at
the man and simultaneously caught the waitress's eye. Both
converged on his booth. At last, he would meet the attorney who
had represented Simpson at trial.

"Hi! I'm Zach Taylor from the public defender's office. You
must be Father Montero. It's nice to meet you after talking on the
phone." The attorney sat down opposite the priest and ordered
coffee with a Super Bird sandwich from Isabelle, the waitress. He
was a regular at the café. "I hope you don't mind if I eat, but I've
got to be in court in forty-five minutes, and I missed breakfast.
Are you going to eat anything?"

"No. I had a bagel earlier," Montero said. "Thanks for meeting
me to talk about the Simpson case. I was with him until the last
moment down at Florence. I'll try to be brief 'cause you're short
on time. I wanted to ask you what you thought of Peter's book,
The Perfect Crime? I assume you read it."

"Yeah. I read it several times. I don't know why he brought
it up at trial." Taylor sounded exasperated. "It just about nailed

his case for the prosecution. It proved beyond any doubt the murder was premeditated. At least, that's how the prosecutor used it. Then when they brought in the other unsolved murders that followed the same modus operandi, it made a convincing argument that he had committed murder before. That really carried weight with the jury. It made a big difference at the sentencing phase of the trial too."

"But that's just it." Montero shook his head. "Why did you let him do so many things to hurt his chances at trial? Why did you let him get on the stand early in the trial and stipulate to all the facts in evidence? That made a defense very difficult."

Taylor quickly got defensive, wringing his hands and shouting, "Look, I tried my best to defend the guy. He was just a terrible client!"

He realized that his outburst had drawn the attention of other customers in the eatery. He lowered his voice and said, "At first, Peter told me that he didn't murder Allister Brown. Then he told me that he planned the murder with none other than the victim himself and Allister's girlfriend, Sarah Parker. I didn't know what to believe at first. He knew about every bit of evidence before the police found it. Then he insisted on taking the stand and verified it all as accurate. I mean, who does that at their own trial?"

"Why in the world would he do that? No wonder the trial went so quickly."

"I tried my best to prevent him from testifying at all. But he threatened to fire me and defend himself if I interfered," Taylor responded as his food arrived. "He was like that: convinced he knew what he was doing. I even went to the judge and asked to be removed as counsel because my client was torpedoing the case. The judge refused to release me from my role because he said the trial was too far along. So I had to stay on and try to defend my difficult client."

Montero couldn't believe what he was hearing.

Taylor continued. "Yeah. He put up essentially no defense and passed on all chances to delay the proceedings. And remember, the prosecutor had fast-tracked the trial as part of his 'Get Tough on Crime' campaign. He wanted to wrap it up in time to put him over the top in the special election last year. It worked, and he was elected district attorney. Poor Peter. He had no idea he was walking into a political opportunity for the DA." Taylor began to wolf down his sandwich. "And the judge was up for reelection too, so he cut us no slack at all to prove he was tough on crime."

"When I talked to Peter, he kept repeating that he hoped his friend would come out of hiding and announce he was alive all along." Montero tried to read Taylor's expression. "What did he tell you about that?"

"Well, that really threw me." Taylor raised a finger as he stuffed food in his mouth. "He insisted all along that he was innocent, but he knew all these details about the crime. His fingerprints were everywhere and on the knife itself. Even the police detective, Lori Sanchez, admitted that it looked like someone had set the guy up. It was too complete, too perfect."

"Yeah," the priest said. "I understand she didn't think he did it, but the circumstantial evidence was overwhelming."

"I used that at the trial to introduce doubt by putting her on the stand. She said it was too perfect, and that seemed to sway the jury a bit. I thought we had a chance with that opinion on our side."

"So what happened?"

"Well, when the prosecution was finished and we began our defense, Peter started to act really nervous." Taylor looked chagrined for a moment, raising his eyes to see if Montero would say anything. "He said he had been talking to the victim every week since his arrest. But his friend didn't answer the phone the last few times when he called. So he panicked."

"Really? So he was in contact with Allister during the trial?" Montero looked confused. "How's that possible?"

"It's complicated, but the long and short of it is that he was free to make calls the whole time. He was in the county jail because he couldn't make bail, but he could still freely use the phone." Taylor furtively looked around the restaurant, as if what he was going to say was a secret. "The calls were always for a few minutes exactly at 3:00 p.m. on the days in question. So he talked to someone. He didn't just make up the calls."

"What did you do? It seems that the phone calls supported his story. At least you could have used them to introduce some doubt in the minds of the jury."

"Oh, believe me, I tried. But that was when Peter became desperate. That was when he showed me his manuscript. That blew me away and blew his defense completely."

"Why? It seems that it gave you proof that there was more to the story. That at least some of what he told you must be true."

"Well, it set up a problem. You've read the book, right? It laid out the murder in detail. It showed that it was not only planned but also premeditated. It tells how they went to the blood bank to give blood so that a sample of Allister's blood would be on file. They even had a genetic test done to essentially fingerprint it."

"Why would he do that? It seems very unusual," Montero asked.

Taylor took another bite of his sandwich. "They did it to prove it was Allister's blood. Then they collected more of his blood over the next few weeks to get enough to spread around his apartment.

You know, to show that he had been attacked at home the night of the supposed murder. And it was a lot of blood. So much that no one could survive that kind of blood loss." He paused to eat more of his sandwich. "It was clever, though, you have to admit. If there wasn't going to be a body, they provided proof of who was attacked by leaving blood that could be identified. That made the lack of a corpse less of a problem for the prosecution." He sipped his coffee and wiped his mouth with his napkin.

Montero flipped through his copy of *The Perfect Crime* as Taylor spoke. "It was really well planned and executed, I'll say that." Montero looked around the restaurant trying to spot Isabelle. She seemed to have gone into hiding. Then he saw her by the kitchen and flagged her down for more coffee. She gave him a dirty look like he was tying up her booth.

"Well," Montero continued. "He wanted me to find out what happened to his friend. Why wasn't he answering the phone? Where was he?"

"I looked everywhere for him." Taylor raised his eyebrows. "To make it convincing, the friend had to disappear for the duration of the trial, or they would be found out. Probably left town because where would Allister stay if his apartment was a crime scene? And Peter's apartment was cordoned off as a secondary scene, so he couldn't stay there." He waved to the waitress, making that writing motion people do to show that they want their check. "And Allister couldn't go to his job at the library in Tempe if he was dead, right? So all I could think of was to look for the girlfriend, Sarah Parker. She had supposedly left Phoenix a few weeks before the murder."

"But I don't get it. Why would she disappear completely if they had all planned this crime together? I thought they were all old college friends."

"Hell, I don't know." Taylor looked frustrated again. "Well, to make a long story short again, I never located the guy or the woman. I wanted to introduce the phone calls at trial to float the idea that there might be an accomplice. Create doubt, right?"

"Oh, I see. Yeah, that could help his case if you could spread the blame or deflect attention. But then, he would still be guilty. Just not alone."

"Well, you see the problem?" Taylor paused to see Montero's reaction. "I only had a day left, and I finally convinced Peter that we shouldn't bring up the phone calls since that could go either way. So we went to court, and I was finished with my last witness. Then the judge asked me if the defense rested, and I said yes." Taylor's eyes widened as he made a face showing disgust. "And Peter held up the book and waved it around. He said we had to see the book. What a fool! By waving it around in court like that, he ensured the book would be looked at. The judge had us approach the bench and decided it was significant new evidence that he had to share with the prosecution. They asked for a continuance to study the new material."

"But can they do that? Just take the book into evidence? I thought you could keep that sort of thing out of court."

"Not normally. Since the defense offered it in open court, the judge felt compelled by law and politics to let the other side have it. They then presented it to prove premeditation and, in those short days of delay, they uncovered the other disappearances back in Berkeley where all three of the friends had lived during college." Taylor devoured the last of his sandwich. "Those cases fit the MO of this case and suggested that, taken with the current murder, they showed the pattern of a serial killer. I objected, but the judge overruled me. All I could hope for then was that the manuscript evidence would prove to be the basis of an appeal someday. In any case, the damage was done. Any doubt the jury might have had vanished, and they found him a threat to society. Guilty as charged. Death by lethal injection." He pushed back his empty plate as if for emphasis.

"Well, I'll be . . ." Montero was surprised. "But no one proved he committed the other murders, so how'd they bring them into the trial?"

"Hey, it was the special election year, and the whole trial suddenly blew up. I was overwhelmed by the new turn of events and couldn't respond fast enough. Every TV station suddenly showed up when the media heard he might be a serial killer, even national reporters from CNN and Fox News. We were overrun by reporters. The trial became a circus, a show trial. We were essentially done."

Taylor pulled back the sleeve of his jacket to reveal his watch and looked scared. He jumped up. "I've got to go. I'm late for Judge Brennan. She'll rip me a new one." Then he realized what he had said. "Oh, sorry, Father. Call me if you need more info, OK?"

"Wait," Montero said. "One last question?"

"OK, but make it quick."

Montero was puzzled by how quickly justice had sprung forward in this case. "How come Peter was executed so quickly after his conviction? It usually takes years before an execution."

Taylor gave Montero an irritated grimace. "That has been a mystery to me too. But Peter fired me right after the trial, and he had no lawyer for all the months when he should have been filing appeals. I guess by making no objections at trial and making no appeals, time ran out on him until it was too late." He looked troubled. "Anyway, I've gotta go."

He threw down a business card and fled out the door, tattered briefcase under one arm.

Montero was upset by the new information. He had to think, to put it all together. He ordered a piece of apple pie and more coffee. *It just doesn't make sense. I don't think Peter was a murderer. There must be more to the story.*

He opened up his copy of *The Perfect Crime* and skipped to the pages that described how to collect and disperse blood evidence at the crime scene. Simpson had described the procedures for collecting and handling blood in great detail, even listing laboratory methods used to sample blood evidence and protocols that police would use to investigate the scene, all in the context of the fictional murder he had created. The manuscript was so detailed and comprehensive that it was no wonder the jury, upon hearing about the precision of the text, had concluded *The Perfect Crime* was actually a plan to carry out Brown's murder.

After reading for fifteen minutes, Montero had had enough. He set the volume down, walked from the booth to the front door, and stepped outside into the fresh air. His feelings of revulsion and sadness slowly dissipated.

After a few minutes, he reentered the restaurant and caught his reflection in the glass of the door. He saw a worried man, bags under his brown eyes, a rugged, clean-shaven face marked with concern. He hadn't slept much the previous night because he had kept turning over Simpson's fate in his head. Today he looked like the forty-year-old man he was.

He ate the apple pie and reread part of *The Perfect Crime*. Taylor was right: the manuscript was a blueprint of how to conduct a perfect crime, using a fictional murder as the basis for a procedural mystery. *Very interesting. Very compelling.*

Perhaps that was why he found Simpson's case so intriguing. In his previous life, before choosing to become a priest, he had been a soldier and later a policeman, so he knew a lot about crime and investigations. That experience, and his understanding of people he had met over the years, signaled to him that something was not quite right here. Something did not add up. And he had made Simpson a promise, a promise that he must fulfill. He remembered a line from an old Robert Service poem: "A promise made is a debt unpaid." He was committed to solving this puzzle.

He pulled out his cell phone and keyed in the number of the Phoenix Police Department. When an operator answered, he asked to speak to Detective Lori Sanchez. She was the only person who had suggested the crime scene was indeed too perfect.

Chapter 3

April 4, 2014

Montero and Detective Lori Sanchez met at the same Denny's the next day. Tall and slender, Sanchez carried herself with a sense of assurance that Montero thought might come from her police training and several years on the beat in Los Angeles before joining the Phoenix police force. She wore her long brown hair parted down the middle, her clear skin unencumbered by makeup. Montero thought she was strikingly beautiful, with wide-set eyes, no more than thirty years old.

When Sanchez approached him, he held out his hand to her and said, "Thanks for meeting me here, Miss Sanchez. Or is it Mrs.? This place must be a little out of your way."

"It's Lieutenant or Detective," Sanchez said, shaking his hand. "Although, Father . . . you *could* say I'm married to my job these days." She scrunched up her nose. "I don't know why I said that. It doesn't really matter." Her voice had a slight edge to it, like she was hoarse from talking, a little rough but not husky.

"It must be my collar," Montero said, releasing her hand. "It unsettles some people to talk to a priest. It brings out all sorts of odd things. Today, just think of me as a concerned citizen."

"OK, sure," Sanchez said tentatively, sitting down.

"I want to ask you a few more questions about the Simpson case," Montero said, waving the waitress over. They'd talked about the case over the phone the day before.

Sanchez ordered coffee. "I'm glad we're meeting here," she

told Montero. "The other cops don't usually eat here."

Montero tipped his head, waiting for her to elaborate.

"After I testified at the trial, I got in trouble with my partner and some of the others at the station. They said I sold out the DA. They weren't pleased when I said that Simpson might have been framed." She paused and keenly eyed Montero.

"I suppose you're wondering why I care so much about this case," he said, sliding the bowl of creamers toward her.

Sanchez nodded. "Yes, why are you interested?"

"A lot of things," he didn't answer directly. "What makes you think he was framed?"

"Right from the start, I thought the crime scene had been staged. Our work was too easy. Too much evidence pointed in the same direction. We never find crime scenes where all the evidence can only be interpreted one way. The only fingerprints in the whole place belonged to Simpson and Brown. I figured someone must have wiped everything down before leaving the prints. They left nothing to confuse us. That never happens."

"Isn't that what Peter described in his book? A perfectly set-up crime scene? You read it, didn't you?"

"Yes. But I didn't have to. I could already tell something was fishy."

"Had you seen this kind of thing before? Set-up scenes?"

"Sure, when I was in LA. Frame-ups. They were usually silk stalkings. You know—crimes of the high and mighty."

"Yeah?" Montero said, his expression urging Sanchez to continue.

"One time there was this lawyer who wanted to get his business partner out of the way, so he stuck him with stealing from their firm. But he messed up. He created a crime scene that made me suspicious. Like this one."

"I'll try not to keep you too long," Montero said. "I was

wondering . . . what was your impression of Peter?"

"I was directed to look for the witness he said was missing, so I interviewed him, and I immediately got a gut feeling about him. He was so naive. I mean, he talked about the crime as if it were a freaking *theory* or something. Who does that?"

Montero raised his eyebrows.

"I don't think Simpson killed anyone," Sanchez continued. "He was clearly not the type."

"That's the impression I had as well."

"But the prosecution brought up the murders—missing-persons cases, technically—in California where the FBI profiler said Simpson could have been one of those rare serial killers who staged his crime scenes according to some inner vision, like the Brown murder scene." She shook her head as she said, "He might have fit that type. It would have been quite a stretch. But it didn't seem right to me. I'm still not convinced he murdered Brown, much less those women in Berkeley."

There was a huge crash from the kitchen door where two waitresses collided, knocking a tray out of the hands of Isabelle, who was again their waitress. She swore at the other waitress, and they traded insults at the top of their lungs. A busboy tried to pick up the broken dishes and food, stepping between the two women to do so. A manager came out from the office and hustled the women into the kitchen to avoid a confrontation in front of the customers.

"And what about Allister's girlfriend?" Montero glanced at his notes. "Peter said she and Allister had been together a long time."

"Sarah Parker," Sanchez said, nodding. "Now *she's* an interesting one. She and Brown had lived together in the apartment Brown was supposedly murdered in. The first thing we heard during our investigation was that she frequently argued with him.

Sometimes they would have these huge fights. According to their neighbors, she'd get really loud and accuse Brown of cheating on her. She'd throw things too. A neighbor called the cops once, telling them it sounded like someone was being murdered next door." She paused. "Murder, huh? That's kind of ironic."

Neither Montero nor Sanchez said anything for a few seconds.

"So . . . what happened?" Montero finally asked.

"I checked out the police report to see what it was about. Apparently, they got there and found her yelling at Brown. She'd really roughed him up, even gone so far as to hit him with a hammer." Sanchez chuckled. "Talk about a hell of a temper. I don't know how she talked them out of arresting her."

"Really? None of this came out at the trial?" Montero asked.

"I don't think so. Why? What are you thinking? Another person with motive?"

"Not necessarily. It's just that Peter never mentioned their fights."

"He probably didn't know about it," Sanchez said, smirking. "I mean, how many guys do you know who'll brag about their girlfriend beating on them?"

"How far did you go to locate Parker?"

"Not very far. Me and my partner only had a few days to look for her during the continuance of the trial. I was working another case then, but my boss asked me to put some time into locating her. It seems that six weeks before the so-called murder, she moved out of the apartment and supposedly went to live in Los Angeles, no forwarding address. She didn't have many friends, but we talked to the few she had, and they said they hadn't heard from her for a couple of months before the murder. Without a forwarding address, we couldn't locate her in LA." Sanchez paused as if she wondered what Montero's angle was. She sipped the last of her coffee.

Montero nodded. "OK, so you couldn't find *any* clues to her whereabouts?"

"No. We didn't find her laptop, cell phone, or even her car, a blue 2006 Honda Accord. It hadn't shown up anywhere, even with a BOLO out, which means . . . ."

"Be on the lookout. I know."

"She showed no credit card use, had no bank account." She leaned forward with her elbows on the table. "Now *that* was odd." She looked conspiratorially at Montero and then ducked her head. "Shit! I hope he didn't see me. He's from the station."

After a while, a policeman who had been paying his bill stepped out the door, and she continued.

"Parker had an account where her paychecks were sent, but the account was closed six weeks before the murder was supposed to have occurred. She withdrew about two thousand dollars in cash. We thought maybe she was afraid Brown would follow her to LA, so she took the cash and hid. At least, that's what it seemed like at the time. Who knows? There was something odd going on around all that, if you ask me." She checked her watch. "Then I got pulled off the search. I testified about the crime scene, and my boss treated me like I was toxic." She grimaced and sat back. "After that, he put me on an embezzlement case for three months. I spent whole days staring at invoices and record books for a case that later got thrown out on some shitty technicality."

Montero shrugged. "I think we've all been there at least once." He thought for a moment. "Shortly before Peter was executed, he was adamant that something bad had happened to Allister and Sarah. He said that was the only thing that would have kept them from coming forward at the right time." Montero stopped to think for another moment and then continued. "I recall Peter saying he and Allister had often made fun of Sarah for wanting to run away and get married. He and Allister joked all the time about 'doing a Vegas' with Sarah. I guess he could have meant driving up there."

"Why would the guy want to marry a bitch who hit him with a hammer?" Sanchez blurted out. Then she slapped her fingertips over her mouth and closed her eyes. "Sorry, Father. My language slips once in a while."

"Don't worry. It happens all the damn time." He grinned. He was used to the way people swore. He had done it quite a bit himself before he had become a priest. But it wasn't that he had quit altogether; he just kept it in check.

"I think I'm swearing more lately," Sanchez said. "It must be the kind of people I associate with. You know—the dregs of society. Not that I think of all of them like that. It's just the way we talk down at the station. Everyone's on edge. Too many perps and not enough free time." She snickered at her last statement.

"It sounds like you've got a lot on your plate."

"Always." Then Sanchez said, "Well, I need to get going. I'm wrapping up a robbery case and am due in court this afternoon."

"Is that what you do most of the time? Robberies? That sort of thing?"

"Not really. Lately, I've been looking into gangs and drug smuggling. I work with Narcotics quite a bit."

"It takes a lot to keep Phoenix safe, I guess."

"Hey, listen. I've got to get back, or my partner will get suspicious. But if you need anything else, just call me. I'll try to help." Sanchez rose to leave. "It just bothers me that we may have missed something. You know?"

Montero stood up too. "Thank you, Detective. I appreciate your help."

"No problem."

They shook hands. As Sanchez turned to leave, Montero asked, "Is there any way I could see a summary of what the police found out about those missing people? Is any of it public record?"

"I don't know if it's public or not," Sanchez said. Then she hesitated, seeming to consider whether she should help him out. "Since the case is closed, maybe I can get you that summary. I'll see what I can do." She dug out her business card and scribbled her cell phone number on it. "Call me on this number, not the station phone. They might hassle me if they think I'm still working the case."

Chapter 4

April 6, 2014

Two days later, Montero drove along Highway 79 on his way to the State Prison at Florence to see another lost soul on death row. This was to be his first meeting with this man, and he hoped it would go well. Some prisoners took out their anger on him, thinking he was just another person against them. Others just needed someone they could trust and in whom they could confide their fears. Sometimes they would try to convince him that they were innocent. He knew it was because they thought he wouldn't care about them if they were truly guilty. Guilty or innocent, it didn't matter to Montero; he was there to help them as much as he could. In some ways, he hoped today's man was guilty. It made his job easier. No one wanted to see an innocent man executed.

Just before Montero turned into the prison complex, his cell phone rang. It was Sanchez.

"Good morning, Detective. How are you today?"

Sanchez responded brightly, "I'm good, Father. Thanks for asking. Say, are you going to be near the station anytime soon?"

"Why? What's up?"

"I have something for you about the case."

"Oh really? I can make it there this afternoon, if you'd like. I'm down Florence way now, but will be done here by noon."

"Good. How about we meet at three at Salvador's on McDowell? That's a pretty low-key place. Do you know it?"

"Yeah. They have pretty good roast chicken there."

"Three, then?"

"Sounds like a deal. See you then." Montero put the phone down and prepared for his meeting at the prison.

*****

Salvador's Grille, in Montero's opinion, was the premier Guatemalan restaurant in Phoenix. One of the bigger restaurants in this part of the city, it had a bar and two large rooms with booths and tables. It was always packed during lunch or dinner. But by midafternoon, it was quiet enough to have a conversation.

Montero arrived early, took a stool at the bar, and kept an eye out for Sanchez. He was still wearing his black pants and shoes from the morning's duties but had swapped his black shirt and cleric's collar for a plaid short-sleeved shirt. He wanted to blend in. While he waited, he ordered an iced tea and made small talk with the bartender. He had only been sitting there a few minutes when Sanchez walked through the front door, talking on her cell phone and carrying a manila folder. He caught her eye, and she waved.

Sanchez was dressed the same way as she was the last time he saw her, in black slacks and shoes, a blue uniform-style top, and a lightweight tan jacket. She carried her Glock tucked into a holster on her belt. Still on her call, she followed him to a booth in the back of the restaurant where they wouldn't be seen. She ended her call and ordered a Sol beer. To her surprise, Montero ordered one too.

"What's with the look?" Montero asked. "I'm a man of God, not a saint. Besides, it was really tough in Florence today. Let's get some chips and salsa too. I'm hungry."

"OK. Here's what I got," the lieutenant said after their server left. She opened the file folder and swept the room for unwanted eyes. "I made a copy of the main file from our investigation. Just the police work, no supporting forensic reports . . . correction, I copied as much of the file as I could get away with. I'm sure the information would all be discoverable by FOIA request anyway, but it would take you three months or more to get it." She pulled three photos out of the file and passed them across the table to Montero. "I even got you pictures of the three friends. You know Simpson," she said, pointing to the first photo. "And here's the supposed victim, Brown, and the girlfriend, Parker. Brown's pretty good-looking."

Sanchez read from the file. "It says here that he's six one, has blue eyes, brown hair, a light complexion. He was an aspiring writer like Simpson, worked at the university library, low pay. I guess he was waiting to be discovered?" She read ahead in the file before continuing her summary. "I don't know. He had a nice enough apartment. The lease was under Parker's name. I suppose she earned more, so she was the one to qualify for the lease requirements, at least initially. You can read the details yourself." She handed Montero the sheet on Brown, and he quietly perused it.

Sanchez went on. "Parker used to be a writer but turned to teaching high school English. She graduated magna cum laude from UC Berkeley in English. Wow! Must have been pretty smart." She dug through the pages of the file. "Let's see . . . what else? OK—here. She taught at a high school in the city, was off for the summer when this all went down. The school hasn't heard from her since then. It's like they both just disappeared." Her voice drifted up at the end, as if asking a question.

Montero compared the photos. Brown looked like any other twenty-six-year-old man who had an education and was of poor means. He had smiled broadly for the photograph, and Montero thought he looked genuinely happy. Parker was an average-looking woman of about the same age. Brown hair and eyes with a big smile too. She appeared to be tall and slightly chubby. No, not chubby. She had some muscles on her like she worked out. Her smile looked forced somehow. There was something about her eyes that projected sadness. He was good at spotting unhappiness. Maybe it came from his time at his last job.

"What else do you have for me?" Montero shoved the photos aside and reached for the file. "Ah, you copied practically the whole thing. Very good. Field notes about the crime scene too." He stopped. "Wait a minute. How did you pull this off?"

"Don't worry. I was careful. I made the copies last night after my shift when hardly anyone was around." Sanchez smiled patiently before she said, "But don't go showing this stuff to anyone."

Montero flipped back and forth between two reports. She smiled at his concern. "Hey, Father Montero, you look like you've looked through one of these reports before. How's that?"

"Let's just say I've worked on some cases over the years. And call me Guillermo if we're going to drink beer together." He flashed a smile before returning his attention to the file. "This is good stuff. I'll have to study it tonight. What made you risk getting this for me, by the way?"

"It's simple. I got a lot of shit for testifying that I thought the Brown crime scene was staged, and I didn't like the way my boss treated me for that. I guess I feel like I need to find out whether I was right or not, and if I was, it would sure help my cred in the department. I guess I want to prove I was right."

Montero seemed to understand. He kept peering at the file. "It might help vindicate you, you mean." He looked to see her reaction to his statement.

She didn't respond.

"Well, then," Montero said, "I'll go through this material as quickly as I can and get this back to you in a couple of days."

"Take your time. When you're done, just burn or shred it so no one comes across it later. OK?"

"Sure, sure. No problem. Say, did you ever find out anything about Brown and Parker going to Vegas?"

"Vegas? Let's see . . ." Sanchez looked at the ceiling, trying to remember what she had read. "No. Not a thing. At least, not after the murder. I checked all the work we did on tracking her. Pretty strange if she's alive. It's odd that she hasn't used her credit cards at all."

Montero had just gotten to the part of the file where the police summarized what they had found about the missing persons in California when he said, "So they really didn't find any bodies in those cases either."

"No. That was why the Berkeley PD classified them as missing persons as opposed to murder cases."

"How'd the DA think to link those cases to Peter?"

"Believe it or not, one of the DA's staffers was doing his law degree at Berkeley at the same time the disappearances occurred. Seeing the dates when the friends were there must have triggered his memory."

Montero exhaled loudly.

"Yeah, I know," Sanchez said. "Talk about serendipity. And bad luck." She ordered another beer and then stared expectantly at Montero. He didn't look up from the file. "Um, by the way," she said. "I'm off duty till morning. So I can have my limit of fifty beers . . . just in case you're wondering."

Montero kept reading.

"Guillermo?"

"Huh?" Montero glanced at Sanchez. "Oh, no worries." He read from the file. "Lucy Johnson . . . ."

"She's one of the missing Berkeley women, right?"

"Right. Peter said that he and Lucy had been dating when she disappeared."

"How did he seem when he told you about it?"

"Genuinely upset. Said he was still shocked."

"Weird. What are the chances of dating someone who mysteriously disappears?"

"It sure made him look guilty in the prosecutor's eyes." Montero looked evenly at Sanchez and said, "So are those California cases related to Allister's murder or not?"

"I don't know enough about them to say. It would take some more digging."

"Then where do we start? Do we get going on tracking down Allister and Sarah or on learning more about the Berkeley cases?"

Sanchez's beer arrived. Montero asked for more chips and salsa.

"Yeah. Let's think about how we can learn about those Berkeley cases. And how do we track down Sarah Parker?" Montero thought about it a little.

"That's a problem. Let's see . . . maybe we should approach this like we were on the run. Put ourselves in their shoes, you know?"

"Yeah, OK." Montero said. "Let's say we believe Peter's version of events, and Allister and Sarah planned to wait until close to the end of the trial to show their faces. That means if we were Allister and Sarah, we'd have to lay low for a while. No eating at, working at, or hanging out at our usual places. No using our credit cards or driving our car. They didn't have two cars, did they?"

"Not according to the file. Apparently, she drove the car to work, and Brown rode the bus to get around town. We know Parker had a couple of grand in cash from closing her bank account. We don't know if she shared it with Brown, but for now, we'll say she did." Sanchez looked pensive.

"Is the BOLO for the car still in effect?" Montero asked.

Sanchez's phone rang. She winced when she looked at the screen and let the call go to voice mail. "Yes, but it's an old request," she said in response to Montero's question. "So it's less and less likely it'll get any attention. Only the automatic license analysis functions would notice it." Her phone rang again. "Damn," she said, standing up. "I gotta take this."

Montero looked ahead in the file but decided his eyes were getting tired from concentrating on the typed pages. He gave his eyes a rest by looking around the room at the other people who had come in for a late lunch or an early beverage. He noticed the sign announcing that happy hour began at 3:00 p.m. He checked his watch, and sure enough, happy hour was now underway. He wondered if all these happy people had gotten off work early or if they were retired. Certainly the older gents at the bar tables were in that category, playing cards and laughing loudly.

Sanchez returned to the table. "I'll have to go soon," she said. She took a drink of her beer. "Let's look at the car angle some more. You can't really get around the metro area without wheels. They could've purchased a car with cash if it was really cheap. You can't rent a car without handing over a credit card."

Montero asked, "If you give a card for a rental and pay with cash, does the rental company actually run the card, or do they just record it? You know, like a hotel usually doesn't run the card until you check out."

"It might depend on the company," Sanchez said, scribbling in her notebook. "I should be able to find this out without raising a flag at work. I'll see what I can do."

Montero looked at the file again. "Well, going back to our scenario, if I was going into hiding for what could be several months, I'd buy a car, not rent one. It would be cheaper. I'd buy it with cash and only pay cash for any gas or service for it. But a purchase would still create a paper trail because the vehicle has to be registered within thirty days of the purchase, right? Maybe we can look to see who bought a car around the time of the murder by seeing if it was registered soon afterward. It might be worth checking if those records are searchable."

"Should be," Sanchez said. "I'll look up new registrations when I get back to the station. They may not have bothered to buy insurance, so I'm not even going to go in that direction."

"Next, we'd need a place to stay. Right? We probably couldn't afford a motel for very long. If we paid cash for a month-to-month apartment lease, most landlords would be happy, so no paper trail there. That means we're out of luck in that department." Montero finished his beer and looked around for their waitress.

"We've covered transportation and lodging," Sanchez said. "How about communication? We wouldn't go without cell or internet access. Evidence has already packed up Simpson's and Brown's phones. The other detectives would have checked for Brown's cell phone usage, but I don't know if they would have looked for a contract for him. His and Parker's accounts have to be listed somewhere. You know, one thing people forget about is their cell phone contracts. Those are usually for two or three years. Maybe we can track Parker through hers."

Montero sat up quickly and slapped the top of the table. "Brilliant thinking, Sanchez. They may still be paying for their phone service somehow, maybe even getting their bills in the mail. If the bills came by mail, can we find out if there was a forwarding address? Wait—the simplest thing for them to do would be to file a change of address card with the post office. Did Parker do that? What if . . . ?" He looked excited. "What if mail kept going to Brown's apartment after the murder?"

Sanchez's face broke into a broad smile. "That's something I can check out right now. I think the apartment's still empty because nobody wants to rent a place where someone was murdered. I remember *that* from my interviews with the neighbors. The building manager said he wouldn't be able to rent it for at least a year, not until everyone forgets what happened there. He whined that it was costing him money. Wait a minute." She stopped talking and held up her hand as if trying to remember something. "When I was there, I saw some junk mail by the door. No letters. That means they had their first-class mail forwarded somewhere. The question is, where? I'll see what I can find out. I doubt whether anyone asked about the forwarded mail of a dead man, even the other detectives."

Sanchez's phone rang again. She sprang up from the table and said, "I have to go." Then she excitedly said, "I'll let you know what I find out."

Chapter 5

April 7, 2014

The next morning, Montero stayed home to read the rest of the Brown murder file. He poured himself a second cup of coffee and settled into a chair in his living room, where he caught the morning sunshine and had a great view of Camelback Mountain. He opened the file and turned to the investigative summaries of the Berkeley missing-persons cases. Berkeley Police Department Detective Louis Carter, the lead on the cases, had penned all three. Montero decided to call him, and after being transferred a number of times, he finally reached him.

"This is Carter," a man said gruffly.

"Hello, Detective Carter? My name is Father Guillermo Montero. I'm calling from Phoenix, Arizona."

"Hello, Father," Carter said, his voice losing its edge. "How can I be of help?"

"I was hoping you might be able to provide information concerning one of my parishioners." Montero was fudging his relationship with Simpson a bit, but he told himself it was the only way to pique the detective's interest. "I ministered to Mr. Peter Simpson, the young man recently executed for murdering his best friend, Allister Brown. Do you remember the case?"

"So he got the death penalty, did he?" Carter asked. "I wasn't sure that would happen since they never found a body."

"You remember the case, then?" Montero asked.

"Yes, Father."

"Good. I understand that you shared information about Berkeley missing-persons cases with the Phoenix district attorney—specifically cases about three women who went missing while Mr. Simpson was attending college in Berkeley."

"Um, yes, I believe that's right."

"Good. Now, maybe you could clear up something that's been bothering me."

"If I can, yes."

"Are you *sure* your missing-persons cases were related to the Brown murder? I only ask because your cases weighed heavily on the jury's decision to convict Mr. Simpson. Swayed them."

The detective hesitated. Then he said, "Look, Father, I argued that the cases had similarities, but I did *not* say they were related. I *never* thought the DA should have brought up our cases at that trial. My captain had me ready to fly down to Phoenix to testify. He said he wanted to support the Phoenix PD in any way he could. He figured contributing to their case would help us solve our three outstanding cases. Get them off the books."

"You should know," Montero said, "that Peter maintained his innocence right up to the end. He was convinced Allister would come forward at the last minute, according to some plan they had. For some reason, Brown didn't show up."

"*Okaaay*," Carter said through a laugh. "So it's like Brown was dead or something, right?"

"Not exactly."

"These guys can really drive you crazy, can't they?"

Montero forced himself to smile and said, "Well, yes. They can, believe me." He let that settle before he continued. "It may seem bizarre to you, but I thought Peter was telling the truth when he said he didn't kill his friend. I'm keeping an open mind about his guilt. That's why I called you. I've talked to a detective down here who says the crime scene looked too good, too set up to be real. So if you could . . . ."

"You must have talked to that Lieutenant Sanchez. I chatted with her a few times. She was convinced it was a setup."

"She's the one."

"You want my help to clear your conscience. I get it, Father. I'll tell you what I'll do. Since you were the guy's priest, I'll get you some information about the Berkeley crime scenes, whatever I can without giving out certain details we need to keep quiet. That work for you?"

Montero couldn't believe his luck. He heartily agreed to keep the information confidential.

"There's something I think you should do in the meantime," Carter said. "Contact a reporter named Dennis MacEvie over at the *Oakland Tribune*. He talked to a bunch of people who knew the women who disappeared, wrote a series of articles about the cases. He's read between the lines to try to piece together the facts, stuff we can't do because it's speculation . . . call him. If you still have questions after that, get back to me. But right now, Father, I have a report to finish. I'm on a deadline."

Montero thanked Carter and ended the call. Then he punched in the number for MacEvie and left a voice message.

He had just started writing some notes when his phone rang. He was pleased that it was a call from Sanchez.

"Guess what, Father, er . . . Guillermo?" Sanchez said excitedly. "This morning, I got the forwarding address for Brown's mail. It's to one of those Mailbox Plus shops. The manager said the box was opened on June fourth of last year. That's just two days before the murder. He said a woman set up the account and paid cash for three months in advance."

"Interesting."

"Now get this: I showed him Brown's and Parker's pictures, and he said Parker was for sure the woman who rented the box. He remembered seeing her and a man come in once to collect the mail, but he couldn't say if Brown was the man he saw."

"That's amazing work, Sanchez. You hit the jackpot." Not only had they already found the mailbox address, but they may have also found evidence that Brown was still alive after his so-called murder.

"There's more," Sanchez said. "No one has picked up mail since early October. It just sat there until the box got full. At the end of December, the manager rented the mailbox to someone else and boxed up any mail that came afterward in case the woman came back. He still has the mail, even though he has notified the post office to stop delivery. He said we could have it if we got a court order."

"How come no one thought of this during the investigation?"

"Why would a dead man forward his mail? Maybe our investigators thought they had a slam dunk, so they didn't look any further. We still have no proof that Brown was alive after the murder happened. What I want to know is why Parker was in Phoenix on June fourth and not in LA."

"Maybe the mail will give us the answer."

"Yes, but there's a problem. I can't exactly go to my captain and tell him I need a search warrant, can I?"

"No, I suppose not. Is there anyone who could ask for you?"

"The case is shut down. There's no way anyone would touch it."

"That *is* a problem." Montero silently thought about the new information for a few moments. "Well, at least we can put together a timeline of sorts with what we have."

"True."

"Sarah closed her bank account on April sixteenth, six weeks before the murder. Then she moved to LA, but she set up the mailbox in Phoenix on June fourth. Two days later, Allister was supposedly killed. On the sixth, someone picked up mail and continued to do so until early October."

"Right. One more thing: Let's insert Simpson's last successful phone call to Allister, on October tenth. That means Brown and Parker hid out, separately or together, until early October. After that? They disappeared."

"Never to be seen or heard from again."

"Then we have no other information to include until the execution on April second. Do I have it right?"

"So far, so good."

"So what did you learn about the California cases?"

"I talked to the detective who ran those cases out in Berkeley. He put me on to a reporter named Dennis MacEvie. The detective remembers you, by the way."

"Oh. I remember talking to him. He was very helpful and friendly. Seemed to know his stuff."

"He had glowing remarks about you too. He had a sort of awe in his tone of voice."

"OK. Now I know you're exaggerating."

Montero's phone beeped. "Hey, I'm getting a call from Oakland, probably the reporter calling me back. I'll let you know what he says."

Montero disconnected from Sanchez and accepted the incoming call. He and the reporter talked for an hour. When the conversation was over, he felt completely drained. MacEvie had conveyed a vast amount of information about the three Berkeley cases, the results of months of legwork spanning four years. He had interviewed several of the missing girls' friends and associates and pulled together conclusions about what had happened to them, some of them unusual. While they had talked, MacEvie had sent Montero an email to which he had attached his articles and additional research notes. He emphasized that he was aware the information wasn't complete and not all of it was verifiable, which was why the police had found it of limited use when he had offered to share it with them.

MacEvie went on to say he was giving Montero this information with the hope of getting the scoop on what was going through Simpson's mind during his last days on death row. It would be a quid pro quo arrangement. If Montero broke his vows and spilled Simpson's story, MacEvie could write an award-winning article about the death of a serial killer.

Disgusted, Montero told him to forget it and ended the call.

Chapter 6

April 8, 2014

Sanchez, bearing a six-pack of Sol lager, arrived at the adobe-walled Hacienda Montero for dinner at seven o'clock. The spring air was still hot. The day's temperature had reached ninety-eight degrees, unseasonably warm for April, even in Phoenix. Sanchez had changed out of her work attire and into a tank top, shorts, and flip-flops.

Montero led her to the back patio where he was roasting pork chorizo and early sweet corn on his barbeque grill. Various dishes held beans, tortillas, pico de gallo, and other components of the meal. He was wearing khaki trousers, a University of Arizona Athletic Department T-shirt, and well-worn leather huaraches.

At first, they just made small talk, most of it lamenting the apparent early arrival of summer heat in the valley. "I refuse to turn on the air-conditioning until June," Montero said. "I don't care how hot it gets. Now, in the car, that's different. I'll take my comfort earlier because it's much hotter there, especially if you have to sit in traffic. How about you?"

"Well, Guillermo, I grew up here, so I'm used to the heat, maybe more than you. I deal with it by dressing like this . . . ." She held out her arms to show off her outfit. "And hiding in the shade as much as possible. By the way, how long have you been in Phoenix?"

"I came here five years ago to do my ministerial mission. Before that, I lived in El Paso. Talk about hot! It was brutal sometimes, but nothing like it is here in midsummer. Wow! In July, you really *can* fry eggs on the sidewalk."

"El Paso? Are you from there originally or just there for work? I don't meet many people who grew up there."

"For work. I grew up near Albuquerque and moved there after high school for a job. It was pretty nice, and I got to know some good people. How about your family? Was your dad a cop? Because I don't run into too many woman detectives these days."

"My dad was a prison guard at Florence before he went into security. So I saw what he did on the job. He'd tell me about some of the convicts he guarded—the good, the bad, and the ones he thought might have been innocent. That got me interested in hearing about the crimes they committed and how they got caught. It influenced me. I received a scholarship to study criminology at Arizona State. Did well. So then, I enrolled in the police academy. Right about the time I was finishing up there, one of my instructors moved to LA. He told me to look him up after I'd put in a couple of years on the Phoenix police force, so I did that and wound up working three years in LA."

"What brought you back here?"

"My parents were getting on. They needed help, and since I'm their only kid, I came back. I'm not complaining, though. I like it here."

Soon, the chorizo was done, so Montero expertly collected the meat with his spatula and arranged it on a platter alongside the ears of corn. Then he and Sanchez settled at the outdoor table to eat.

"This is a great place you have here," Sanchez said, biting into a tortilla. "That's quite a cactus." She pointed to a large saguaro cactus. "It must be pretty old."

"Some people baby their cats or dogs," Montero said. "I baby my cacti. I'll show you my cactus garden after dinner."

"Gee, I can't wait," Sanchez said with a grin.

When Montero and Sanchez left the table to tour Montero's xeriscaped yard, the late-day sun was beginning to descend behind Camelback Mountain. The yard was landscaped with carefully selected shrubs and flowers that could survive the scorching desert heat. He was especially proud of his cactus garden featuring several varieties of the plant. He told Sanchez that his garden created a peaceful atmosphere that soothed his soul.

Red sandstone paving stones with sand filling in the cracks between them led from the garden to a side door of Montero's three-bedroom ranch-style home. It was way too big for one person, but he liked his extra space. The living room featured a large theater system with state-of-the-art THX theater-style sound. He had converted one bedroom into a home office and kept another as a guest room. The guest room closet was full of his camping gear. He had a two-car garage but unpacked moving boxes took up a good third of it. "Someday, I'll finish moving in," Montero said.

After the tour, they went back to the patio and got down to discussing the information that MacEvie had sent. Sanchez motioned toward a new file on the table to Montero's left and said, "Guillermo, tell me everything that's in there."

"I'd be glad to." Montero summarized what he had learned. "There were three different events, almost a year apart. All involved women who disappeared from their apartments at night, apparently without major signs of violence, except in the case of Lucy Johnson. The other two, Naomi Jones and Tina Serano, appear to have just vanished. In all three cases, the women lived alone, were students, and knew at least one of the three people we are investigating."

Montero pulled out pages that contained photographs of the

three women, all quite pretty. "The first one was Lucy. She dated Simpson during his sophomore year for about three months. They were still dating when she disappeared, so he was the natural suspect. On the night in question, he happened to be out of town on a field trip for a class, so he was later ruled out as having no opportunity. There was no indication of any problems between them.

"The second missing woman, Naomi Jones, dated Allister during his junior year. He met her in an English class that he and Sarah were taking. That was before he started dating Sarah. Naomi had her own place and just vanished one night with no indication of where she had gone. No signs of a struggle, but the crime scene was odd. It looked like her apartment had been wiped down of any trace of fingerprints and other evidence. Obviously, there wasn't much to go on.

"Now, Tina Serano's case was a bit different. She worked at a local Italian restaurant as a waitress and apparently knew our three students from their visits there. She was a history major who was in her fifth year of studies. No one knows what happened to her. She was last seen leaving the restaurant one night and apparently never made it home. Her car was still in the parking lot where she'd parked it the night before. The police thought she'd gotten into her car and then something happened. They didn't find anything much in the car, though. No blood, no fingerprints except hers, just a broken fingernail and a piece of fabric torn from the dress she'd worn to work."

"What I want to know," Sanchez said, paging through the file, "is how in the hell the DA could have possibly thought these cases were related to the Brown case? The only things they have in common are superficial evidence that the crime scene had been cleaned up and the absence of a body." She turned the page. "All counters in the kitchen at Lucy's home were wiped, and some blood was removed with Clorox. That got everyone's attention and was similar to other crimes where a knowledgeable killer destroyed evidence. Fingerprints were wiped down at Naomi's home too." Sanchez leaned back in her chair and stretched her arms up over her head. In spite of himself, Montero admired her sleek form.

"Those missing-persons scenes weren't so unusual," Sanchez continued. "Any thorough kidnapper or murderer would do the same things. But again, no bodies were ever found in any of these cases, so they're a bit of a mystery."

Montero leaned on the table while he sorted through the pages in his file. "So . . . the Berkeley cops investigated the three friends because, in one way or another, they knew each of the victims. MacEvie thinks there's a pattern to the relationships. He worked the pattern angle for some time, talked to everybody who knew the three victims or the three friends around the time of the disappearances.

"MacEvie said that Simpson met Parker just after Lucy disappeared. They apparently dated for a while, and that was how she met Brown. By this time, Simpson and Brown had become roommates and had started to spend a lot of time writing together. In fact, one person who knew them said he suspected they may have had a ménage à trois for a while. He saw both guys making out with Parker at a party but put it down to extreme drunkenness at the time. I guess that's not so unusual at that age.

"The next spring, Brown met Jones in a class. They started dating, and he frequently stayed at her place, but he kept his apartment with Simpson. That summer, Naomi disappeared too. Her friends thought she'd gone back East, where she was from. Apparently, Parker began dating Brown exclusively after that, according to the same source. Simpson moved out so she could move in."

Montero got up from the table and went inside to pour two glasses of sangria. He motioned for Sanchez to follow him to the den, where they could sit in softer chairs. Sanchez picked up his file and her notes and went inside. "Yeah, that shit happens when you hang out in a close group," she said while they walked. "I had more than one boyfriend move on to a friend of mine. Somehow, you never see it coming. Did that ever happen to you?"

Montero cleared his throat. "Well, I wasn't always a priest," he said, giving her a knowing look. He changed the subject. "Brown and Parker were still together during their senior year. Peter had a few girlfriends, but no one serious. He took criminology classes in addition to his literature classes. He had always wanted to be a writer, like Brown. That was what brought them together: writing—especially mystery stuff."

"That would explain why they had an interest in criminology classes," Sanchez said, nodding. "OK. That makes sense. Now, I have a question for you, Guillermo. If they were doing all this writing and studying, how did they support themselves?"

"Peter worked in the campus bookstore. Brown worked here and there and eventually landed a night security gig at one of the campus libraries. A job with all that down time would be perfect for a writer."

"If you can tolerate the boredom," Sanchez said.

"Sarah had no family support, so she worked a lot of different jobs while in college. Let's see . . . she was a waitress, a motel housekeeper, a night shift employee at a pharmacy. You name it, she did it. During the summer, she taught writing and literature at a camp for school-age kids. This must have been difficult work for her because the administration reprimanded her three times for yelling at the kids. She got fired during her last summer there. They said it had something to do with her negative attitude. As hard as she worked, though, she still graduated with a hefty student loan debt. Unable to find a teaching position right away, she stayed in Berkeley and worked whatever odd jobs she could find."

"When, during all of this, did she and her friends get to know Tina Serano?" Sanchez asked.

"The summer after graduation. Then Parker got a teaching position in Phoenix at a high school, and they all moved down here. Peter started working consistently right away, but Brown only occasionally subbed at the university library and spent the rest of his time writing. Parker supported him and his writing."

Montero sat quietly while Sanchez rounded up the dishes from the patio. He took over when she started loading the dishwasher. "I guess I wonder how much of the reporter's information is dependable," he said more to himself than Sanchez, "and not just speculation. And it seems that Peter didn't tell me everything he knew about the cases in Berkeley. He said he only knew Lucy, but he clearly must have known the other missing women too."

"Yeah, I have to ask myself what I should believe."

"And then there's his attorney. I talked to him a few days ago. I think he's holding something back too."

"So . . . that's what we've got," Sanchez said with finality, draping a dish towel over the handle of the stove. "Listen, I'd better get going. I have to get up for an early day tomorrow. Have to prep for a trial that starts the day after tomorrow. Thanks for the great meal." She patted her flat belly and said, "I should run a few miles before work."

She stepped over to Montero and gave him a perfunctory hug good night. "I never thought I'd hug a priest named

Guillermo," she said with a laugh.

***

The next morning, Montero felt inspired to go for a short jog around the neighborhood. It felt good to run a little, but it was getting warm already, so he cut it short.

In the afternoon, after he had spent the morning at his parish office, he revisited MacEvie's notes concerning Simpson, Brown, and Parker's romantic involvement. MacEvie had sworn he had a solid source to back up his claim that the threesome had been known to spend the night in the same bed and often entertain other female sexual partners. But Parker didn't always welcome these interlopers. One night, she'd literally thrown a woman out of the apartment because she had spent too much time with Simpson. Parker had been jealous of the attention she was paying him and asked the woman to leave the party. On other occasions, she had become hostile toward another woman having sex with Brown. She loved both Simpson and Brown and could not share them beyond a certain point.

MacEvie thought that Parker became jealous of other women if they were too interested in whomever she was dating at the time. She had apparently had a real conflict with Johnson. Her displeasure escalated until one night she instigated a catfight in a bar. Then she fell in love with Brown, apparently with Simpson's blessing. Later, she seemed to push Simpson out the door so she could have Brown to herself. When Jones had come along, she had hung out with all of them for a time, including other mutual friends, on a strictly platonic level, and then had started dating Brown. Then, just like that, she had disappeared.

MacEvie had told Montero there had been a rumor that Brown occasionally had been seeing Serano before she vanished.

One of her coworkers had seen her talking to someone in the parking lot the night she disappeared, but that coworker never revealed him or herself to the police, so there was no real proof that it had ever happened.

Montero jotted down a few more notes about the case and then got back to his paying job. He had to review his proposed budget for the next year. If he could get it approved, he would be able to keep up his visits to inmates at the Florence prison, his calling. Many priests did not want to conduct the visits. They required a long drive and could be depressing at times.

He texted Sanchez, telling her to call if she wanted to talk more about MacEvie's information. She texted back that she might be free to meet the following afternoon. Her night would run late because she had something big going on. One of her cases was ready to break.

Chapter 7

April 9, 2014

Sanchez straightened up and adjusted her top before she turned the corner to reach the Mexicali Bar and Grille, a big hangout for members of the Westside Glendale Lokos Gang. Sleek Harley-Davidson motorcycles and their riders dominated the on-street parking in front of the bar, so she had to strut through a gauntlet of tobacco- and weed-smoking, leather-clad bikers to reach the door. She encountered two guys who thought they had a chance with her and tried to grab her ass as she went by but got their hands slapped away instead.

On this night, she was no longer conservatively dressed Detective Sanchez with the Phoenix PD, but a hardcore biker chick revealing more flesh than she was comfortable with. Her tight short shorts threatened to expose more than her tan lean thighs, while her long V-neck tank divulged enough cleavage to get her in trouble.

While dressing at the station, Sanchez had gone for the bad hot chick look, pulling her hair to one side of her neck and applying long eyelashes and dark, nearly purple lipstick. She had checked herself in a mirror before she left and decided she looked more like a cheap hooker than anything else. *But hey*, she had thought, *the guys I'm trying to fool won't look past the boosted C cup anyway.* Her new look was not wasted on her partner. When she had exited their unmarked car parked on a side street, he had given her the thumbs-up and made a lewd comment he would later regret. She would get even with him, provided she survived the upcoming meeting with her confidential informant.

The high heels of her ankle boots clicked on the concrete sidewalk. A hint of lacey socks peeked above her ankles to obscure the extra magazine of ammo she had hidden in her right boot. Her main weapon was her usual concealed-carry .45-caliber compact Springfield XDS semiautomatic, which she had holstered in the waistband of her shorts at the small of her back. She had put on a button-front vest, which she left open to better conceal the gun, but instead, her constant tugging at her top to keep the XDS covered inadvertently flashed more breast than she wanted. She figured it was better to show some skin than to let on she was packing a hand cannon.

This wasn't Sanchez's first time undercover. In LA, she had had to make her bones by doing a few stints on cases in the prostitution and drug worlds. There were some close calls, but she had managed to control her fear and revulsion well enough to get through it. But that had been a few years earlier, when she was still naive about what could happen to her if her cover got blown.

Sanchez approached the front door to the bar. She took a deep breath to contain her fear and marched past several men wearing leathers and biker club colors who stopped talking to watch her go by. She climbed two steps to the open doorway where loud Mexican rap music poured into the street. She stepped inside, and a heavily muscled bouncer immediately gave her a perfunctory pat-down along her sides and looked in her little handbag.

It was dark as sin inside and packed to the seams with black-clad and tattooed humanity. Even the women had covered their skin in bluish-black or colored ink in all kinds of pictures, words, or graphic patterns. In some ways, Sanchez felt relieved. Most of the other women there were even more scantily clothed than she was. But she also realized she was probably the only person there with no ink showing.

Sanchez pushed her way to the bar, trying not to make eye contact with anyone while still scanning the room for her CI, Eduardo. He was an average-looking Hispanic guy affiliated with the Westside gang. He was her insider to the gang's recent expansion from drugs into gun smuggling and sales. The gang had crossed a line into violent activity lately, which she thought meant they had changed their business model to more cross-border trading. That might mean they had partnered up with a Mexican cartel. She hoped to find out from Eduardo if this was true and hopefully have him point out a few of the players to her if they were here.

She pushed up to the bar and had just ordered a Dos Equis beer when a Hispanic woman with an elaborate cross tattooed on her chest got in her face and shoved her to one side. She had apparently gotten too close to the woman's man, who was leaning on the bar. Sanchez's first reaction was to shove back, but she didn't want to create a scene, so she just took her beer and moved away.

She finally spotted Eduardo at the back of the room, wearing a Cardinals T-shirt, black jeans, and an NYC ball cap, leaning against the wall and getting very friendly with a woman. She made her way over to him, carefully threading across the dance area while fending off roaming hands. Eduardo didn't see her coming until she shimmied up next to him. She grabbed his arm to turn his attention away from the other chick, who was practically pasted on his chest and kissing him like they were old, intimate friends.

When Sanchez finally caught Eduardo's eye, he jumped like he had received an electric shock. She wasn't sure if it was because he recognized her or if the other woman had grabbed him someplace personal, but the woman suddenly glared at her with the look one gives a menacing insect that's about to be smashed with a rolled-up newspaper. Sanchez realized the woman was the possessive type and backed off to let Eduardo find a way to disengage. She moved to the back wall where there was a semblance of cool air drifting into the room. She leaned on the wall close to an older woman who was also enjoying the cooler air. They didn't say much, just acknowledged each other and sipped their beers.

She kept her eyes on Eduardo, who broke away from his paramour of the evening and left her standing along the wall, still glaring at Sanchez and now mouthing words at her that were probably not complimentary. The finger gesture seemed to sum up her intent.

Eduardo took Sanchez by the arm and pulled her out the back door onto the loading dock in the alley where spent beer kegs were stacked and other merchandise temporarily stored. He shoved the door closed behind him so no one would follow. No one was supposed to come out there, but it was the only quiet, private place to talk on short notice.

He pulled her down the dock ramp and over to the back of the alley by the dumpsters, speaking in a hushed voice, "I can't talk much now. Maria's going to get mad if we're out here too long."

Sanchez shook off Eduardo's grip and said, "Well, then you'd better tell me what you know real quick. I don't want to keep you from your true love." She smiled and leaned in close to him to tease him as she emphasized the word *love*.

Eduardo rolled his eyes, making it clear that her sarcasm was not lost on him. "So, I found out the Westside guys are goin' into business with some guys from Sinaloa. They're bringin' guns across the border both ways and need a local gang to handle the US side and the distribution."

"The Sinaloa Cartel from Mexico? Moving guns? How do they get them?"

"I don't know that. All I know is there's a big deal goin' down soon. I don't know when or who in Westside's in on it. Maybe Valdez and others." He was really jumpy. "Look, I gotta go," he said. "We'll talk more later. OK?"

"So, who's the girl? She your girlfriend?"

"No. We've only hooked up a couple of times. I told her you're my sister-in-law and you needed to talk about a problem at home. I hope she doesn't get too mad. She already thinks you're trouble."

The back door of the bar swung open, and a big man in a muscle shirt stomped onto the loading dock. "Hey! What you doin' here?" he yelled at Eduardo. He marched over to them with his arms out to his sides like he expected a fight and said in a rough, low voice, "What you doin' here? No one's supposed ta be out here. House rules."

He came close, and Eduardo backed up a bit, leaving Sanchez to deal with the bouncer or whoever he was. He walked up to her and appreciatively looked her over. Then he looked at Eduardo. "This your chick? What you doin'? She givin' you a blow job or somethin'?"

"Nah. My *friend* and me was just talkin', man."

"Well, beat it then," he growled. "Maybe she and me gonna be friends now."

Sanchez didn't want to get into a fight, and she certainly didn't want to be the big guy's friend, so she tried to act out the tough biker chick role. "Hey. Leave us alone, man. We're just talkin,' like my friend said. Why don't you go hassle someone else?"

The man came closer to menace them.

Sanchez stepped forward and warned, "Don't mess with me, dumb ass."

For a big guy, he moved fast. He reached out and slapped Sanchez on the side of her face, catching her completely off guard. The blow sent her reeling backward against the dumpster, and she bounced off it right into his arms. Stunned, she tried to twist out of his grasp, but he had one arm around her waist from behind and lifted her nearly off the ground with her left arm pinned to her side. She struggled to regain her wits, but she couldn't breathe right.

Eduardo yanked on the guy's arm, but he received a hard right cross to his face, sending him down on his butt. Sanchez tried to hit her attacker with her free elbow but couldn't land a real blow because of the way she was being held. The guy slapped her again hard with his free hand and then started to paw at her breasts.

The back door of the bar opened again, and this time, two heavyset men stepped out onto the loading dock and lit cigarettes, apparently to talk. They were surprised to see the three-way fight in the alley. One looked at the big man holding the struggling Sanchez and asked in thick Mexican Spanish, "What the fuck you doin', Alberto? We're supposed to talk now."

Alberto was in the act of pulling up Sanchez's top when he saw the pistol tucked in her belt. He was surprised. For a second, he loosened his hold on her and reached for the gun. That was enough time for her to twist around and land her elbow in his face.

Then everything happened in just seconds. He let go of her so he could pull the gun free and shouted, "Gun! Gun!" as she twisted free, leaving the gun in his hand. Sanchez spun around and grabbed for the gun, getting both her hands on it. She pushed it down and tried to twist it free. Alberto got his second hand on top of hers and started to bring the gun up, overpowering her, pointing the gun at her leg. But he didn't have his finger on the trigger yet. He was a lot stronger than she, and she knew he would soon wrest the gun away. All she could think to do was drop down, lower her head to his hands, and clamp her teeth down on his right thumb as hard as she could.

Alberto shrieked with pain and pulled his hand away from her, nearly knocking her teeth out. In that instant, she jerked the gun around so it pointed at his belly and pulled the trigger. The bullet drilled into his guts, and he dropped to his knees, letting go.

Sanchez backed away holding the XDS in both hands, aiming at Alberto's chest. That was when Eduardo shouted, "Look out!" and took off at light speed down the alley, picking flight from his subliminal mind's choice of fight or flight.

Something whizzed past Sanchez's face, startling her into the immediate awareness that someone was shooting at her. The hair on the back of her neck and everywhere else stood up and warned of danger. In what seemed like slow motion, she turned toward the loading dock where the sound of a gunshot had come from and the two Mexicans had been standing. A second and third bullet zipped past on her left side as she slowly turned to face the men, who she now noticed had filled their hands with black semiautomatic handguns, which they were determined to unload in her direction. Sanchez raised her weapon in both hands, squaring off like she would at the target range, and returned fire as lead flew by her on all sides. In slow motion, she watched each shot fire from the muzzles of the men's handguns, heard the bullets whizz past, and then heard the lead strike the big dumpster behind her.

Flash, zip, clang. Flash, zip, clang. Over and over.

In the same slow-motion scene, she felt her own gun with each shot, slowly pulling the trigger, feeling her XDS jump up as the bullet left the muzzle, hearing the big .45 boom, feeling the kick in her hand, and then seeing her bullet strike the concrete block wall behind the men. She couldn't imagine why her first two shots went wide and to the right, but somehow her brain corrected, and she saw one man jerk back, his fingers still working the trigger as he slowly fell backward onto the loading dock.

Lead kept flying past Sanchez. But then something hit her hard in the left shoulder, causing her to spin around to her left. To her surprise, her left arm suddenly went limp and fell to her side. She marveled at the event, taking an instant to realize that she was shot but felt no pain at all. But bullets kept coming at her, so she turned back to shoot at the last threat to her life, now holding her XDS only in her right hand. She aimed in slow motion and fired at the man, *boom, boom, boom,* until his head jerked, and he flew backward to join his buddy on the deck of the loading dock. She kept pulling the trigger in slow motion, but the *booms* had stopped, and her gun was empty.

She lowered her arm and looked around the dark, empty alleyway. Nothing alive and standing except her. No remaining threats. She raised her right arm and saw that her magazine was empty, the slide of the pistol now locked open, awaiting a new magazine. Out of habit, she pressed the release button, and the empty mag fell noiselessly to the ground. *Funny . . . no sound,* she thought. Then it dawned on her that she couldn't hear anything, only shouting coming from far away.

She looked at her gun. Normally, her left hand would have come up with a fresh mag by now, and she would release the slide, ready to shoot again. But her left arm just hung loosely at her side, and blood ran from another hole in her hand she hadn't noticed before. *Oh yeah*, she thought, *I was shot. That's why my arm isn't working.*

She looked down at her now exposed shoulder, as her top had torn free in the wrestling match with Alberto. Blood dripped out of a round hole and ran down her breast into her bra. *Shit! I'm bleeding.* Then her shoulder and hand started to throb.

She dropped the empty gun to the ground and reached her right hand behind her back under her tank top. Her back was wet and sticky. She tried to turn around to look over her shoulder, but that really hurt now. That was when she noticed Alberto lying on the ground in a pool of blood, his eyes closed. *I'd better check on him.* She dragged her tired legs over to where he lay and tried to squat down beside him to check his pulse. But her legs gave way, and she wound up sitting next to him, observing that he was still breathing, just unconscious. She sat with her legs crumpled under her, her good arm propping her up in a sitting position. She began to shake uncontrollably.

Then the sound came rushing back into her head, and she heard someone running toward her. A man was shouting, *"Sanchez! Sanchez!"*

In her confused state, she realized that Sanchez was her. Or was it she? She could never remember which was correct.

She looked up as the man, someone she knew named Bordou, ran up to her with a big black Glock in his hand. He was her partner, and he would help her.

Bordou said something to her, but she didn't understand the words. His lips moved, and there was sound as he pulled her toward him and looked at her shoulder. When he pulled his hands away from her, they were covered in blood. He waved one of his bloody index fingers up in front of her nose and moved it back and forth for some reason, she knew not why. She felt cold, so she leaned into him to borrow some of his warmth.

Then two other people, cops she knew, not sure of their names now, ran up the alley, shouting. One went to check on the men on the loading dock and to keep people from coming out the door of the bar. She watched the other man come to check on Alberto, who was slowly bleeding out on the pavement.

Bordou spoke into a radio and then reached around and somehow managed to pick Sanchez up in his arms. She couldn't imagine how heavy she must be to carry. She felt tired and her arms were heavy, and they wouldn't move at her command now. She rested her head on his shoulder, exhausted, as he ran with her down the alley to the side street, talking to her all the way. The last thing she remembered was flashing lights coming down the street and a siren somewhere far away and dull, but also nearby. She closed her eyes.

Chapter 8

April 10, 2014

Montero spent the better part of the morning with his superior, the dean of the vicariate for the Greater Phoenix area, which happened to include much of the state. Montero's parish was especially set up to serve the inmate population in the state-run institutions. He didn't have a territorial parish like most priests. In fact, he was what was called a secular priest since he was not associated with a direct order of the church. He was considered out in the world rather than within the church itself. This meant that he had taken the vows of chastity and obedience but was not bound by the vow of poverty and other restrictions that monks and many others within the church followed. Because of his prior military and police experience, the dean viewed him as the best qualified for the job, something he usually enjoyed anyway. He had seen both sides of the criminal justice system and could empathize with the inmates better than most.

It was already lunchtime when he finished the meeting. He checked his cell phone and saw he had neither a text nor voicemail from Sanchez. He called her and got her voicemail. He texted her while he ate lunch and then hid out in the church library to go over parts of the Berkeley cases.

He had sketched a time line on a single page of notepaper. On it, he wrote that Parker and Brown had been serious for four years, based on what MacEvie had told him. Parker had feelings for both Brown and Simpson and may have held the three of them together with her income and lesser drive to write. Montero thought it was odd that they knew all three missing girls. Two of them had been in the same classes with at least one of the friends, so maybe that was the reason. He thought it was interesting that the police didn't have any suspects. Then again, without finding a body in a university town, they may not have invested a lot of resources in the cases.

Then he became curious about whether these sorts of disappearances were common in university towns across the country. Since there were two large universities and several smaller colleges in the Phoenix urban area, he thought to look there first. He decided to ask Sanchez if she could find out if any students had disappeared in Phoenix. He dialed her cell number but got voicemail again.

At the end of the day, he drove home, stopping at the Azteca Market en route. He picked up a few fresh vegetables to go with the leftover chorizo, along with some beer. Then he got back into his white Toyota pickup for the drive home. He flipped on the radio to local news as he entered traffic and just caught the end of a broadcast:

" . . . at the Mexicali Bar and Grille last night. The gunfire erupted from an altercation at the rear of the establishment when three members of a local gang apparently attacked a police-woman. The officer has been taken to the emergency room at John C. Lincoln Medical Center suffering from multiple gunshot wounds. Three men were also shot at the scene, one of them fatally. It is believed that a drug sale may have been involved.

"On a lighter note, the children at the Valley Child Care and Learning Center certainly were surprised today when . . . ."

Montero pulled his truck out of traffic in order to listen to any more news about the shooting. He heard nothing new. Then he dialed Sanchez's number, afraid that the policewoman in the shooting might be her. No answer.

He pulled back into traffic, aggressively crossing all lanes until he was in the left turn lane at the next intersection. When he spotted a break in traffic, he spun the steering wheel and floored the gas to execute a wild, tire-screeching U-turn across the center lane of the boulevard. He cut off an older couple's car as he turned onto McDowell Road. He drove west too fast for traffic and reached the hospital thirty frustrating minutes later.

He ran to the front desk and asked what room Officer Sanchez was in. The nurse wouldn't tell him at first, but after insisting that he was her friend and her priest and simply must see her, she relented and sent him to the third floor. He found her alone in a private room. A police officer standing nearby began to intercept him. Seeing the priest's collar, he let him enter the room, saying Sanchez might not be awake now. Montero said he would sit with her anyway and pray.

Montero entered the room and saw that she was, indeed, asleep. She looked bad: her face was bruised, and her right eye was swollen shut. Her left shoulder and left hand were heavily bandaged. She had two IVs in her arm, one dripping blood into her vein, the other a clear liquid. He pulled up a chair, took her hand in his, and silently said a short prayer. He kept holding her hand while he prayed again, this time out loud.

Sanchez's left eye fluttered a bit, and she opened it to look at him. She tried to smile, but moaned in pain instead. "It must be worse than I thought if they sent for a priest," she said, wincing from the effort.

"I only just heard about you on the radio, or I would have come over earlier. Are you all right? On the news they said multiple gunshot wounds."

"I got hit pretty good here in the shoulder and again in my hand. The rest is just from fighting a guy who blindsided me." She tried to sit up. "Hey, can you give me that glass of water?"

He handed her the glass. "What happened? You texted something about your case breaking yesterday. Were you on a raid?"

"No . . . no raid. I went to a bar, a gang hangout, to meet a CI. I was undercover. My CI and I went out back to talk and, well, I guess someone saw us go out there and got suspicious." She paused and seemed to be replaying the scene in her mind. "Then a guy came out the back door and asked what was going on. I tried to play it cool. Told him to mind his own business. You know, the tough chick thing. He popped me one in the face and grabbed me like I was a piece of meat or something, one arm around me, holding me so tight I couldn't get at him. That's when he gave me this shiner. He started to cop a feel of my boobs, so I elbowed him in the face." She took a sip of water. "Shit, did he get mad. Then he saw my gun in my butt holster, so I was forced to make a move. There were two other guys . . . um, two other guys . . . ." She shook her head as if to clear her mind. "I don't remember all of it now." Then she began to shake. Tears appeared. She couldn't go on.

"Hey, Sanchez," Montero said with as much enthusiasm as he could summon. "You're OK. You're going to be fine, good as new in a few weeks. You did what you had to do. It's all right." He thought about what it must have been like for her to have to fight for her life like that, scared, outnumbered, and alone. *Thank God she survived*, he thought. He asked, "What did your CI do?"

Sanchez made a face and said, "That son of a bitch." She looked at Montero askance. "Look, I'm going to swear in front of you sometimes, OK? It's just who I am." She tried to smile. "Yeah, that son of a bitch took off at the first sign of trouble and left me there to deal with those shits. What an asshole! Wait until I find his miserable ass. You know?" She winced. Montero screwed up his mouth, then said, "You're right. He *is* an asshole." "Well, the guy got ahold of my pistol, and we grappled for it. Then I guess I shot him in the guts. Then these other two guys produced handguns and just started firing in my direction, like they were in some Tarantino movie—not aiming, just pulling the trigger. I got a lucky shot at one of them right away, but I had to shoot it out with the second guy. I was scared as hell, let me tell you." Sanchez stopped talking and began to self-consciously tear up.

The door of the room burst open, and a tall, blond policeman entered, followed by two more officers. The first one boomed out a loud greeting: "Well, there she is, Lieutenant Wyatt Earp Sanchez! The lone survivor of the shootout at the OK Corral! By the time I got into the alley, there she was, standing tall and blazing away at these two bad guys. Lead flying everywhere, ricochets all around. I'm surprised anyone in the neighborhood survived at all." He laughed and pointed at Sanchez. "That's my partner, ready to take on the whole Sinaloa Cartel by herself."

Sanchez looked at Montero and fired back at the greeting while wiping away her tears, "And that's my lazy partner, Jeff Bordou, over there. A day late and a dollar short, as always." Then she asked, "What took you so long to get to the alley, Bordou? Did you wait to see if we'd run out of ammo?" She smiled and tried to point her finger at him but didn't quite make that happen. Then she said softly, "Thanks for getting me out of there, you big stud."

Bordou strolled over to the side of the bed and beamed down at Sanchez. "It takes more than a few bullets to take the sass out of you. How're you feeling?" He noticed Montero's collar. "Oh, sorry, Father." He stepped back. "I didn't know you were a priest. I'm Jeff Bordou. Sanchez and I pair up on cases sometimes, which is the same as saying I have to look after her to keep her out of trouble."

"I'm Guillermo Montero. Pleased to meet you." They shook hands, and Montero turned toward Sanchez, who was struggling to keep her eyes open. "I'll leave you to your friends, OK?"

"Thank you for visiting and praying for me. It felt nice. Come back later, if you like—if I'm awake, that is." She tried to smile.

Worried that Sanchez's injuries might leave her maimed or hurt her career, he hunted for her doctor. He finally left the hospital only after the doctor had satisfactorily assured him that Sanchez would make a full recovery.

***

Over the next two days, Sanchez underwent two additional surgeries, one on her hand and one on her shoulder, to ensure that there were no more bullet fragments lodged near her shoulder blade. That bullet had just missed her lung and had come close to injuring an important bundle of nerves. A few millimeters one way or the other could have permanently interfered with the movement of her arm.

She was exhausted the whole time while she was in the hospital due to the surgeries and the several interviews she underwent with different people within the Phoenix PD. There were many questions because two of her attackers had died from the shooting, one at the scene and one in the hospital the next day. Internal Affairs conducted a harsh interrogation that drained her emotionally and set her recovery back.

She finally went home after three days, loaded with pain medications. She weaned herself off Percocet after another week and then relied only on Extra Strength Tylenol for pain control. Her serious shoulder wound was healing as well as could be expected.

***

Montero stopped in on her first day home and every day for the rest of the week. He ran errands for her or just chatted with her awhile. He helped her get through the shock of her near-death experience and listened to her struggle with the deep moral challenges caused by her shooting two men to death. She also had weekly appointments with a police psychologist.

Her good friend and coworker, Maria Sandoval, and other friends from the PD cooked for her and helped around the house. Montero met Sanchez's parents, who frequently came by to help out. They all had dinner together once that week, and it went well.

By the second week at home, Sanchez was already tired of being the object of constant attention. She had received about all the help and advice that her mother had to offer, so she asked her parents to only come by occasionally, like they used to. She insisted that she could do everything for herself and even took them for a drive just to show them she was OK. By the end of that week, her parents had honored her wishes and only dropped in once every three days.

Montero talked to Sanchez about the Simpson murder after she got home and settled into a routine. She had lobbied with her captain to let her come into the station a few hours a day to deal with issues related to the shooting. But she couldn't really focus on Simpson yet, and Montero continued with his own investigation.

Chapter 9

April 17, 2014

Montero made a number of telephone calls to local newspapers to see if there were many unsolved missing-persons cases involving young people on or around Arizona's college campuses. He tried the campus papers first, but found that the city papers covered that type of story more often. He told the reporters he contacted that he was looking for any cases in which an individual had disappeared without leaving a trace, like the women in Berkeley. After some digging, he found out there had been two unusual cases over the last two years in the Phoenix area. Upon further investigation, he determined that one of the missing persons was a college kid who had ducked out on his rent. The second case was closer to what Montero was looking for.

In 2012, a twenty-year-old woman named Tracy Mickelson, a sophomore at the University of Arizona in Tucson, went missing without a trace. She was enrolled in the English literature program and was taking a class that was cross-listed at Arizona State University. In fact, it was a comparative literature class that was taught at the ASU Tempe campus two nights a week, and she drove up from Tucson to Tempe, just south of Scottsdale, to attend. She regularly drove from UA to ASU and back in the same night.

One Tuesday night, Mickelson drove up to Tempe for class and was never seen again. Her roommate didn't report her missing until three days later. The first night Mickelson didn't come home, her roommate suspected she had hooked up with a guy she had met in class. On the second night, her roommate began to worry; they had made plans, and it was unlike Mickelson to stand her up. When her roommate still hadn't heard from her on the third night, she knew something was wrong, so she had called the UA police department to report her missing. UA police had looked for her car around campus and then contacted Arizona state patrol to see if she had been involved in an accident. Nothing had been reported. They then contacted the ASU campus police, and the next morning, ASU officers found Mickelson's car in the campus parking garage near the library. This suggested she had never left campus. Forensics found nothing unusual inside or outside of her car.

Montero drove over to ASU in Tempe to talk with Officer Thomas Smith from campus police. Smith brought him up to date on the case. When he finished meeting with Smith, he walked to the campus library to make some notes in his ever-thickening file. He found the campus refreshing as he walked past the modern buildings, palm tree-lined open spaces, and green lawns, which defied the climate of this arid state.

At the library, he added the latest information to his timeline, showing all events that might be related in any way to the three Berkeley friends. He made it on yellow-lined paper and now had to tape two pages together to make it all fit. He knew this was primitive, but as far as he was concerned, it helped him to arrange all the pieces he had gathered so far.

SIMPSON CASE TIME LINE

2006–2007   UC Berkeley   Freshman Year
Peter Simpson, Allister Brown, Sarah Parker
start college at UC Berkeley in English.

2007–2008   UC Berkeley   Sophomore Year
Simpson dates Lucy Johnson.
Johnson disappears from her apartment.
Parker meets Simpson in class.

2008–2009   UC Berkeley   Junior Year
Parker dates Simpson.
Parker meets Brown via Simpson.
Brown dates Naomi Jones.
Jones disappears.
Parker dates Brown.

2009–2010   UC Berkeley   Senior Year
Parker moves in with Brown, Simpson moves out.
Simpson dates other women.
Graduation.

2010–2011   Berkeley   After Graduation
Friends look for work in Berkeley.
Tina Serano disappears.
Parker accepts teaching job in Phoenix.

2010–2011   Phoenix
Friends move to Phoenix; Parker begins job.
Brown and Parker live together.
Simpson finds job at bookstore.

2012   Phoenix

            Brown gets job at library.

            2/25   Brown and Parker have fight at
                    apartment; police called.

            3/13   Tracy Mickelson disappears from ASU
                    Tempe.

2013   Phoenix

            4/16   Parker closes her bank account and
                    moves to Los Angeles.

            6/4   Parker rents mailbox in Phoenix.

            6/6   Brown murdered?

            6/8   Simpson arrested for murder.

            June-September: Investigation of the murder.

            10/5   Trial begins.

            Early October: Last mail pickup from mailbox.

            10/10   Last telephone contact between
                    Simpson and Brown.

                    Simpson tells lawyer he is in contact
                    with Brown.

            10/12   Simpson gives his book to the judge.

            10/20   Trial ends.

            10/28   Simpson sentenced to death.

            December: Final judicial review complete.

2014   Phoenix

            January: I meet Simpson at the Prison.

            4/2   Simpson executed.

Montero looked over his handiwork and thought there had to be lots of things still missing. He sat back and decided that he had gone as far as he could for the day. He packed up his notes and walked to the parking garage to retrieve his car. Only then did he realize he was standing in the parking garage from which Tracy had vanished. Or at least where her car had been found. He looked around. It seemed a safe enough place. Maybe she had never made it back there. He supposed no one would ever know what had happened.

On the way home, he decided to swing by Sanchez's condo to see how she was doing now that she could go into work a few hours a day. It was a beautiful day, and he stopped to pick up a six-pack of Sol beer in case Sanchez felt like talking.

When Sanchez opened the door, she was still wearing her work outfit. "Don't mind if I do," she said, helping herself to a beer. "This is much appreciated." She had just arrived home and unloaded a few groceries into her refrigerator. She took a beer with her into the bedroom, and a few minutes later, Montero heard the shower running.

He stood at the entry to her living room and looked around at the décor. It was a bit sparse, like she hadn't really settled into the place yet. *She's worse than I am*, he thought. He inspected the photographs on her bookshelf. There was a photo of her as a young girl outdoors with her parents at what could have been the local arboretum with lots of barrel cacti behind them. There was another of her dressed in a cap and gown with a friend at a graduation, maybe college. Then one of a smiling Sanchez in a police officer's uniform, probably after graduating from the police academy.

A few steps away on the wall were a few documents, diplomas, and a commendation from the Phoenix police chief for doing a superior job on a case. There was also a framed pistol range target with ten bullet holes all within the nine-point ring. Underneath it were dated signatures of witnesses to the amazing shooting feat and a pistol expert badge. *Damn good shooting.*

The sound of flip-flops echoed down the tiled hallway, and a smiling and refreshed Sanchez stepped into the room wearing a T-shirt and shorts, one arm in a sling. "*Whoo!* That feels better!" she said, trying with difficulty to pull her long hair up into a ponytail.

Montero tipped his head toward the pistol range target and said, "You're quite a good shot, Lori. Ten shots within the diameter of a fist. Great grouping."

"Yeah, thanks, but I need to keep up at the shooting range if I'm going to stay on top of it. That target was from my best day at the range."

They drank another beer and complained about the early summer heat and the usual other topics that all Phoenix residents share. Then Sanchez talked about how she was still answering questions at work about her recent shootout. "It's getting old, if you know what I mean." The department psychologist had her talk about it constantly to try to purge her of thoughts about whether it was right or wrong. Montero assured her she had done the only thing possible under the circumstances.

Still standing in place, she finished her beer and pulled another out of the refrigerator. "Want one?" she asked Montero.

He shook his head.

"Internal Affairs gave me a clean bill of health, so I hope most of this crap is over. My captain let me get back on the drug case I was working when all this went down." Sanchez glanced at her injured hand. "He said I had to work it from the office until he's certain I'm fit to get back in the field. I'll have to take Bordou with me, then."

She and Montero each settled into a chair in her living room. "Bordou has been looking for my CI for me, with the idea that he might have better luck talking to Eduardo than I would, since he's hiding from me. He could let him know that I'm a little less likely to beat his ass now that a week has passed by." She snickered. "I guess I can't blame him for running when the shooting began, but where is chivalry in this modern age?"

"He was probably scared as hell they'd find out he was snitching to a cop and bury him in the desert somewhere." Montero chuckled. "So . . . what have you learned about the men you shot?"

"Oh, those guys. I was right about them. The guys on the loading dock were members of the Sinaloa Cartel, all right. One of them is an enforcer in the Phoenix area. The guy I shot in the guts belonged to a Phoenix gang named the Westside Glendale Lokos. At least, that's what they call themselves. The names change frequently. They're an offshoot of the local Lokos Posse. Through them, Westside has access to drugs, guns, and cash."

"How many street gangs are there in the metro area now?"

"Oh gosh. Dozens. Most aren't real big, but a few are larger and are connected to LA gangs and other outfits. Westside is an up-and-coming gang that's getting into lots of drug sales and enforcement. Some say they want to directly hook up with Sinaloa to gain recognition by getting heavy into gun violence related to drug and gun shipments and providing local enforcement for the cartel. A bad sign."

"Who are you concentrating on?"

"The Phoenix gangs. If Sinaloa wants to expand its business into Arizona, it's going to need a lot more local shooters to do their business."

"I didn't realize the local gangs were that violent. On TV, you just hear about their turf wars and robberies and stuff. I counsel some gangbangers in my work, but mostly I see them after they've graduated to bigger crimes and wound up in prison."

"Well, these Westside guys want to go big time, and fast. They're largely Hispanic men from the neighborhood who want to be somebody. You know what I mean? The gang lets them do that. But these days, they have to pump a lot of lead to stand out and get noticed."

"So how does your CI fit into the picture?"

"He grew up near Carl Hayden High School and knows some of the gang members who deal drugs there and at other schools in the area. Westside's making a play to sell drugs at the local middle school and other public places near there. We, of course, want to stop that activity, as well as shut down their recruitment efforts. I was at the Mexicali that night because my CI had information about a new deal going down between the Westside gang and the cartel to help with guns and human trafficking to move girls south."

"By south, you mean Mexico."

"Yeah. Sinaloa does it once in a while now. But most of the kidnappings have been intimidation cases. You know—they grab the mayor of a small town near the border and threaten him to ease up on police enforcement so they can operate freely in his town. Lately, they've grabbed policemen and others, sometimes even the wives and daughters of officials, to get their way. You never hear about it in the newspapers because so few kidnappings are ever reported. As you probably can imagine, this has a chilling effect on law enforcement when you know it could be your daughter who is grabbed and raped or simply killed to force your hand."

"I never thought it would get this bad here in Phoenix. I

know El Paso deals with some of the same problems. It's probably gotten worse since I left."

"I hope to meet with my CI tomorrow and see what new info he has for me. That is, if I can fit it into my schedule of meetings about the shootings. It looks like most everyone is now convinced that I shot those men in self-defense."

"And how are you dealing with it now?" Montero looked her in the eye. "OK?"

Montero had helped her work through the shock of having taken another person's life. He thought Sanchez was doing all right. He worried that she would develop Post-Traumatic Stress Disorder from the ordeal because it had been so sudden and terrifying. So far, he had not seen any signs of it, but PTSD was often delayed. Sometimes it didn't show up until much later when the person was in a similar stressful situation. He had warned her of this and told her he had experience with PTSD himself from the days when he was in the army. He had served in Desert Storm after he enlisted and later became a ranger. He had surprised her with this information, but it helped explain to her why he was so familiar with weapons and death. He also had told her that after the military he was a cop in El Paso for a few years. That was why he knew so much about police procedures and reporting. He hadn't really explained why he had left the police force to become a priest. That was still a private matter between him and his God.

Chapter 10

April 19, 2014

We got a hit on that BOLO for Parker's car today," Sanchez excitedly relayed to Montero. "I reposted it two days ago when I came back to work so it wouldn't get completely lost. I also extended it to a couple of other agencies, and that paid off. It was picked up at the border patrol station in Nogales, Arizona, on one of their license camera sites where they digitize the data and put it up on the computer network. Anyway, the car was spotted near Nogales, and highway patrol picked up the driver an hour ago. They're holding the driver for us until we get there. You doing anything you can't just drop and go for a drive?"

Montero said he would be free in about a half hour, which happened to be how long it took Sanchez to reach his office and pick him up. When she got there, Montero insisted on driving his truck to spare her strain on her shoulder, which still wasn't up to par. After a brief back-and-forth about how she was OK to drive, Sanchez relented, and they headed south in the Toyota.

They drove out of town on I-10 toward Tucson to take Highway 19 to Nogales, Arizona, across the border from the bigger city of Nogales, Mexico. The air was blistering hot and formed a mirage on the pavement ahead of them as they cruised along in air-conditioned comfort. The CD player blasted out an Alejandro Sanz tune as they rode through the desert. Sanchez unconsciously tapped a foot to the energetic beat. Montero turned down the volume of the music so they could talk.

They drove to the border patrol station where the driver was being held. The officer on duty led them back to the holding cell, where an agitated Mexican national named Carlos Gonzales was waiting. Montero thought he did not look happy. Sanchez went into the interview room to talk to him while Montero sipped sour coffee in the observation room.

"I am a businessman, not a criminal," he said. "Why are you holding me like this? I cross the border at least once a month to deliver crafts and jewelry to shops in Phoenix. I don't have time to be locked up like this, for no reason whatsoever." His English was very good, and it was clear to Montero he was the businessman he claimed to be.

Sanchez explained to Señor Gonzales that the police had a BOLO out on the car he was driving, which was related to a murder in Phoenix, and they thought an important witness was still driving it. The patrol officer had already verified the license plate, XRS8932, and the VIN number. It was the vehicle they had been looking for.

Gonzales told her that he had bought the car from a woman a couple of weeks earlier in his hometown of Puerto Vallarta on the west coast of Mexico. The woman had told him she wanted to sell it for cash since she did not have a bank account. He had needed a better car for the long drives up to Phoenix, so he had bought it. He said he collected jewelry and handicrafts from local artisans and sold them to hotels and tourist shops in that area and up here in Arizona. His contact in Phoenix was Emilia Flores, who owned the Artistas Mexicanas shop downtown. She would vouch for him since they had done business together for three years. He said he was still driving the car with the Arizona plates because his registration had not been finalized in Mexico. He had a temporary license in the window to prove he was telling the truth.

What caught Sanchez's interest when she read over the title for the car was that the woman who sold it to him was named Sarah Brown, not Sarah Parker. Gonzales showed Sanchez a photocopy of the woman's driver's license he had made at the time of sale. The license photo was Parker, all right. He said she also had showed him a marriage certificate from Puerto Vallarta to show that she had married a man named Brown, explaining the change in her last name. Gonzales didn't have a copy of that document, and he began to fret that maybe he should have made one.

Sanchez told Gonzales that his ownership of the car was not in question; she needed to locate the woman who had sold it to him. She asked if he knew where she could find Parker. He said all he knew was that she was then staying at a small hotel called The Iguana Verde in Vallarta.

Sanchez sat with Gonzales for fifteen minutes, getting his contact information and any other help he could provide on the woman's location. Then they both left to go their separate ways. Sanchez and Montero got in his truck and headed back to Phoenix.

"Lori, you handled that very well. You treated Gonzales like a human being. Cops have a bad rap for treating everyone, even witnesses, like criminals."

"Well, thank you, Guillermo. I appreciate a compliment once in a while. I can use your support. Just before I left the station, the captain reamed me a new one for renewing the BOLO. He said it wasn't my case, so I should keep out of it." She made a face to show her reaction to her boss. "I think we now know where Brown and Parker have been hiding since October—in Mexico. That's why we didn't have any hits on their credit cards. They were out of the country. It doesn't explain the weekly phone calls, but they could have been made to a burner phone in Mexico."

Montero agreed. He traded the Sanz CD for Paulina Rubio's new one, and "Me Gustas Tanto" blasted from the speakers. Sanchez gave him the thumbs-up.

"That would explain a lot," he said. "But what do you think of her getting married and the name change? It's too bad Gonzales didn't have a copy of the marriage certificate. It would more or less prove that Allister wasn't murdered last June and that he was still alive and living in Mexico. I wonder when they got married."

"Gonzales said he couldn't remember the exact date but was pretty sure it was a few months ago. They got married in Puerto Vallarta. He looked to see if the certificate was real. He recognized the city administration's seal on the paper. We have something we can use to follow up now. If we go there, we can perhaps find her. And, hopefully, Brown as well."

"Can you get your boss to let you go down there? Would he want to find Parker?"

"I don't know. It's a closed case, so he may not want to do anything. All I can do is try to convince him. Wish me luck." She turned away and looked out the window at the passing desert landscape.

"Good luck. But if I know you, you'll find a way to make things happen even if you can't go down to Puerto Vallarta yourself. Am I right?"

"Don't worry. If I can't go, I'll at least find out what happened. I've got a backup plan."

Chapter 11

April 20, 2014

The son of a bitch turned me down! He won't let me go down to Puerto Vallarta to find Parker! How in the hell can I figure out what happened if I can't follow my leads?" Sanchez was on a rampage, stomping around Montero's back patio in the evening light and letting off steam she had held in all day.

"You know, Lori, when I first met you, you didn't talk like this. If you swore, you would say, 'Excuse me, Father,' or 'I'm sorry, Father.' Now you let it fly like a sailor on shore leave." Montero's disappointment showed in both his tone of voice and the concerned expression on his face. "You have to burn off this anger."

"What do you think I'm doing right now?" She stopped pacing and turned to face him with her free arm raised in an isn't-it-obvious gesture.

"And accept that things just didn't go your way."

"Oh shit. I mean . . . I'm sorry. I really am, Guillermo. I don't mean to swear so much. But it just burns me up to have a good lead and not be able to do anything about it. Captain said I'm only on partial duty until I'm fully recovered. So I can't travel, to Mexico or anywhere else. I can't really go into the field on active duty yet." She kicked a rock with her right foot in anger. "It's just very, very frustrating."

"Well, he has a good point there. You're not fit to defend yourself yet. And in Mexico, even working with the local police, you would need to be fit enough to do that. Who knows what you could walk into? And it's not your jurisdiction. So don't be mad at him for that, OK?"

Montero led Sanchez to a chair and convinced her to sit down. "Did you ask about contacting the local authorities to follow up on the marriage certificate and the hotel Parker stayed in? They can do a lot of the legwork for you—if they're asked nicely."

He had caught her attention and raised his eyebrows. Montero had some experience in working on cross-border cases from his time on the El Paso PD. He looked at Sanchez to see if she had worked that out yet. He thought that she looked very tired and distraught today. She had recovered physically quite a bit since she had been shot. But she complained of not sleeping well and being tired all the time. Montero knew that these were signs of stress brought on by the shooting, and they were normal. But the wrinkles on her brow and the stress in her voice made him concerned that she was not getting over the psychological shock as fast as she should have been. If she was having bad dreams, it was a sign that PTSD might be around the corner.

"Say, Lori? You know, since I've known you, I don't think you've talked about going on a date. Is there anyone special in your life?"

Sanchez snapped her head up in surprise.

"We never talk about stuff like that, so I just wondered."

She looked right at Montero and said, "You must have gotten that from my mother. She's always asking me if I ever meet anyone interesting. Oh Guillermo, that is too much." She began to laugh loudly and pointed at him. "My God, she got to you, didn't she? What did she say? Did she ask you about my dating life when I was in the hospital?" She stared at the priest with her mouth open as she held back her amusement. Montero stood there and smiled. He had finally found her funny bone. He had not seen her laugh for weeks as she had tried to recover, and it was good to see her laugh. She needed to lighten up a bit and ease herself into department work again.

"Guillermo, women my age and in my job don't date. We're too busy building our careers. Anyway, I haven't met many men who interest me lately. I meet lots of bad men—criminals, perpetrators, and losers—so my selection of dating material is rather limited. So if you run into my mother anytime soon, you can tell her that. Besides, I have a few good friends to keep me out of trouble."

She went over to Montero and patted his shoulder. "Look, I know that you're worried about me, and I appreciate your concern, OK? I'll get better. Thanks for cheering me up. I really need that lately. You help me a lot. Just don't go setting me up with any nice single guys. Tell my mom that too."

She stepped away a little and changed the subject. "Now, how about some dinner? We can whip up some tacos here, or we can go out for the special at Salvador's. Roast chicken tonight, I think."

They spent dinner talking about her strategy to have the Puerto Vallarta police look into Parker's location. Montero reminded her to approach the subject gently because it could reopen the Simpson case, depending on what she found out about Parker and Brown. And that could have serious implications, especially since it had been the high-profile case that had gotten the DA elected last year. He would not want people to know that he may have convicted and executed an innocent man. And the police chief would not want his department to appear as if it had screwed up the investigation. The stakes had risen as Sanchez and Montero worked out a plan.

***

Sanchez went to the station the next day and made a number of phone calls to learn the most effective way for her to elicit the assistance of the Puerto Vallarta police force, called *la Policía Turística* or the tourist police. They were the ones who interacted with foreign visitors in the city. There were other police forces, but the tourist police were the point of contact that made the most sense to handle a missing-persons case.

She made a few calls to see how often they had worked with American agencies and found them quite willing to help her if they could. It required the right type of authorization. However, the formal channels might require three or four months to navigate.

Sanchez inquired further of a detective on the Phoenix PD who had worked with Mexican city cops before, and he said she should not open an official investigation between the two departments because of the politics involved. Instead, he suggested that she find someone on the Puerto Vallarta police force with a connection to Phoenix. He advised that it would be better to make an informal request for help since no Mexican laws were likely broken, and she was only requesting information that was largely public. She asked around and was surprised to find that there was an officer on the Phoenix PD who had a cousin in the Puerto Vallarta tourist police. He would be happy to talk to his cousin when she was ready to launch an inquiry.

Sanchez arranged a meeting with her boss, Captain Bill Teller, and told him she could gain a lot of information if she could contact the Puerto Vallarta police and make an unofficial request. If it was done in a low-key manner, the odds of gaining cooperation were good.

He listened and complimented her on her legwork. He told her she could make the initial contact and see where that took her. By now, he too had become curious about what had happened to the Parker woman. But he said he had no funds for her to make a trip down there, no matter what she found out. He required her to run any news she learned by him right away since the results could be politically sensitive. He emphasized the latter point.

Sanchez got things started by having the local cop call his cousin in Puerto Vallarta, Officer Juan Hermoso. Once he explained things to his relative, Sanchez made contact, and Hermoso was very helpful. Within two days, he emailed a copy of the marriage certificate to her.

She asked him to see if a woman named Sarah Parker or Sarah Brown was registered at the Iguana Verde on the waterfront. Hermoso said there was no one there by that name, but a woman fitting the description that Sanchez had sent him had been there recently.

Sanchez examined the certificate and discovered several pieces of useful information. First of all, the names on the license were Allister Brown and Sarah Parker. They were married on October 12, 2013. That matched the timing of the Simpson trial and was just two days after the last phone call between Simpson and Brown on October tenth. The two lovebirds had given a temporary address of a boarding house in the nearby town of San Francisco. That was apparently where they were staying at the time. She decided to ask Hermoso whether he could find out if the couple was still there.

He came back with the fact that the town was in another state of the country—Nayarit, not Jalisco, where Puerto Vallarta was located. He had no authority there. But he did make a phone call to the boarding house. The manager remembered the couple but said they had left last year.

Otherwise, Hermoso could do no more.

Sanchez sat at her desk and contemplated the new information. Now she knew where Brown and Parker had gone to wait out the murder investigation and the trial. She had proof that Brown was not murdered in June of last year, and therefore, Simpson was innocent. Most of all, she finally had proof that she had been right all along, not a traitor to the department or the DA, but correct in her assumption that the Brown murder scene was a setup.

But where were they now? The only way to continue her quest for the truth was to follow up on their trail in Puerto Vallarta. She had to get to the bottom of the mystery. If she couldn't travel to Mexico herself, then she would need to implement her backup plan.

She keyed in Montero's number.

***

Sanchez arranged to meet with the CI in her drug case the next day, just after lunch, when there would be less traffic and fewer prying eyes, if that was possible. They met at the Tacorita on Baseline Road. She had her friend Maria Sandoval, an undercover cop, eating a burrito at the counter. Sandoval was her backup if anything went south.

The CI appeared right after Sanchez found a seat in the red vinyl booth at the back of the restaurant. He had a ball cap pulled low over his face. He slid into the other side of the booth and looked up at Sanchez. He had a huge welt on the left side of his face like he had either been punched really hard or he had fallen flat on his face from drinking. Sanchez guessed it was the latter.

She spoke in Spanish. "You look like hell, Eduardo. What did you do now? Fall off a bar stool?"

"I don't remember what happened, but it still hurts like hell," he replied in Spanish. "Did you bring the money?"

"I have some money, but you have to earn it first. You know that."

"Sanchez, you're a real bitch. You know that? The way you shot up those cartel shits is going to come back on you someday. Someday soon. You need to be careful. Those people have long memories. They strike back. They'll find out it was you and come after you."

"Thanks for the warning, but I can handle myself." Sanchez smirked at him, perhaps seeming too confident.

"Not against these guys. They'll stop at nothing. You, your family. Just look out." He put a hand on her wrist as he said this.

She pulled her hand away. "Well, let's get down to business. What do you have for me?"

"I got more about the Westside guys and what they got going with the cartel. They wanna be the main action in Phoenix for speed and marijuana. Other drugs too on the south and west sides. They been recruiting from other gangs to get their numbers up for the deal. They pulled a lot of *la raza* from other gangs in town. The cartel is in on it. They're providing a lot of hardware from somewhere. It's like *Fast and Furious* in reverse, guns coming up from the south."

"How many guns? What kind are they moving?"

"I seen some AKs is all, but I think they were full auto. Handguns and ammo. That's what I seen. I didn't want to ask too much."

"Are the guns here already, or are they still moving some?"

"Some're coming up each week. Not so many each time. They come with the product trips. You know, with the drug shipments. Maybe some are separate. I don't know more."

"And what else do you have?"

"I got people dealing at the high school. You know, the fancy one: Carl Hayden. One student there is the main salesman in the school. I got his name too, for the right money."

"Eduardo, you know how it works." Sanchez spoke sternly and gave him a hard stare. "You tell me what you got, and I decide how much it's worth. OK? This is pretty good info, and I owe you for last time. But I'm keeping some back because I think you knew there would be trouble last time we met. Did you?"

"I didn't know nothing. But when I saw those guys, I had to leave quick!" Then he leaned forward. "Why did you shoot my friend in the *cojones?* Everyone's afraid of the woman cop who shoots too low for comfort. You know?" Eduardo laughed uncontrollably for a minute, then realized a few people were looking at him.

"What do people in the gang think happened? Do they know it was me, a cop?"

"Yes. They know it was a cop from the TV news." He snickered. "But you? No. No one saw who you were, just a *chica* trying to buy some crack or something. The big blond cop got there real fast, so they thought he shot everyone. Only my friend knows it's you, and he's in the hospital at Florence or somewhere. No one knows where."

"OK. Let's have the names. Gang members first."

Sanchez wrote down the list of four names—three gangbangers and one student. Then she slid a pack of bills across the table to Eduardo, more than usual, and thanked him for keeping her name out of the shooting as far as the gang knew. Eduardo noticed the bonus and nodded.

"Eduardo, you did good. See if you can find out when the next guns are coming, OK? Keep in touch."

They parted company, and Sanchez paid the check. She went outside and walked down the street and around the corner to where Bordou was waiting for her in an unmarked car. She slid in on the passenger side while they waited for Sandoval to disengage. "They haven't made me for the shooting yet," Sanchez said. "But Eduardo may need watching—in case they find out he knows who was involved."

Sandoval climbed in the back seat, and they pulled out. "So?" Bordou asked. "A burger and a beer at Jimmy's?"

Both women nodded.

Chapter 12

April 26, 2014—Puerto Vallarta, Mexico

Montero walked over to the large outdoor sculpture and stared in amazement. It was a bronze statuary scene with bizarre, life-size man-creatures dressed in flowing robes climbing a tall ladder that led skyward to some unseen heaven. Tourists were posing for photographs next to one of the bronze characters, and children were playing tag around the base of the sculpture. This was just one of many interesting attractions along the walking street, called the Malecón, in Puerto Vallarta. It ran the length of the downtown shopping district and led to the central square where the cathedral, the Church of Our Lady of Guadalupe, rose to dominate the area. The whole town was located on the seashore of the Bay of Banderas, a huge ocean embayment on the Pacific coast, miles across. It was a beautiful town. *No wonder so many tourists flock here for vacation*, he thought.

Montero walked toward the square where the *Policía Turística* had their town office. He was wearing blue jeans and a plain light-blue short-sleeved shirt with his clerical collar attached. He wasn't sure if the collar was appropriate, but he was comfortable wearing it. He was going to meet Officer Juan Hermoso to follow up on his findings regarding Parker.

When it was clear that Sanchez would not be allowed to make the trip, she had talked Montero into taking a few days of vacation to come down and see what he could find out. This was the Sanchez 'backup plan' in action—for him to make the trip. It was OK by him. It was important to him to discover what had really happened to Brown and Parker.

He had been to Puerto Vallarta—or PV, as the tourists called it—when he was a young man. He found it to be one of the truly great resort towns of Mexico with a combination of art, food, culture, and people that was hard to find anywhere else in the country. And the fishing was exceptional in the right season.

Hermoso was a friendly man with a huge smile that seemed to be a permanent feature of his personality. He was in his mid-thirties and had several years of policing experience under his belt. His facility with English and his pleasant demeanor made him a natural choice to head the department when the city had decided to revamp its tourist police force. He was the type of man the mayor wanted to interface with the many *Americanos* who frequented the city.

Montero liked Hermoso right away, and he suggested they begin their meeting by eating lunch together—a good way to develop a personal bond.

The two men walked two blocks to a restaurant situated above a row of artisan shops near the market. They sat on a balcony overlooking the River Cuale, where the sea breeze cooled them as they each drank a beer and ate a simple meal of Dorado fish.

"So you say this Parker woman has been missing for the better part of a year?" Hermoso asked, speaking Spanish with a local flair.

"Yes, that's right."

"Well, based on what I've found out, she must have lived up the coast in San Francisco much of last year. At least, until she got married here in Vallarta. I don't know where she went after that. It appears she lived here in the city for two or three weeks about the time she sold the car to Mr. Gonzales. But I haven't been able to learn more."

Montero had already heard this much over the phone when he and Hermoso had set up his visit. "But so far, you have no real information about where Allister Brown has been during this time, correct? Except that they were both at the boarding house up the coast. I wonder where he has been and where they are now."

"Yes, that's the big question, is it not? I can't go up to San Francisco to investigate further unless there's something that becomes a matter of police business. Understand?" Montero nodded his head. "But you are free to drive up there, of course. It's a short drive, maybe half an hour, or a little more. The people there are quite friendly and should be able to help you. They do not have any police there because it's a small town. They have no real crime, although I've heard that one of the drug gangs is beginning to work that area, like many towns that are popular with tourists. The gang mostly sells drugs to tourists and doesn't move large shipments through there, so it is safe. You understand? There is little need for police work there."

"Yes, I understand you. I think I'll drive up there this afternoon. I already checked into my hotel, The Iguana Verde."

Hermoso raised his eyebrows.

"Yes, the same one. It's nice enough and is within walking distance of the Malecón. I will have to rent a car next. Do you know where I can get a reasonable deal? I'm here on my own dime, so I need a bargain."

"My friend, you are in luck," Hermoso said. "It happens that I have a cousin who is in the car rental business. I assumed you would need a car for a day or two, so I told him you were coming. If you like, I can walk you over to his office, just to be sure he gives you his best price. Then when you come back to Vallarta, we can meet again to discuss what you have learned. This is good?"

***

The drive to San Francisco was pleasant and sunny. Montero drove up the coast road to Nuevo Vallarta, where much of the new resort development was taking place, and beyond into verdant farmland and small villages. He arrived in the unassuming town of San Francisco by three in the afternoon. He drove around to get a feel for the place. San Francisco was located on the beach, but it had originally been built as a traditional town, not as a tourist destination, so much of it was laid out in blocks running from the main square located several blocks from the sea. This was an advantage during tropical storms, when the waves coming from the open sea could be dramatic. Even on normal days, the waves were high and steady, which explained why it had become a hot spot for surfers from the States.

Montero asked a man on the street where the boarding house, La Casita, was located. When he pulled up in front of it, he found it was a wood-frame family home with a few small bedrooms added for guests. It was painted in bright green with white trim and looked like it had seen better days. Two huge scarlet bougainvillea shrubs added a burst of perfume and a splash of color on each side of the front porch.

The manager of the guesthouse was Señora Rosa, a tiny, kindly woman with ancient skin, the result of many days spent in the sun. Montero had no way of telling how old she was, guessing she could be sixty or eighty, depending on what she had done in her long life. She was a kind and passionate soul with a bright mind beneath her braided white mane. She had good teeth that she displayed often as they talked. The señora invited him into her living room to sit in front of an electric fan that was spinning vigorously, but nonetheless, it was still stifling in the room. She brought him iced tea, and they settled in to talk in her native Spanish.

"This man and woman, this Allister Brown and Sarah Parker, they were very nice. They argued sometimes, but what couple does not have some troubles? They were here for two or three weeks, or maybe a little more. They came in October. I have the register book here because I knew you would want to know the dates . . . . Let's see. Yes, they arrived on October twelfth, and she checked out on October thirtieth. I remember her checkout date because it was the day before the Day of the Dead celebration. She did not want to be here for that day. You can understand."

Montero nodded his head. "Did she give you any idea where she was going? Did she go to Puerto Vallarta?"

"Yes, I think she did. She went to Vallarta to be somewhere happy. The Day of the Dead is celebrated there with parades and parties. It celebrates the lives of the dead, this holiday. Did you know? You do not celebrate it the same way in your country. There it is about the devil and scary things for children, yes?"

"Yes, it is true. We do not have Halloween as a holiday to celebrate the spirits of our dead relatives like you do. With us, it's all about scary costumes. I grew up in New Mexico, so I was aware of the holiday, but most Americans do not understand its significance."

"So I wonder why you have come here to find this couple. They seemed like nice people. Have they done something wrong? Are they in trouble with the law?"

"It's complicated. They are witnesses in a missing-persons case in Phoenix, Arizona. Mr. Brown was expected to testify at a trial, but the police could not find him in time to testify. Now there are still questions about the missing person."

"And why is a priest involved? Why you? Did you know this man?"

"No, I never met him. But I knew his friend very well. His

friend went to prison because they could not find this man Brown." Montero tried to simplify the legal aspects of his search as best he could—a difficult thing to do in a short conversation.

"When was the trial? Why couldn't they have him travel from here to the trial? I don't understand."

"Because he was here, and no one knew that. His friend was relying on him to come to the trial, but he did not come or let the court know he was down here the whole time."

"When was the trial, then? Maybe he sent a message and it was lost."

"The trial went from October fifth to October twentieth."

"Oh, I see. But that was about the time of the accident. Let me look . . . yes, I wrote it down here in the register because it was so tragic. It happened on October fourteenth, right before that poor girl was killed. She was found dead on the beach on October twentieth, just a mile or so from here where the forest comes down to the edge of the sea. It was a big mystery—what happened to her—because that sort of thing never happens in this area."

"Wait!" Montero sat up straight, nearly spilling his iced tea. "A young woman died here? How did she die? Did the police investigate?"

"*Sí, sí.* At first, the police thought she had drowned while swimming in the sea. There had been a storm, and the waves were rough at that time. They ruled it an accident at first because of that."

"What can you tell me about her?" Montero asked.

"She was camping alone, a foolish thing for a woman to do anywhere, I think. But she had been camped there for more than a week. I met her once by accident. She was with Allister Brown by the beach, and they were talking very quietly by themselves.

And more than that, I think. I did not think it was right for him to be there with her like that. But I am an old woman. What do I know of what young people do these days?"

"You mean that Allister knew the woman?"

"Well, they knew each other quite well, I think. That might be why Miss Sarah had an argument with him the next day. She was very angry about him doing things. I could not understand all of what she said, but she was very loud when she was angry. It was something about a woman."

"What was the woman's name? Do you remember?"

"No, I don't remember, not now. It was months ago. But you could ask Señor Muñoz in the village. He writes a local newspaper for our community, and he wrote an article about it when it happened. You should see him before you go. He has an office in the big blue building by the square. He can tell you about these things."

Montero got up from his chair, preparing to leave. "Oh, one last thing. Did Parker still have her blue Honda Accord when she was here? She sold it in Vallarta a number of weeks ago."

"So she went to Vallarta after all? Yes, she drove away from here in it."

"Thank you for your kindness, señora. You have been most helpful."

Montero saw that it was already after four o'clock, but he thought he might get lucky and still catch Muñoz in his office. He got in his car and drove the few blocks to the town plaza, with its dozens of huge shade trees and a few old men sitting on park benches in the trees' umbra, talking and playing cards.

He parked on one side of the plaza and walked across it, passing a dozen young children who were playing in the water fountain at the center of the square. They were splashing one

another across the fountain, laughing wildly and sloshing water
everywhere. An old woman who tended the children looked up at
him as he went by. He smiled at her and said, *"Buenas tardes,"*
causing her to smile back at him. He continued on to the street
where the blue office building stood brightly in the afternoon
sun. He climbed up its concrete stairs, also painted blue, but
worn down by many feet over the years.

He knocked on the door of a small office bearing Muñoz's
name, to no effect. He looked in a dusty window beside the door
to see if anyone was about but only saw a few empty chairs, a
table, and an antique wooden desk, the kind with many small
drawers and vertical slots where one could stuff notes to sort
them by topic. The slots were overflowing with notes from many
years of scribbling, the collected memory of a scholar named
Muñoz. Montero wrote a note and tucked it in a crack at the edge
of the door. Then he went downstairs to have a cool lemonade at
the quaint café next door. He made notes about what he had
learned from Rosa.

A short time later, a man came up to him and asked if he
was Father Montero. The man was tall, thin, and looked quite
distinguished in his light suit coat. A twinkle in his eye signaled
an intelligence that came from years of observing the world and
the strange creatures inhabiting it, especially the human variety.
He looked Montero over, observing his initial reactions and
perhaps came to the conclusion that he would like this priest. He
smiled and presented a frail hand in greeting.

"Yes, señor. I am Guillermo Montero." He saw his note in
the man's hand and stood up to greet him. "And you must be
Señor Muñoz. Please sit down. Would you like some lemonade?"

Muñoz took off his jacket, folded it over the back of a spare
chair, and sat on the chair across from Montero. He ordered a

Tecate beer. "I prefer a cold beer at this time of day. Life is too short to drink lemonade when what you really desire is a beer." He smiled at the thought. "How are you? I see from your note that you have talked to Señora Rosa about the death of the young tourist last year." He held up Montero's note. "What can I help you with, Father?"

Montero absorbed Muñoz's well-spoken Spanish, evidence of a university education. "Señora Rosa told me there was a young woman who drowned in October. She also said that you wrote an article about it. Is that true?"

"Yes. I wrote two articles, actually. I publish a gazette for the town, which covers happenings on this side of the peninsula. It is only a few pages every week, but it is the only paper we have, and I list events, sales, birthdays, and important news for our local people. I only print a hundred copies because most people pass the paper on for others to see. I am retired and find it keeps me busy as well as connected to people in the community. But you didn't come all the way to San Francisco to hear me ramble about my paper, did you?" Montero waited patiently for Muñoz to continue. "I'll make copies of those two articles for you."

"Would you mind summarizing them for me now? If you have the time, that is."

"Father, I have nothing else that I must do just now." He smiled and sipped his beer. "It all began because the woman, an American named Jill Claymore, was camping on the beach near the point on the south end of the bay. She had been there for a week or more before she died. I think she must not have had very much money because she never ate in cafés or rented a room. The townspeople, those who got to know her, were concerned about her camping all by herself. You know, we have some criminals in this area who sell drugs—mostly to tourists, if

you believe the local people, but also to some of us here."
He looked at Montero to see his reaction. "She was found one
day by a tourist who had walked around the point to try the surf.
She had washed up on the beach, having apparently drowned. The
police were summoned and concluded from the marks on her body
that she had, in fact, drowned and been carried up on the beach by
the waves. There are some rocks in the shallows that she must have
been dragged over because her body was badly scratched and
bruised. They sent her body to the coroner in Tepic."

"Tepic," Montero said thoughtfully.

"It is the seat of government for the state of Nayarit."

"But Puerto Vallarta is closer."

The old man eyed Montero. "You do not yet know the
geography of this part of Mexico or the Byzantine nature of the
government bureaucracy that both serves and burdens our people."

"It sounds complicated."

"Yes, it is. But here we are in Nayarit, State and Vallarta is in
Jalisco State. Even though Vallarta is closer, it is part of a
different government system." He sipped his beer, immensely
enjoying it. "Anyway, after a few days, the coroner released a
report that the woman had not drowned; she was smothered. No
seawater in her lungs. So someone threw her body into the sea
after smothering her with a pillow or something like that. They
could not tell much else because she had been dragged over the
rocks and was in the seawater for some time. The police never
discovered who might have done it."

"I suppose after that much time it would be difficult to tell
much because any evidence of a crime would be destroyed."

"Yes. And we had the big storms again after she was found, so
her campsite was nearly washed away. There was little the police
could do. There were a few locals who had seen her with various

people, but no one seemed to have a motive. They located her parents in California somewhere and sent her body to them."

"So that was that," Montero said. "I understand the woman knew Allister Brown. At least, that is what Señora Rosa told me. She had seen them together once in the village."

"She told me about that. Miss Claymore had a few male admirers, and apparently, he was one of them. One day, I was in the cantina the same time he and Sarah Parker were there. I witnessed Miss Parker accusing him of visiting Claymore's camp. He insisted he had only been surfing with her, but she said she didn't believe him and stormed out of the place. She was really angry. Anyway, soon after that, he had the accident."

"What accident?"

"Didn't Rosa tell you? I assumed you knew all about it. About a week before the woman died. Let's see . . . they found her on the twentieth, so the accident was on the fourteenth. Yes, that's when Allister died."

Montero leaped up from his chair, knocking over his glass of lemonade. "What? He's dead? Are you telling me he died in October?" He couldn't believe what he was hearing.

"Yes. It's true. I thought you knew that." Muñoz used a napkin to wipe up some of the spilled lemonade.

"Oh, my Lord! What a shock. I had no idea." Montero sat on his chair and tried to control his emotions. It was a real shock and it overwhelmed his thoughts. *How could this be true?*

"Some other surfers actually saw it happen. Allister Brown died while trying to surf in the big waves made by a storm. He was surfing, riding a really high wave too close to the point, where there are some big rocks. He lost his balance and went down right under the wave. Witnesses said he fell all wrong, head first. His head hit the rocky bottom, and he broke his neck. He supposedly died instantly. The story made it into the Vallarta newspaper. We don't have that many surfing deaths in Mexico. But sometimes tourists attempt waves that are bigger than they can handle, and they can be injured easily. A girl broke her neck down at Sayulita earlier this year too. She was lucky to survive."

"And did the coroner verify that it was an accident?"

"Yes. But there was no question that his was an accidental death because people saw it happen."

"Was his body sent back to the States?"

"No, his wife buried him here. She was very upset and hardly talked to anyone for weeks."

"You're talking about Sarah Parker, right?"

"Yes. But by that time, she was Sarah Brown. They'd gotten married only two days before it happened. It was unfortunate."

Montero sat there without saying anything. He had to take it all in. He pulled out his notes and checked his time line. *If Allister died on October 14, then that would explain why he didn't answer Simpson's last telephone calls from prison. He was dead by that time. That explains a lot of things.* Then he said, "I don't know what to say. I came down here expecting to find Allister Brown alive. I had no idea he was dead. Maybe I should go and look at his grave just to be thorough about it. Is the cemetery near here?"

"Certainly, my friend. I did not know that you were unaware. We can walk there from here in five minutes if you like. Just follow me."

They walked three city blocks to a churchyard and the small cemetery behind it. They sauntered to the rear of the cemetery where there were newer-looking headstones, and Muñoz stopped in front of one with a sloping face. "Mrs. Brown wanted a headstone but did not have much money, so she bought this one."

Montero looked down at what could only be called a

pauper's grave, it was so humble. The stone read, "Allister Brown, 1987–2013." He knelt down and bowed his head to say a prayer for the man he had never met. They paused there in silence for several minutes, and then Montero decided he had to take a photo of the grave and the headstone. Sanchez would want it as documentation.

"His death would be recorded in Tepic? The state capital?"

"Yes, it has to be. Is it important?"

"I think I will need to go there to verify all of this for the people that I am working with. Is that a long drive from here?"

"Yes, about two hours if there are no trucks on the road. The offices already will be closed by the time you get there. But you could call and ask to have the certificate sent to you. It would be slow but much simpler for you."

"Let's walk back to your office. I need to get copies of your articles if you will make them for me, and then I should get back to Vallarta. Maybe I can drive up to Tepic tomorrow."

"Yes. That would be sensible. And if you are looking for company on that drive . . . ." Muñoz kindly looked at Montero. "I have a small errand that I could do in Tepic. You know, you have to take this same road tomorrow too."

Montero brightened. "That's an excellent idea. I would love the company. And you would, no doubt, know your way around the city better than me anyway."

They returned to Muñoz's office, and he made copies of the articles, plus of a local map. They agreed on a time to meet the next day.

Montero was driving back to his hotel in Puerto Vallarta to clean up for dinner when he received a call from Hermoso that he would not be able to meet him that night because of a family emergency. He said he would explain tomorrow, and they would definitely have dinner then, possibly at his house, if his wife agreed. Montero took a shower and decided to eat in the hotel restaurant because he was feeling tired from the day's travels and discussions.

He tried to call Sanchez to tell her his findings about Brown's death, but she did not answer. He left a message, giving her a brief summary of the news. He fell asleep while waiting for her to return his call.

Chapter 13

April 27, 2014—Puerto Vallarta, Mexico

Montero received Sanchez's call in the morning.

"Allister Brown is dead! I was shocked at the news," he said. "To die in an accident just two days after being married is terrible luck."

"I'm more than shocked," Sanchez said. "I don't understand how it could happen. In your message last night, you said it was a surfing accident of some kind?"

"That's what I was told. He went out to catch a wave, and it was too big for him. He got too far ahead of the curl and plunged head first into the beach, broke his neck. There was nothing anyone could do. They said he shouldn't have tried such big waves. Señor Muñoz said there were a few witnesses, so there's no question that it was an accident."

"Talk about shitty luck. But you said there was another girl killed there in San Francisco, right?"

"Yes, she was smothered, according to Señor Muñoz, and then thrown into the sea. The police have no idea who could have done that."

"Wow. So much for my image of a sleepy little fishing village." She was surprised.

"It's a nice little town. I'd come here on vacation if I could, but I'd try fishing, not surfing. The waves are too big."

Sanchez was silent for a few moments and then asked. "Any

indication that Brown or Parker was involved in her death?"

"I have no idea. Apparently, there was little evidence to work with, and no one had anything against the girl, except maybe Parker since she argued with Allister about Claymore. The police ruled her out as a suspect."

"Did you follow up with the police? Do they have any leads?"

"Yes and no," Montero said. "The detective I spoke with said it was a closed case. There was too little evidence to work with. I'm driving up to the state capital, Tepic, this morning to get copies of the death certificates for both people."

"Can you get a copy of the coroner's report for Brown?" Sanchez asked. "Otherwise, we may have to go through official channels, and you know what that means."

"OK, I'll try."

"But Guillermo, I don't understand." Sanchez said. "If Brown was dead and Parker was in shock, I still don't see why she didn't call in to let Simpson know about it. She could have saved him at the trial."

"That troubles me too, Lori." He said. "Even if she was in shock . . . . Well, later she could have saved his life."

Montero then called Officer Hermoso to set up their dinner plans. Hermoso said that he should come over to his house for dinner. His wife would cook seafood from the bay, and they could talk after the meal. They set the time for 7:30 p.m. to be sure he was back from Tepic with time to spare. That settled, Montero drove to San Francisco to pick up Muñoz, and they continued on to Tepic.

They arrived in the ancient, bustling city at 11:00 a.m. and went to the state records office straight away. Montero was frustrated because they had to wait in line for nearly an hour in the hot, airless corridor only to find out that death certificates were not available in that office but in the auxiliary records office located across town. By the time they reached that office, it was closed for lunch, so they ate a nice meal at a nearby café. Muñoz left Montero at the café to run his errand, promising to meet him at the coroner's office at 3:00 p.m.

When the office opened at two o'clock in the afternoon, Montero placed an order for copies of both death certificates and waited. At three o'clock, he received the copies and raced on foot over to the coroner's office just as the clerk was ready to leave for the day.

Montero explained what he needed, but the clerk told him that it was impossible: the office had closed at three, and besides, Montero would have to fill out the proper forms before they could release an autopsy report. It would be better to have a police department or another government office request the report because they were considered for official government use only. The clerk handed him seven forms and pointed out which ones needed signatures and how many copies of each would be required. Montero asked if he could fill them out right then and have the clerk retrieve the report anyway.

"No, señor. It does not work that way."

Muñoz arrived at that point and asked the clerk if there was any way he could persuade him to stay open a few minutes longer. Then he took Montero aside and asked him how badly he wanted the reports. Then he privately talked to the clerk for a few minutes, and the man became very nervous. He told the two visitors that they should wait a few minutes outside the building.

Montero wondered why they were waiting, but before long, the clerk appeared at the door. He opened it a few inches and put out his hand as if to shake hands with Muñoz. Muñoz passed a small packet to the clerk; the clerk passed him a large manila envelope.

The door closed, and Muñoz said, "Let's get out of here."

When they got to the car, Muñoz handed the manila envelope to Montero. Inside were copies of the two coroner reports. "You owe me five hundred pesos," Muñoz said. "That is about forty US dollars. Oh, and you can buy me a beer when we reach San Francisco." He smiled and added, "My friend, no one fills out all the forms the clerks want if they don't have to. It is much simpler to do the man a favor, and he will do you one in return." He laughed at Montero's expression.

Montero joined in the laughter when he realized what Muñoz had done. The bribe was well worth the money. They had a beer when they got to San Francisco and read the reports. Then Montero drove on toward Puerto Vallarta.

When Montero was about twenty minutes outside of Puerto Vallarta, his cell phone rang. It was a very excited Hermoso on the line. "Father Montero, I have very good news for you. We have found your Sarah Parker. I had my men search for her in recent police reports, and I passed around a copy of the photo you gave me. We got lucky. I will meet you at the hotel and pick you up."

True to his word, Hermoso was waiting in his patrol car at the hotel when Montero pulled up. They sped off toward the outskirts of town and pulled into the parking lot of a large hospital. Montero asked if Parker had been injured, and Hermoso said yes. They rushed to the elevator, and Hermoso pressed the basement button. Montero began to suspect what was about to happen.

When they walked down the corridor to the door marked *Depósito de Cadáveres*, Montero stopped Hermoso outside the door. "You mean to tell me you found her and she's dead?"

"*Sí*. It was a surprise to me also. One of our clerks found her record in the computer. She died only two weeks ago, and her body has not yet been claimed or disposed of. So we are in luck to still have the body to work with."

Montero stood dead still in the corridor and stared at Hermoso. Hermoso realized that this information might be a shock for Montero. "What? You do not look happy, my friend."

"Well, I wanted to ask her some questions." Montero sighed. "And I feel sorry to hear when anyone has died. How did this happen?"

"First, let us enter the morgue and sign in. Then we will look at the file and identification papers. We will be able to view the body after that."

They entered the anteroom, showed identification, and signed in. They then took the coroner's file and sat at a table on one side of the room. The file contained a police report on how her body had been found and information about the death scene.

Hermoso summarized the findings for Montero. Parker had died in a drowning accident on April eighth. She had allegedly fallen from the rocks along the steep ground south of Playa de los Muertos, a popular beach south of the hotel district on the other side of the river about a kilometer south of where they had had lunch the day before. There were rocks there that some people dove from. The local boys knew where the deep water was, but an inexperienced person could easily hit bottom or the rocks. According to the report, she may have been walking along the footpath above the rocks and just fallen in the dark. Two or three people fell there each year. The city had put up a railing and fence to prevent people from going there, but they just went around the obstacles.

"So did she drown, or did the fall kill her?" Montero asked.

"She apparently hit her head hard enough to knock her out. Then she must have been in the sea for a while because she had some water in her lungs, but not enough to think she was completely underwater."

"What does that mean? Then how did she die?"

"Guillermo, I'm not sure. But it looks like she died from a combination of things. They think that they found her about a day after she had fallen. If someone had found her earlier, who knows? Maybe she could have been saved."

"Seawater does a lot to degrade the evidence," Montero said, "but I see no reason to suspect anything other than what the coroner has found. How about identification? How did they identify her?"

"See for yourself, Father. She was wearing one of those butt packs with all of her identification in it when she fell. Here's her driver's license. She is definitely your woman. It is an Arizona license, and the name on it is Sarah Parker, with a birthdate and address. This looks like the same address you showed me earlier. Here are other papers—a library card, a credit card in her name—and some cash in dollars and pesos. The rest is a city map, cosmetics, and other personal effects. I will have the clerk make photocopies of the papers for you. With this kind of documentation, there can be no mistake about her identity. What do you think, Guillermo?"

"It all looks good. And the time of her death fits with what we know about her selling the car. I wonder where she was staying. Can you check the local hotels to see if they have any missing guests who match her description?"

"Yes. We will do that. But it might surprise you to know how many young tourists do not return to their rooms for a few nights if they meet a person at a bar. You know what I mean. This happens often during spring break, when people are so drunk they even forget where their hotel is. Hotel managers don't know if they have left early or have just found a new party for a few days."

Hermoso closed up the file and went over to talk to the clerk. When he came back, he said they could now go in to see the body.

Hermoso and Montero followed a man in a white lab coat into the examining room, which contained a wall full of locker doors on one side. The man walked to one of the doors, opened it, and pulled out a long traylike drawer that had a covered body on it. Hermoso went to the drawer and pulled back the white covering from the upper portion of the body.

The dead woman looked unusual because her skin color was very different from that of a living person, no matter how pale they were when alive. The body was that of a woman of average height, a light complexion, full lips, and freckles on her cheeks. Her brown hair had been removed and placed at the side of her head, a result of the autopsy. It was hard for Montero to tell her age, but she looked older than her twenty-six years, possibly because of her time in the seawater. Her body was flabby, which caught Montero off guard because he had had an image in his mind of Parker being more fit based on the photo he had seen of her with Brown that had been taken a few years ago.

Hermoso pulled the covering down farther to reveal the rest of her body, something that might have seemed insensitive to most people, but when looking at dead bodies, nothing was private. They saw more signs of her being overweight and scars on her abdomen.

Montero was curious. "What kind of operation did she have to get these scars?"

They called the technician over to ask him, and he went to get the pathologist, who was in the next room doing paperwork. The doctor came in, introduced himself, and offered his help.

They explained their question, and he looked at the body. Then he looked in the file to see what the coroner had to say about it. Then he said simply, "C-sections. She had two children this way some years ago, maybe three and six years. You can see that they were American procedures by the stitching that was done. And they are older because the scar tissue is old."

Montero asked, "As far as you can tell, how old is she?"

The doctor looked at the file again. "This says she is about thirty years old. But looking at her teeth and the elasticity of her skin, I would say a little older than that, maybe thirty-five or thirty-seven. It is difficult to know. What does her driver's license say?"

"Twenty-six," Montero said.

"Really?" The doctor looked at the body again for a few moments. "No, I would argue that she is no younger than thirty-two, probably thirty-five as I said. I will discuss this with the examining physician tomorrow when he comes in to work. Thank you for asking this question. We want to be as accurate as possible on the report." The doctor left the room.

Montero pulled out the more recent driver's license photograph he had of Parker. He held it up to the face of the dead woman and called Hermoso over to look at it. "Juan, take a look at this. I may be crazy, but they aren't the same person."

Hermoso looked back and forth between the woman and the photo several times. "They're close. It is always difficult after the autopsy because the hair is removed. But the eyes don't look right. This woman has darker eyes than in the photo. Eye color does not change after death. Here, you look while I get the doctor again to ask this question."

Montero had the same reservations. The doctor reentered the room and quickly looked at the eyes and the photo. "Yes, they look different, but photos can be off. The license says she had light-brown eyes, and this woman has dark-brown eyes. Maybe there was a mistake when they gave her the license. I do not know." He looked at the technician and asked if the coroner had run fingerprints on the corpse. Then he said to Hermoso, "We will rerun fingerprints in the morning and do a complete ID kit, including teeth and other parameters. We will take it to a higher level to be sure who she is, if that is satisfactory to you gentlemen?"

Hermoso thanked the doctor and walked out of the room with him, leaving Montero with the body. Montero's mind reeled with the possibility that this dead woman had been killed and her death made to look like that of Sarah Parker. *What in the world had happened here?* he thought.

When Hermoso came back, he said that they should go, adding that he would follow up in the morning to make sure the fingerprints were checked.

They left the hospital and drove back to Hermoso's home, where they had a wonderful dinner of lobster and red snapper. Señora Hermoso, Clara, was most gracious and entertaining. But neither of the two men could keep from thinking about the woman in the morgue. After dinner, Montero thanked both of them for their hospitality, and Hermoso drove him to his hotel.

Once in his room, he called Sanchez immediately and downloaded everything he had learned in the last two days. Their telephone call ran late into the night.

Chapter 14

April 28, 2014—Puerto Vallarta, Mexico

Montero waited for thirty minutes in the corridor outside the morgue while Hermoso observed the fingerprinting and ID procedure. Soon, Hermoso told him they had the prints, nearly intact, certainly enough to use to compare with the prints of the real Sarah Parker. He had already asked his captain for permission to contact the Phoenix Police Department for Parker's prints. Hermoso wanted to know if Montero could unofficially get the prints from Sanchez. "It would save us a great deal of time," he said.

"Oh, I see," Montero replied. "Yes, I think we can make that happen. Do you have the prints on a file so I can email them to her? I can call and ask what format is needed."

Montero dialed Sanchez and reached her quickly. She said he could email her the fingerprints as a JPG file. Then he told Hermoso, "Yes, we can do that. Give me the file to send, and she'll take it to the forensics department to make the comparison. She said they certainly have the right thumbprint on file because Parker had that taken when she got her license to drive a multipassenger vehicle, probably for school outings. She's checking other databases that might have Parker's complete set of prints." Montero sent the file off to Sanchez shortly after that.

Montero suggested that he and Hermoso should go to the site where the woman's body had been recovered to look for additional evidence. He knew it was unlikely they would find anything because it had been two weeks since her death. They did so to be thorough, but found nothing useful.

In the meantime, the tourist police forensics team dusted all the contents of the woman's purse for fingerprints. They didn't find a single one, not even one from the dead woman. They couldn't explain it.

Montero and Hermoso returned to Hermoso's office a few hours later. His men had begun the search for any hotels or guesthouses where any guests had gone missing two weeks before. So far, there were no hits. Two places reported rooms that had been vacated about that time with no personal effects left behind. But that was at the peak of spring break, and many, many people had been in the city at that time.

Hermoso suggested that they might find out who the dead woman was by comparing manifests for incoming and outgoing flights from Puerto Vallarta. He sent an officer to collect the flight information, but with twenty-three airlines and nearly seven thousand passengers flying in and out of the area on an average day, it would take several days to go through the records.

At 2:00 p.m., Sanchez called Montero to say that the single print of Parker's thumb did not match the dead woman's print. She had asked the department forensics staff to try for a match with national databases, and so far, that had returned no hits.

"Guillermo, it's possible her fingerprints aren't on record anywhere," Sanchez said. "She may not be in the databases at all. We are also specifically checking with the Berkeley PD to see if they happened to get her fingerprints when they were questioning her about the missing persons there. Detective Louis Carter said they had no reason to take her prints, but he would check out other avenues as soon as possible. He's in court today, so his time is limited."

Montero relayed the information to Hermoso, and they broke for a late lunch at a small café near Hermoso's office. They sipped their beers as they ordered roast chicken.

"Father Montero, this is very disturbing to me. If that woman is not Sarah Brown, then we have what looks like a murder on our hands. How else can we explain the fact that the identification papers were planted on the corpse?"

"And how do you place the evidence with a body after it falls into the water?" Montero asked. "Someone planted the evidence first and then pushed the woman off the cliff."

"So it appears. But why are there no prints on any of the articles in her purse? That seems peculiar, doesn't it?" Hermoso hit the table with his open hand and shook his head.

"My friend, that is the one thing that is bothering me." Montero waved the pen he had been writing with in the air. "We have seen the same type of tampering with evidence in some of the other cases related to these three friends, both in California and in Phoenix. To me, it seems like a similar setup, like the MO in the missing-persons cases we've been looking into."

"At the very least, it suggests that this woman's death was planned with some care. It was premeditated murder."

Montero's cell phone rang, and he answered. "Well, Sanchez, I wish you were here with us. We are drinking beer and eating very tasty chicken over a working lunch. And the weather is pleasant, unlike the heat of Phoenix." He paused and smiled at Hermoso as Sanchez let him know how much she wished it were him back in the desert heat and not her. "Yes, I'm rubbing it in." He listened for a minute and then put the phone down.

"Sanchez found a complete set of Parker's prints on paper, but it will take two or three days to get them into the electronic system to make a comparison. Parker had to be fingerprinted for a job she was hired for several years ago at a children's summer camp near Lake Tahoe. They did a complete background check there because she was going to be dealing with kids. Otherwise, there have been no matches of the dead woman's fingerprints in any of our national databases."

"And the dead woman's prints did not match anything in your databases in the States? I believe we will have to keep her on ice as long as it takes. Some of the officers are already calling her *la mujer de hielo*, 'the woman of ice.' Someday, maybe we will find out who she really is."

***

Sanchez had been working on two tasks over the last three days. She had followed up on her drug trafficking case and had begun a deeper inquiry into the disappearance of Tracy Mickelson at the Tempe campus. She told Montero she would have some news on both fronts when she talked to him later in the day. But now she was rushing to meet with a student from Carl Hayden High School.

She had arranged a clandestine meeting with a student named Carlos Batista. The arrangement was for her to pick him up behind the O'Reilly Auto Parts store on Van Buren Street. She was to approach in her unmarked car, and he would get in and join her for a quiet drive so they could talk.

She arrived at the agreed-upon time, but there was no sign of Batista. She trolled the area for a few minutes and then noticed a kid hiding behind a dumpster who looked like her subject. When she pulled up to the dumpster, he dove through the open right back window and told her to keep moving. He certainly looked the part of a gang informer, wearing a hoodie, a Cardinals ball cap pulled down to hide his face, and blue Converse sneakers with untied laces. He stayed completely out of sight, so much so that Sanchez wondered what he was doing in the back seat. Occasionally, he popped up and surveilled the street as if he were on the run from vigilantes. "I can't let no one see me," he said. "They'll rat me out if they catch me with a cop. And then I'm a dead man."

His dramatic interpretation of events shook Sanchez a bit, but she knew he was imagining the worst outcome. "Hey, we're just going to talk a little. Don't worry. You aren't so important that they're watching you all the time. Unless you already screwed up somehow." She turned in the seat to look at the boy. "Did you do something dumb? Otherwise, you got no worries, OK?"

Batista sat up in the back seat but stayed low as he scanned the street. "You don't know these assholes, sister! They got eyes everywhere."

"We've got a few minutes. Why don't you tell me about this guy, Marco, who you buy drugs from? How did you meet him? How does it work?"

"He's a real bad son of a bitch. Once, I saw him beat the crap out of a guy for not selling enough weed. It was real bad. I met him through the other guy who dealt at the school. Then the cops arrested that shit, and I had a chance to take his place. But I just saw the money, you know? It was worse than I thought. They expect a lot a sales. They tell me how much I got to sell, and if I don't do it, they . . . well, they can be real motherfuckers."

"So Marco is in Sinaloa or Westside?"

"Westside. They're real bitches, you know?"

"OK, so you buy your drugs from Westside, right?"

"Yeah, from a guy named Lope," Batista said. "He took over from Marco when he went up North."

"Do you ever meet the Sinaloa guys?"

"Don't know. One time, I saw a guy who coulda been Westside, maybe Sinaloa. Was with Lope. Like he was keeping an eye on him. He scared the shit out of me, man. He had tattoos and scars everywhere. Carried an automatic."

"What was his name?"

"Lope called him Boss. But he said, 'José,' when he answered his cell once."

"Who else at school bought from Lope?"

"A few kids that he knew. He was a nice guy. Real suave, you know? And he talked to this one teacher. I think she knew him from before me. I can't be sure."

"Which teacher? Was she selling drugs too?"

"I dunno. She was just a teacher. But it might have just been to score some weed. I would be scared shitless to sell to a teacher. I don't trust 'em." Batista stopped to think. "I don't know her name. She had brown hair and looked kind of plain, you know?"

"Could you recognize her if you saw a picture?"

"Maybe. I haven't seen her for a while."

"When was the last time you saw Lope?" Sanchez asked.

"Last week. Had to pay for a stash."

A beat-up Honda Civic with darkened windows slowly drove by Sanchez's sedan, and Batista looked afraid. "Hey! I better get goin'. Someone'll see me if I'm not careful. Let me out here. Now!"

"Sure. I'll want to see you again soon. See if you can find out the name of the teacher and if she sold drugs too, OK?"

"OK."

Sanchez pulled over next to a bus stop, and Batista jumped out and was gone.

She drove back to the office to write up her report. She had a feeling that she was getting somewhere on the case. A few pieces were falling into place about the distribution channels for the Westsiders' drug operation. After more prep, she might have a surveillance crew catch a few of the players in the act of dealing drugs. That might nab her someone higher in the chain of command or more knowledgeable about the organization. It was a slow process, and she had to be patient.

Then she checked her messages and found three texts from her mother. She realized that in all her focus on work, she had neglected her family. That was a problem she had: working too much and then trying to make it up later by fussing over her parents. Then work would take over her life again. Her father understood how her job worked, but her mother didn't understand that much of it was out of Sanchez's control.

She picked up the phone to call her mom. Maybe she could make them dinner tomorrow. After just a few minutes, her parents agreed to dinner. Sanchez ended the call and tried to figure out how she could make it happen with her busy schedule the next day.

Chapter 15

April 29, 2014—Phoenix, Arizona

Sanchez collected her papers before her meeting with Captain Teller. She had just received an email list of the people who had been at the ASU library in Tempe on the days before and the day when Tracy Mickelson had vanished from the campus. She was looking for the name of a man, Barry Martin, whom the campus police had suspected of other petty crimes on campus. He was also a person of interest in a more recent sexual assault on a student a month ago. He had been on campus for more than a year and may have been one of two men who had assaulted another girl at a party around Christmastime. She wondered why he was on campus at all, but apparently the women had been afraid to testify against him.

Although Martin's name was on the list, any student might have been at the library every day studying, so his presence was not a particular indicator of any mischief. He just hung out there a lot. Two other students on the list had popped up as potential suspects. They were listed as sex offenders on the statewide sex offender registry, although neither had been charged with any crimes in the last two years. It was odd how many offenders there were on the college campus. But there were a lot of young and unsuspecting women at colleges, so they were logical places for that type of man to haunt.

The list was only possible because the university had upgraded the security system for the library two years ago. The new system required students to swipe their ID cards through a scanner and check their bags and any other large objects to be X-rayed upon entry into the building. This created a record of when people came and left the premises. Mickelson had left the building at 10:05 p.m. that night. Martin had left just after that, which looked suspicious. The other men of interest were not in the building that night.

The campus police had interviewed Martin after seeing his name on the list. They had also asked eleven other people who had left the library around the same time if they had seen any suspicious activity that night. Nothing unusual had been reported. Martin had not parked in the garage, so he had no reason to be in there when Mickelson had disappeared.

The campus police had reviewed recordings taken of vehicles entering and leaving the garage that night. They had seen Mickelson drive into the garage at 7:00 p.m. but not leave, which was confirmed when her car was found parked inside. Many other cars had come and gone, but that was normal for the campus. Several had left shortly after 10:00 p.m., but again, nothing about them looked suspicious. As a result of the disappearance, the campus had added video cameras to the levels of the parking garage and improved the lighting as well.

Sanchez ran her eyes over the list on her computer and saw nothing new for the three days that the entry log covered. She noticed that a second file had been attached to the email. She opened it and found that a separate listing was available for employees who passed through a different security station. Then she found something new. One of the employees who had been at the library that night was Brown. He had checked in at three o'clock that afternoon and checked out at 9:55 p.m.

Sanchez called over to the campus police office and asked to speak to Officer Thomas Smith, the man she had been talking to about the Mickelson case. She asked Smith to look up Brown's employment information. Smith searched on the computer for a while and then told her that Brown had been a part-time employee from October 2012 until June of last year. He apparently had taken two classes as part of the benefits package available for part-time employees—both in the humanities program—one in anthropology and one in the English department. In fact, the English class was the comparative literature class taught in the spring of 2013 that Mickelson had taken when she had driven up to Tempe from Tucson on the night she went missing. She thanked Smith for his help and said goodbye.

Sanchez tried to put the new information together with what she already knew. *That's no coincidence*, she thought. Since both Brown and Mickelson had left the library at about the same time, it was likely that they had gone for a drink after class or went somewhere to hook up. Mickelson didn't move her car, so they would have gone somewhere close by on foot or in another vehicle, since Brown did not have a car. Nothing would have been open on campus at that time of night. That meant they must have gone off campus.

Sanchez called up a map of the area on Google and checked for restaurants and bars near the library, finding a few places they could have walked to that night. And if they had done that, then Mickelson might not have come back to the garage until later, maybe even midnight. The possibility that Mickelson *had* come back to the parking garage later at night made it worthwhile to look at the rest of the video. The campus police had done this initially but hadn't found anything incriminating, so it could be a waste of time to pursue. But she needed to be thorough. After all, she knew more now than they had when they had conducted their investigation, like the fact that Brown might have been involved.

She called Smith again, apologizing for troubling him. She asked if he could send her the complete video file for the garage so she could look at more of it. He told her it was an analog tape and even if it was in digital form, the file was too big to send via email. She could, however, come over to his office to view it. He said he would be happy to set it up, and they arranged a time for the viewing.

***

Sanchez walked to Smith's cubicle at the back of the large workroom. He greeted her and led her to one of the small cubicles along the side of the main room. "I have the video set up for you in here. Meanwhile, I have to attend to a few things. I'll be back in about twenty minutes."

She sat down and cued up the tape on the screen. It covered the twelve-hour period from 6:00 p.m. to 6:00 a.m. She began watching the tape at ten times the normal speed to get through the material that did not interest her. She reached 9:00 p.m. and then began viewing at a slower speed, dropping to normal view for each vehicle that passed the entry station after that time. As she watched, she made notes of anything that looked suspicious.

At ten o'clock, there was a lot of activity as many people left the library and picked up their cars from the garage. Then little happened. Sanchez sped forward on the tape and only saw four cars leave the ramp between 10:30 p.m. and 11:30 p.m. Then she saw three cars leave right around midnight. She figured that must have been when the restaurants on the nearby street closed.

She was getting bored when she saw a compact car enter the ramp at 12:26 a.m. It quickly went by, and she could not make out much about it. But a few minutes later, the same car left the garage. This time it had to stop at the electronic gate and wait for it to open before proceeding. It was a Honda Accord with Arizona license plates. Sanchez sat up and adjusted the focus so she could get a better view of the grainy screen. She hoped to be able to read the license plate of the car. Her attention was on that part of the image as she played with the controls.

"Who's that?" Officer Smith said, having returned. He was looking at the face of the driver who was now identifiable on the screen.

Sanchez shifted her gaze from the license plate to the face and gasped. "I know that person!" Then the hair on the back of her neck stood up, and she shivered. "My God! That looks like Sarah Parker."

"Who's Sarah Parker?"

"She was the girlfriend of Allister Brown, the guy who vanished last year. She was at the parking garage late that night. Here, let me back up to show you her entering the ramp." Sanchez reversed the tape to show Smith the arrival.

"Did she come to pick Brown up or something? But that should be at ten when the library closes."

"No. See, she was alone in the front seat when she left. Let me verify this license number against the one we had for the BOLO on the car." She dug through her notes and found it. "Yes. It's the same car, Sarah's 2006 Honda Accord, XRS8932. And she's driving it. What in the hell was she doing there at the library after midnight?"

Smith became animated with the discovery of the new clue. "Let's get a printout of those images. They're legible, but one of our guys is real good at cleaning up video, so if you want, I'll ask him to see what he can do." He rushed out of the room to find the other man.

Sanchez sat staring at the screen. *What am I looking at here?* she thought. *Why is Parker on campus? Was she following Mickelson or Brown? Why would she do that?* Then it occurred to her to check the timing on the other information she had on Parker. She went back to the early investigation of Brown and Parker right after Simpson was allegedly murdered. At last, she found what she was looking for. One of the neighbors had said that the couple had had a really bad fight on February 25 of 2012, and the police had come to investigate. That occurred sixteen days before Mickelson disappeared on March 13. It happened late on the same night as one of the comparative literature classes, a Tuesday.

Smith returned with the video expert, whom he introduced as Jerry. Sanchez got up from the console to let Jerry work with the machine and download a few frames from the video for enhancement. She and Smith retreated to the break room for coffee and discussed their new findings.

Like Sanchez, Smith was a straightforward guy who took his job seriously. He had been on the campus police force for four years after serving five years with the Flagstaff PD. He was considered good-looking by many—tall, blond, and clean cut— with a sort of all-American look to him. He had a ready smile that let someone know when he liked them. He was smiling at Sanchez now, and she liked it.

"Well, Detective, this information gives us a new angle on the case. Perhaps a new suspect—Brown? If he knew the woman and had drinks with her, that could make him the last person to see her alive. I don't know what to make of the Parker woman being nearby afterward, but it could just be coincidence."

"I read it differently," Sanchez said. "Maybe Brown was

seeing Mickelson, and his girlfriend was following him to find out what was going on. If she *was* following him, it would suggest that she didn't trust Brown. It isn't clear from the video why she was there, and we don't know that Brown went out with Mickelson anyway. We are supposing that. Maybe Parker came to pick him up from work, for all we know."

"It would be nice to know if anyone saw Brown and Mickelson together. We could ask at the late-night bars and restaurants if anyone recognizes them. Some of our officers went door to door with Mickelson's photo soon after she went missing, but they got nowhere. It would be a long shot."

"I suppose it's worth trying. But we may not be sure they were together that night, just *some* nights."

"I'll make a point of asking around after work and see if I can turn anything up. We should have the better photos of the car soon. If you can supply good ID photos of Brown and Parker, I can start on that tonight on my own time. I don't think my boss will authorize any department time for it just yet. But if we turn up a connection, then he might want to officially reactivate the case."

"OK. I'll email them when I'm back at the office." She collected her papers. "Thanks a lot for your help, Officer Smith. This really makes a difference." She shook hands with Smith but hesitated a few minutes to chat with him about where he had grown up. He seemed like a cool guy.

"Call me Tom," he said as he smiled at her again and added, "Maybe we could get coffee sometime."

Sanchez blushed a shade and said, "Sure. That would be nice." She walked out the door, then stopped to look back at Smith. He was still watching her, so she waved, and he did too.

Sanchez drove directly back to her office and sent him the

photos. By that time, Smith had sent her the improved photos pulled from the video camera in the parking garage. She felt that she had just discovered something important. The fact that Brown had worked at the library and knew Mickelson was surprising. He was now a common person in at least four cases where women he had known had disappeared. In all cases except one, he could have been involved in their disappearance. And Parker had known most of the missing women, except for Lucy Johnson in Berkeley.

She sat at her desk finishing up other work before leaving for the day. She thought about calling Montero to see if he was free to talk but didn't want to bother him. He had spent the last few days in Texas at a conference and was only getting back into town.

Then her cell phone rang. It was Carlos Batista.

"I gotta see you right away," he said, his voice shaky. "I think they know I been talkin' to you. I seen that José guy with Lope, and they wanna see me 'bout a problem. Maybe they saw us talkin'. I dunno. But what if they want to off me or somethin'? Help me!"

"Carlos, calm down. It's probably nothing. They may just want to talk to you about your sales. Have you been selling all they gave you? Or are you behind?"

"I sold all I could sell. But I have some left, and I can only give Lope that much money. I told him it was a slow week 'cause of the holidays, but he was mad anyway. You think that's all it is? They won't beat me?"

"Carlos, I don't know what they want. But if you run from them, they'll only get suspicious. Maybe you should meet them in public, like at the McDonald's or Safeway. Then if they're mad, they can't do anything."

"That José would kill me right there in public if he wanted

to. But maybe what you say would work. At least they would have to think about it before they cut me."

"OK, there you go." Sanchez tried to sound positive. "Now, did you find out the name of the teacher for me? Who was she?"

"I still don't know. She taught English at the school. That's all I know."

"All right, so set up the meeting. If you can do it soon, maybe I can arrange to be close by to watch in case anything happens. Set it up, and then call me on my cell. After you call me, be sure to delete the number so they won't find it. OK? Call me in half an hour."

She put away her phone and walked down the hall to see if Bordou was around. He was, so she plopped down in the chair next to his desk.

"You up for a little stakeout for an hour or so tonight?" she asked. "Nothing official, but one of my informants needs babysitting during a meet-up he has going. It shouldn't take more than an hour."

"What's in it for me, Wyatt?" Bordou was still kidding her about the shootout.

"If you're good, I might buy you a beer afterward. But no promises. You in or not?"

"Let me know what time, and I'll ride over with you. You goin' to tell the captain?"

"Probably not. Seems like a simple meet. Nothing heavy going down."

The meeting was set to take place at 10:00 p.m., so the duo arrived at Van Buren at 9:30 p.m. They got into position across the street from the McDonald's where the meet was set. They had a good view of the interior of the store from Sanchez's car using binoculars. They didn't want to get too close and spook anyone. At 10:15 p.m., they saw Batista enter McDonald's, buy a milkshake, and sit near the front of the store in clear sight. He had followed Sanchez's instructions on that.

They waited another half hour and started to get restless. It looked like the meet was not going to happen. Then Sanchez's cell phone rang. "What should I do? They ain't coming. Wait, wait! I see Lope in the parking lot. He has José with him."

Sanchez swung her binoculars to the left to see Lope coming toward the door. The other man, José, heavily muscled and wearing a thin mustache, was right behind him. He looked high on something, nervously looking around him. Sanchez thought she saw the bulge of a gun under his shirt at the back of his pants. They went into the McDonald's and got burgers to eat. Then they sat down with Batista.

Sanchez and Bordou watched the meeting unfold. It started out OK. The men just talked and ate their burgers. Then Lope got animated. He pointed his finger at Batista and made a fist. Batista looked scared. He put his hands up in a defensive position and shook his head. He pulled out a wad of money and gave it to Lope. Lope settled down a little and counted the money in a somewhat clandestine way. He put it in his pocket and pointed at Batista again.

Then José stood up and said something to Batista. Batista got up and backed away into the corner. José went over and grabbed him by the shirtfront and pulled him toward the door. Lope looked surprised at this turn of events and tried to get between Batista and the oversize guy. He got punched in the face for his trouble.

That was when a man wearing an apron, maybe the manager, came out from behind the counter and tried to talk to José. He attempted to pull Batista free from the man's grasp. *Bad move, man*, Sanchez thought. *You're going to get your ass kicked.* Bordou started to radio for backup. This was going south fast.

Sanchez started her car and gunned the engine as she felt for the reassuring presence of the Glock on her belt. She pulled her unmarked Ford Interceptor around another car and prepared to pull out of the parking lot and cross the road to the McDonald's parking lot. She had to wait for traffic to clear on Van Buren before she could cross the street. *What's taking so long? I have to go now!*

She pulled out into the first lane, watching what was happening across the street, which was out of her control. It was going down bad. She had to go. She brought the engine to a loud roar, and when the last car passed to open her path ahead, she floored the gas. Her car launched forward like a pent-up slingshot, tires burning a black tattoo on the street as she went.

José had grabbed the man in the apron and slammed his face into the wall. He pulled out his gun and waved it at everyone in the restaurant. He looked at Batista and hit him over the head with the pistol. Then he dragged him outside into the parking lot. Lope tried to stop José but to no effect. José pushed Batista up against the side of a Ford SUV. As Sanchez burned out from her side of the street toward the parking lot, she saw José shoot Batista in the guts twice. He held him up so he could watch him squirm in pain. Then he backed up and let Batista drop to the ground.

José was laughing when Sanchez's unmarked car roared into the parking lot, aimed right at him. He turned to look at the approaching vehicle and stopped laughing. He didn't aim his gun. His eyes were focused on Sanchez at the wheel. He just seemed surprised, eyes wide and mouth open, as the car ran into him at high speed. He flew backward twenty feet, slammed into the side of another car, and fell motionless to the ground. Sanchez's car skidded to a stop six inches from him.

***

Sanchez spent much of the night being debriefed and writing her report. The captain was not amused, but Bordou had said it had been his idea to watch the meeting go down. He had dragged Sanchez along to keep him company. No one believed him, but it gave the captain an out. Sanchez was happy she had not been reamed out on the spot. Now she owed Bordou a few cool ones for covering her ass.

When they had finished, Sanchez and Bordou conducted the initial interview with Lope. He was very cooperative after seeing the kind of people he was doing business with. They got a preliminary statement out of him about what had happened tonight, which confirmed that the big guy was José Battelle of the Sinaloa Cartel. That information bought Lope a free night in jail for his own safety.

Batista did not make out very well. He was rushed to the hospital, where he was in surgery for seven hours. When Sanchez called in to ask about his condition, she was told he was unconscious. He could not talk and might not ever again.

She felt rotten about the whole thing. Destroyed and exhausted, she went home at 6:00 a.m. and fell asleep on her bed without taking off her gun holster or boots.

Chapter 16

April 30, 2014

Montero awoke the next morning to hear about a heroic policewoman's dangerous encounter with the infamous Sinaloa Cartel the night before. He dropped his toothbrush at the news. There could only be one woman who would put it all on the line to run down an assassin while he was shooting his victim. No name was given for the officer, but he knew who it was. He speed-dialed Sanchez immediately. No answer. He finished cleaning up and got in his car to drive to her home. She was in danger.

He arrived to find a police cruiser parked in front of her building, signifying that her captain had realized the potential threat. He pulled up alongside the squad car and greeted the officers, telling them he was there to visit Sanchez. They cleared him to park in her building lot. He knocked on her apartment door, and she smiled as she let him in.

"So . . . how much trouble are you in this time?" he asked as he helped himself to a cup of coffee.

"This time, I'm actually considered a hero by the captain. I didn't shoot anyone, so he was happy about that. And the perp didn't die from the bump I gave him with my sedan. But I put some serious hurt on the bastard. Montero, he just stood there and pumped two rounds into the kid in front of my eyes. I *had* to stop him."

Montero, propped up on the kitchen wall, told her he understood. She came over and leaned on him so he could give her a short hug. She needed some reassurance after her late night. After a moment, she pulled away and filled a travel mug with coffee.

"Well, I have to go into the station now to reinterview the other guy we pulled in last night. His name is Lope. He's the guy in the local Westside gang who runs drugs in Glendale and the west side of the metro area. He also runs the kid who was helping me and got shot. The kid sells at the high school and surrounding neighborhood. He's just out of school himself, a dropout. But he knows the kids who are buying and some teachers who are too."

"Sanchez, you weren't there alone this time, were you?"

"Oh, hell no. I had Bordou with me in the car. We both watched it go down, and he backed me up real good. He saved me a lot of grief with the captain." She did a double take, put down her coffee cup, and stared at him silently at first.

"Oh, I see. You think that I went all PTSD on the guy? What is it with you and PTSD?" She gave him an inquiring look. "No, I didn't have any anxiety or fear. I just had to stop the son of a bitch before he killed someone else. OK?"

Montero threw his hands up and sighed. "OK. I had to ask."

"Hey, I know you worry about me, and that's cool. But I'm OK . . . really." She looked into Montero's eyes and waved her hand in the air as if swatting away a fly.

"How's the kid doing?"

"He's going to make it as long as nothing weird happens." She turned off her Mr. Coffee and stacked some dishes in the sink. "We have a guard outside his room to keep him safe from retaliation and the press. They want the grim photos for the news. You know."

"Did they get your name or photo on the news? I didn't see

it this morning."

"No. I'm still anonymous. But that could change. I don't want the Sinaloa after me." She shuddered at the thought. If they ever found out who had run their guy down, she would be in real danger, marked for death. She paused, then said, "I got new info on that Tempe disappearance, by the way. A breakthrough. I'll tell you about it after work."

They left the apartment together and went their separate ways. Sanchez drove to the station and parked in the basement to avoid any reporters.

She and Bordou walked into the small concrete-block interview room where Lope was waiting. He looked scared as hell, constantly checking out the two-way mirror on the side of the room in case he could see who was watching him. He was handcuffed to a steel ring in the center of the steel interview table. He looked relieved when the two cops entered the room and sat down across the table from him.

"Man, if I tell you anythin', they goin' to kill me real slow and bury me under a cactus. You never snitch on the cartel. They got people everywhere, even in prison. Then one night you're dead, right in your bed." He shook his fist at Sanchez. "No! I ain't telling you nothin'."

Sanchez wouldn't let him play that game. "I gotta tell you, Lope," she said, "you're starting off on the wrong foot. Come on—you're looking at ten years just for being there last night, and you have a parole violation too: associating with a known criminal. That's another five to ten. You've got to give us something, or you'll end up an old man in jail."

"Maybe I can tell you somethin' you can use, but I need to know what I get out of the deal first. What can *you* do for *me*?" He crossed his arms as much as the cuffs would allow and settled into a staring contest with Sanchez.

"First of all, I must warn you that if the boy dies, you go down for abetting a murder. That's ten to fifteen on top of what we already said. So you better have something good for me, or there'll be no deal. *Comprende?*"

"OK, OK. What you want to know? About Westside? Drugs? What?" He straightened up in his chair, his eyes on Sanchez. "But you giving me a deal, right? Or I won't say nothin'."

"Right. You'll get a deal. We have to work out the details with the DA's office. Let me make a call to see what I can do."

Sanchez stepped out of the room to call Clara Alvera in the DA's office. When she reentered the room, she explained that Lope would have to tell her all about the Westside gang's operations and their dealings with the Sinaloa Cartel right now. Then the DA could evaluate what he had to say and how useful it was before negotiating the final parameters of a deal with him and his attorney. She told him to give her a sampling of the detail and content the DA would get for his effort. Lope refused at first, saying he would be dead in a week if he ratted out his gang.

"First off, is Battelle involved in gun trafficking? Tell us how Westside is working with Sinaloa."

Lope stared at Sanchez as if weighing his options. He decided to play the game and hope that he survived somehow. "José was in charge of guns. He had people buy guns at shops and send them to Mexico. He worked with ATF on a few deals. They authorized him to buy guns that he couldn't legally buy at gun shops. You know, full automatic AKs and AR-15s. But not many that way." He paused and looked at the mirror for a moment. "Mostly, he had men buy guns that the cartel changed to full automatic in Nogales or farther south. It's simple to change some of the guns to auto with a single part. I've seen it done. Very easy. He had a special route and other people to do the run to the border."

"How did he transport the weapons?"

"Sometimes in cars or trucks with hidden compartments. Sometimes they just put them in crates on trucks with false invoices. If you know the right people at the border, then no one asks many questions crossing into Mexico. It's easy going south."

"And how about moving people? Is he in charge of that too?"

"No, José just did guns. Other people brought Mexicans north using coyotes and other ways. He didn't get involved in that because it's a big operation that's already set up—"

Sanchez interrupted him. "Wait a minute. When we talked last night, you said a lot of things about José and what he did. You said he even took people south across the border."

Lope shook his head and said he didn't really know about such a rumor. "There was word on the street that he might start taking people south across the border next year. But he only did that once in a while for someone that the Sinaloa wanted to punish in Mexico. He put those people in compartments after they were drugged."

"So kidnapping people to take to Mexico was not his main business? I thought you told me it was."

"No. You must be wrong." Lope stopped talking, sat back in his chair, and folded his arms again.

"Look, Lope. If you withhold information about this and you don't tell me, there'll be trouble. I think you know but are afraid to say. Who are you afraid of, José? He can't hurt you."

"The whole cartel will be after me, you bitch."

"So now you admit there was kidnapping? What is it? Yes or no?"

"Listen to me. I wasn't involved in making the deal, so I don't know what finally happened to her. I was just there to help my boss. OK?"

Sanchez shifted forward in her chair and leaned close to Lope, now intrigued. "What did you help him do?"

"There was a woman that my boss at Westside got for us in a deal. She was a white girl who we had at the house. I thought she was just a hooker, someone on drugs to get her to turn tricks. Westside isn't into hookers, but we had her."

"So you guys don't run any prostitution business in Phoenix? I thought you did."

"No. It was a special arrangement with the Sixty-fourth Avenue Crips. They would run hookers, and we would push drugs in certain areas, so we didn't step on each other's business. I don't know the details. I'm just a soldier."

"Tell me how you got this girl."

"It was about a year ago. Carlos said a woman at the school wanted a special meeting. She wanted to speak to me, alone, right away. She came to me to see if I could make a big deal for some weed. She said she had something to trade for the dope but wouldn't tell me what. She wanted to speak to someone who could deal. I had her talk to Valdez, my boss at Westside. I went with him to the meet."

"What happened?"

"It was real fast. We met outside a Walmart. She wanted to trade ten kilos of grass for a woman she had with her. Boss said no way. It sounded like a trap. But she wouldn't let us go. She said she would take five kilos of grass. Boss still said no. We thought she was crazy or something. Then she took us to her car and opened the truck. There was a blonde woman inside— young, tied up, and unconscious. It was bad news."

"She just had the girl in the trunk? Tied up?" Sanchez was incredulous.

"Valdez told her to shut the fuckin' trunk. We asked her how she got the girl. She wouldn't say, just that she wanted to sell her for marijuana."

"So what happened?" Bordou asked, looking up from his notebook.

"My boss, something strange happened to him. He opened the trunk again and looked at the girl. She was like twenty years old. I think she turned him on. She was sort of pretty, but we couldn't see much of her face with the tape on it."

"And then?"

"Valdez said he'd take her, but for only one kilo. That was all he had in the car anyway. Then the woman got real mad and called Valdez a motherfucker. He punched her in the face and told her he would take the girl and give her nothing, maybe even kill her for her big mouth. Then she acted sorry and said she would take the kilo. So we had a deal. We drove behind Walmart to transfer the girl to our car while she was passed out. We threw a blanket over her and put her in our trunk. Then the boss gave the woman a short kilo. She said nothing more and just drove away. So did we."

"Where'd you take her?"

"We drove around for a while, and Valdez decided what to do. He had to think. It was late at night, so we just took her to the house on Forty-fifth Street and put her in the basement. We untied her, and she woke up then."

"So was she OK? Could she talk?"

"Yeah, but she was in bad shape, on some drug that made her like she was drunk. The boss had two girls at the house clean her up. She looked good all cleaned up. Was hot. Blonde and blue eyes. The boss took her up to a bedroom and fucked her." Lope acted as if it was just business as usual.

"Was she awake for that?" Sanchez was pissed off, clenching

her hands together into fists, but had to keep the interview going. Bordou watched her and suggested they take a break so she wouldn't take a swing at the guy.

"She didn't complain, didn't even make much noise. She was really out of it. We all fucked her. One at a time, you know. Then the boss had us tie her to the bed, and we left her naked so we could fuck her when we wanted." He grinned boastfully.

"You fucking shit!"

Sanchez lunged across the table and punched Lope hard in the face. He didn't expect to see her fist at close range. He blocked the next couple of blows before Bordou could rip Sanchez off him and drag her out of the room. Bordou pulled her close and whispered through his teeth, "Don't say a word. We're going outside."

Sanchez wrestled free of his grip. Bordou told one of the other officers to keep an eye on Lope while they took a break. They walked out to Sanchez's damaged Ford Interceptor and got inside. By then, Sanchez was already beginning to cool down.

"That son of a bitch just said they gang raped a woman, and he seemed to think that was OK. That is just shit, Bordou. Just shit!"

"Look, Sanchez, it *is* shit! I know, I agree," Bordou said. "But we have to keep him talking. I think he's giving us a lot, but we have to get him to fill in the details. You have to calm down."

"OK, OK. Give me a minute to think . . . . We still need to know more about the bitch who sold a woman for a kilo of grass. What a bitch! Just selling someone to get high. I want to get that woman and make her pay."

"Seems to me you've been making a lot of people pay lately."

"This isn't fucking funny. You know what I mean."

"Sure," Bordou said, unconvinced.

"And what did they do with the girl? That was a year ago. What happened to her? Maybe they gave her to the Crips for prostitution. Or what?"

Bordou looked Sanchez in the eye. "OK now? Can you keep it together so we can finish this thing?"

"Yeah. Yeah, I guess."

They went back inside and reentered the interview room. Lope had wiped his bloody lip with Kleenex. He gave Sanchez an angry stare. Then he said to Bordou, "You keep that crazy bitch away from me, or I stop talking now, you understand? Maybe I should get a lawyer now? Maybe that's what I should do."

Bordou decided to take the lead for a while so Sanchez could keep her cool. "OK, she got mad about the girl. Wha'd you expect? But she has it under control now. Let's just do this, and then we'll get you your own cell. You can eat something and then sleep. OK?"

Lope shrugged his shoulders and grunted OK.

"Tell me where the girl is now."

"I don't know. After that night, I didn't see her again, at least not for sex. I saw her at the house a couple of days later."

"What was her condition?"

"The same: kind of druggy. Then she was gone. The men really liked her." He glared defiantly at Sanchez. "She was a real good fuck, you know. Everybody had her a few times. Every way you can, you know?"

"Shut up, Lope, or I'll punch you myself." Bordou gave him a look like he wasn't kidding. "So how come you didn't see her again? Were you somewhere else?"

"No. My girlfriend found out about her and told me she would hurt me if I did her again. She can be a real bitch when she wants. So I had to stay away except for business. Some of the girlfriends didn't like what we did to the girl either. Even the boss got bad vibes from his woman. So he sold her to José for some guns."

"What? Valdez sold her to José? What did he do with her?"

"I think José kept her for sex for a while and got her hooked on heroin. Like they do to most hookers. Then I think he sent her to Mexico on a truck. I don't know for sure."

"And you don't know more about where she was from?"

"No. Some of the guys talked to her when she could talk. She was out of it most of the time. She was a college student somewhere, I think."

"And the woman who sold her to you? Who was she?"

"Hey, I don't know nothin' about her. She seemed like a housewife or something. Not like anyone in the gangs. She wasn't like a kidnap person. I never saw her again. Maybe Valdez knows."

At this point, they broke off the interview and sent Lope to his cell for food and a nap, making sure he would be protected. Then they went to see the captain with what they had learned. It took all afternoon to document the interview.

Sanchez sat alone in her apartment later that night with all of her notes spread out on her kitchen table. She had many new facts and had to put the pieces of the puzzle together. But no matter how she looked at it, she felt she was still missing one or two clues that would tie things up. She felt that the missing woman and the gunrunning case were linked in some way. But how did the pieces fit, and what was she missing?

Chapter 17

May 3, 2014

The next few days saw a few things get resolved in the Westside case. Battelle's condition turned a corner, and he was moved from Lincoln Hospital to the hospital wing of the county holding facility. He continued to improve after the last of his internal bleeding was controlled. He was kept on such sufficient pain medication that he inadvertently gave up some useful information about his gunrunning activities and other matters. He boasted to his new roommate, whom he thought was interested in his heroic days with the Sinaloa, about many things, including what he had done with the kidnapped girl from last year. It turned out the prisoner next to him had worked out a deal to get him to talk in exchange for a reduced charge for the grand theft he had committed. Since Battelle did not talk directly to a policeman, his attorney's protests fell on deaf ears in court.

Lope was held in solitary confinement in a separate facility altogether. He and Battelle were now the star witnesses as Sanchez and Bordou pulled together their case against the Westside gang. They visited all three criminals to ask questions that would help cement the case against several gang members and Battelle. Sanchez's CI came through with some extra information that helped tie up loose ends on the gunrunning portion of the case.

Batista survived after a few days of touch-and-go in the same ward of the hospital. He was stable and able to talk after three days, but he was understandably afraid of retribution when he learned that Battelle was nearby. Sanchez arranged for him to move to another ward once he was in better condition. His room was listed under an assumed name for his protection. He was viewed as an important witness and so was accorded a police guard. This would be the first real interview that Sanchez and Bordou had with Batista since the incident. He was stable and alert, so the doctor agreed to let them talk for a half an hour.

Sanchez approached the side of the bed and asked, "So, Carlos, how do you feel? Stronger today? I hope you're feeling strong enough to talk, 'cause I've a whole lot of questions to ask you." She put a hand on his arm as she spoke.

Sanchez asked him to go over the events of the night when Battelle had shot him. He told them everything he knew, which confirmed most of what they already had seen from across the street and what Lope had told them.

Batista became agitated as he spoke and shook his fist to show how much he loathed Battelle. That led to a sudden pain, and Bordou called for the doctor to check it out. After a brief inspection of the sutures, the doctor said they had to stop the interview for the day. Maybe the next day would be better, at least for another short period. Sanchez prepared to leave and told Batista they would talk tomorrow.

"But don't you want to know about the lady?"

"What lady?"

"The teacher at the school? The one who bought weed?"

"Oh, that lady. Sure, what'd you have?"

"Her name was Miss Parker. She taught English."

"Was her name Sarah Parker?" Bordou asked.

Batista thought for a minute and then said, "I don't know her first name. Just Miss Parker. But she's the one. I asked one of the older boys about her."

"She worked at the Hayden School? Are you sure?" Sanchez couldn't believe her ears.

"Yeah, that's what he said."

"I'll be damned," Bordou said. "She worked there. How did we *not* know that?"

"It never mattered where she worked. I'll have to verify that through the school. It wouldn't surprise me if she smoked some pot. They were all the right age to be into that."

The doctor shooed them out of the room so he could get things done. "OK. That's all for now. Carlos needs his rest, and I may have to add some stitches."

They left and went down to the car. When they arrived at the station, Bordou went off to document their interview with Batista while Sanchez called Carl Hayden High School to verify Parker's employment there. When she got through to the personnel office, they confirmed that Parker had worked at the school from September 2011 to June of 2013. She had been an exemplary employee and teacher.

By the time Sanchez finished working through the papers on her desk, it was already past 5:00 p.m. She decided to call Montero to see if he had time for a beer. She left a message but then decided she would swing by his house anyway since it was on her way home. She pulled into the drive, walked up to the door, and pressed the button for the doorbell. No answer, so she turned back toward her car just as his shiny pickup truck pulled up next to her.

"I got your message. You know I'm up for a beer any time," he said as he lifted a six-pack of Tecate from the front seat.

He pulled the truck into the garage and led Sanchez to the back patio. He gave her a beer and went into the kitchen to find chips and his favorite salsa, a concoction he bought in Tombstone whenever he was close by.

He looked at Sanchez and saw that she was in a particularly good mood. Something was on her mind. "So, Lori, what have you been up to, and why do you have that big smile on your face?"

"Today we discovered that Sarah Parker worked at Carl Hayden High School as an English teacher, and she bought drugs from my informant at the school."

"Really?" Montero let out a low whistle. "That *is* an interesting connection. So what did she buy from the boy? Marijuana?"

"Yes. He said she liked to get some weed every few weeks. But why risk it on her own school campus? If she got caught, she could lose her job, or worse. What a fool."

"Yeah, but I guess it was convenient for her. Most people think they'll never be caught for something so minor." Montero also thought it was stupid for a teacher to buy grass at her own place of work. "Did the kid ID her for you? Did you show him a photo, or did he just have a name?"

"He had a name. I didn't have the photo with me at the time because she's part of the other case. I'll follow up with the photo. We had to stop questioning him after a short while today because he had some pain when we were there. The doctor said we could come back tomorrow."

"You'll need to have him pick her out of a photo lineup to keep it real," he mused. "Do you have any other photos that are relevant to use?"

"Yeah. When I talked to the personnel office at the school, they told me there were five English teachers at the school at the time, and after some pushing, I got her to send me some photos of them from their school catalog. That way the photos were public record already, and she had no privacy concerns. So I have what I need."

"So how is the kid, Carlos, doing? It's bad to get shot in the guts like that. Oh, that reminds me—how's the guy you shot in the alley the other night?"

Sanchez looked at Montero suspiciously. "Why are you asking about that man? Did Bordou say something to you about his wounds?"

"Well, he might have said something last time I saw him. I understand your shot was a little low. Is that true?"

"You men are all the same." Sanchez laughed and shook her head in amusement. "So, yes. The shot was low, and he has one less *cojone* to deal with. It was my life I was saving, so I'm not sorry." Then she smiled slyly and said, "At least none of my fellow cops are hitting on me anymore. They're afraid of what I'll do if they get out of line." Now she looked at Montero, and they both laughed. "I'll never live that down, will I?"

"And he's talking?"

"Yeah, he is. I'm not involved in the interviews, but Bordou is. He said whenever the guy clams up on them, they threaten to bring me into the room, and he starts singing again like a coal mine canary."

***

Sanchez and Bordou arrived at the hospital at ten o'clock the next morning to continue talking to Batista. He was in better shape then and told them he had little pain for a change.

"The doctor told me I can get out of the hospital in a week or so if I don't pull any more stitches. It's really boring in here. And the food sucks big time."

"Well, I thought so. I brought you a treat for your lunch today. I made it this morning. But don't tell the doctor, or he'll be mad." She pulled a small package from her shoulder bag and peeled back the wax paper wrapper to reveal a pork tamale. She handed it to Batista, and he immediately began to wolf it down right from the wrapper.

"*Muy bueno, señora. Muchas gracias.*" He relished the treat. A passing nurse looked into the room and wagged a finger at Batista for eating outside food.

"You've made friends with her, Carlos. I think she likes you. Now, we've got more questions for you. But first, I want you to look at pictures of five women who work at the high school, and I want you to pick out the woman you call Miss Parker, OK?"

She laid out the photos of the women who taught English at Carl Hayden High School, and told him to take his time. He looked at them one by one, lifting each one close so he could see better. He pointed to an older-looking woman with gray hair and said, "This one taught me English the first year I was there. She's Mrs. Marshall. She was good to me." Then he pointed to a photo of a dark-haired woman in her twenties who had a neutral expression. "Here she is. This is Miss Parker." He handed the picture to Sanchez.

She was surprised and looked at the photo carefully, reading the name written on the back of the photo. Carla Hertzman. The woman looked somewhat like the photo of Parker that Sanchez had seen before. She had similar features, brown hair and eyes, and Sanchez wondered if Batista might have mistaken her for Parker. "Look again at the picture. Are you sure?"

"Yeah, I saw her maybe a dozen times. She was friendly but very nervous when she bought the grass." He handed the photo back and continued looking at the others. "No, I don't know her. No, not her." Then he came to the last photo, also of a brunette woman in her twenties. He pulled the photo closer and then said,

"This is the lady who wanted to see my boss. That was last year, but I'm sure it's her. She was in a big hurry."

Sanchez took the photo from his hand and gasped. She looked at the familiar face and turned the photo over to be sure it said Sarah Parker on the back.

Bordou leaned in to look closely at what had made her gasp. "Are you sure about this, Carlos?" he asked. "She was the one who wanted to see Lope last year?"

"Yes, I remember her real good. She gave me twenty dollars, then grabbed my arm and told me not to tell nobody. So I remember her."

Sanchez dug into her file and pulled out the other photo she had of Parker to show Batista. "Here's another photo. Is it her?"

Batista looked at the new photo and compared it to the first one. "Yes, it's her too. But she's smiling in that picture."

"OK, Carlos. I want you to think back to last year. When you met this woman, did you know her name?"

"No. I didn't know any names until I asked the teacher's name at school. I asked who the English teacher was with the dark hair last year. Two guys told me her name was Miss Parker. But I didn't have no picture, so maybe they were wrong."

"And the other woman is the one who bought marijuana from you?"

"Yes, I'm sure of their faces, señora, but didn't know their names."

"Thanks, Carlos. This is very important. We'll have to stop with the questions today so we can follow up. We'll come back tomorrow, and I'll bring you some black bean soup, OK?"

They left the hospital and started to drive back to the station. "This is bad" Sanchez said, "because we need a definite ID on the woman who had the girl in the trunk of her car. I'll call the school and see if we can stop by to talk to the HR person there."

Sanchez made a quick call to the HR department and asked if they could stop by to check something with them. The head of the department said there was no problem, they could come right over if they wanted. So they changed course and drove directly to Carl Hayden High School.

At the school, they went to talk to the HR supervisor named Mrs. Roberts. She, in turn, arranged for them to speak with Carla Hertzman, who was at school and between classes. They sat down with her in a spare room and asked her if she knew Carlos Batista, which caused her to burst into tears. She apparently thought she was going to be arrested for buying marijuana from him. Sanchez explained that they just needed to confirm whether she knew him or not. Hertzman settled down after that and said she knew Batista but had never told him her name.

Then they asked her if she knew Sarah Parker. Hertzman said she had gone out for drinks with her in a group of teachers who did a few things together after work, but that was all. She hadn't been particularly friendly with Parker and had no idea where she had gone after she had left school last year.

The two detectives thanked Hertzman and asked her to call them if she remembered anything, even the tiniest detail that might help them locate Parker. She promised that she would never buy dope or smoke it again. Sanchez thought that was unlikely and felt sorry for the young teacher who certainly wouldn't be inclined to smoke weed for at least a week or two.

Their next stop was at the county jail to talk to Lope. To keep their visit with him concealed from the other inmates, a jailer brought him to a private interview room. Lope was sullen when he entered.

This time, Bordou took the lead. "We have some questions, but let's start with some photographs, OK? We have some pictures of women who might match the one who sold you the white girl. We want you to look at them and tell us if she's in this batch. We may have other suspects later." He laid out the photos of the high school English teachers on the table where Lope could see them.

"Yeah, I think that's her. It was dark and all, but that's her." He pointed to the photo of Parker.

"You're sure? It was dark." Bordou pointed to Hertzman's photo. "The two of them look a little alike. It wasn't this one, was it?"

"No, I'm sure of it. There's something wild about her eyes I can't forget." He pointed to Parker again.

"OK." Bordou sounded encouraged. "Now we need to know more about the transaction. What kind of car was she driving that night? What can you tell us about it?"

"It was a small car. I think it was a Honda. Yeah, a Honda 'cause it had the little *H* on the trunk when we opened it. And I remember the girl didn't smell so good when we pulled her out of there. Like she'd been in there a long time. Sweat and piss. Like the woman didn't take her out to go to the bathroom. That was really bad. It was getting warm during the day at that time of year too. So it would have been hot in the trunk."

"What color car?"

"Dark. Like blue or black. It was kinda dark in the parking lot. We weren't right under one of the lights either."

"Do you remember the date when this happened?"

"It was in early March. I remember because my girlfriend's birthday was coming up, and before we met her, I had time to go into Walmart to buy her a box of candy. She gets real mad if I forget things like that. So about the twelfth or thirteenth of March."

"OK, Lope. You've been a big help. But we still want to talk more about the girl. How was she bound? Tape or rope? Was she wrapped in a blanket or covered up in any way? That sort of detail." Bordou looked down at the table, ready to write what Lope said.

Lope sat back in the chair and looked around the room, as if trying to decide whether he should lie or not. Sanchez caught his eye and said, "Don't even think about covering your tracks. We'll know, and your deal will be for shit."

Lope answered, "She was taped up except for her hands. They were tied with a bungee cord. Her hands were all screwed up from being tied so tight. We wrapped her in a blanket when we pulled her out of the Honda."

"When you moved her, was there any blood? You know? Come on. Give us all the details."

They went back and forth for an hour until Bordou and Sanchez thought they had it all. They wrapped up the interview and left the building.

"Do you believe him?" Sanchez asked Bordou.

He stood at the door of the car and winked at her. "I just don't know. But I know how we can find out."

Chapter 18

May 5, 2014

Sanchez and Bordou peeked into the interrogation room at the Maricopa County Fourth Avenue Jail. It was one with steel chairs that made a long interview very painful for all involved. Sanchez wondered out loud if that was a new idea from the administration to keep cops from interrogating the perps too long. She dashed into the workroom across the hall and got herself a standard molded plastic chair. The guard outside the interrogation room began to object but then said he would have done the same thing. He let the two enter the room, and the interrogation began.

Battelle sat with his leg irons chained to the floor and his handcuffs attached to the steel ring in the center of the steel table across from where Sanchez had parked her chair. Bordou figured out the chair bit too late to retrieve his own slice of comfort, so he sat on the cold steel. He switched on the recorder and pulled out his notepad. He looked at Sanchez to see if she was ready to face off with this character and saw the glint in her eye that indicated she was ready for the contest.

There was something going on with Battelle today. He was self-contained, different from the usual defiant stance he had taken both times he had encountered Sanchez. He sat bolt upright staring at the wall in front of him, wearing his orange jumpsuit, seated on his side of the table next to his attorney, the infamous John Parlance, one of the most highly paid attorneys in the southwestern United States. Parlance was the man who did the cartel's bidding, and Sanchez could tell from his thousand-dollar suit he was well paid for his services. She wished she could interview Battelle alone and in private to extract all the information he had in his head about cartel operations.

They got down to business with the preliminaries, paying all the necessary deference to the attorney present. Sanchez had to check her speech in his presence, which slowed things down considerably. Instead of just asking Battelle anything she wanted, she had to work her way into it in such a manner that she did not incite Parlance to object or interfere with what would have been a simple exchange of information—or at least a trade of insults. After a while, even Battelle was getting tired of the attorney's constant commentary on what was and was not relevant to the deal they had struck with Battelle for his testimony.

"Let's get something straight, Counselor," Sanchez said, glowering at him. "Our deal is for Battelle to cooperate freely with our investigation. You are interfering with that process. If we do not get the level of cooperation that we agreed to, then we will have to conclude your client is not cooperating and is not meeting his part of the bargain. If that happens, we may have to renegotiate the deal or pull it off the table completely. Now, how do you want to play this? Should I call the DA's office and tell them that your client is violating our agreement? Or should we cut the crap and get on with the interview?"

"Detective Sanchez, I find that you are impugning my position as the representative of my client. Such accusations are not at all necessary and are most insulting as well. Perhaps I should be the one who contacts your district attorney to complain about your attitude."

"Go right ahead, Counselor. I'm not the one who has something to lose here. Maybe you should talk to your client and figure out if he wants the deal or not." Sanchez got up and left the room, a move that caught Battelle and Parlance off guard. Bordou followed.

They decided to give Battelle and Parlance twenty minutes to sit on those hard-ass chairs. *It might soften them up a bit.* Sanchez snickered at the thought.

When they reconvened, Parlance made a request. "My client would like to have the leg chains loosened so that he can move his legs into a different position. He is extremely uncomfortable with the present arrangement."

They had to leave the room while the jailer and an assistant came into the room to reposition the chains. Meanwhile, Parlance approached Sanchez and Bordou in the hallway.

"I must compliment you, Detectives, for your strategy regarding this interview. I too have developed a desire to increase the pace of these proceedings, as does my client, who thinks I should be more lenient in my objections to your questions. He realizes that he is in a situation where he must convey the information he has available to meet his part of the deal. And I must compliment whoever selected the steel chairs that we have to sit on. It makes me agree to a quicker proceeding." He paused to look around. "And may I ask where you found that more comfortable chair? Could I have one for the duration of the interview?"

The interview continued for two hours. They were now able to gain Battelle's cooperation, and he detailed several aspects of the cartel's operation to them. The thing they really wanted to learn about was the gunrunning operations in Arizona that Battelle had been heavily involved in.

Sanchez and Bordou took turns leading the questioning. They covered all aspects of the gunrunning trade and filled in a few details that would tighten the case against Battelle. Then Sanchez again took the lead. "Let's talk about human trafficking now. Not the smuggling of people into the States from Mexico, but the kidnapping and transport of people from Arizona into Mexico. What can you tell us about kidnappings in Arizona?"

Battelle settled back in his chair to answer. "We do this sometimes when we have trouble with people not doing their job. I don't know of many takings. Local bosses who think that someone stole from a shipment or from the cartel usually do them. They decide what to do. Suppose one of the crew on a drug shipment takes a few kilos of marijuana for himself. If the boss finds out he took something, maybe he will make him pay it back. If it's gone or sold to someone else, the boss may just shoot the *ladrón*. If he can get it back or pay for it somehow, then maybe they won't kill him. But if he says he won't give it back, then the boss might take his son or his wife until he does right by the boss. If he doesn't, the boss might kill the hostages or sell them in Mexico—if they have any value, that is."

"So what you're saying is that those kinds of decisions are made by the local boss?"

"Yes, it doesn't happen too often. But it's usually because of a thief or a snitch. Only the boss decides."

"How about the capture and torture of police chiefs or mayors in some of the small towns along the border? We have heard that some of them have been kidnapped to make them do what the cartel wants. Is this true?"

"Yes, I've heard it has happened. But I don't know about that personally. I only know what I've heard. This happened to the mayor of Martin near the border. He refused to tell his police to let our shipments go through his town. He was told to have his police disappear at the right times. But he wouldn't listen, so one night, his wife disappeared for a while, and the men had some fun with her. When she came back, he decided to help us as we wanted." A look of satisfaction appeared on his face as he answered.

"You really don't think this is wrong, do you, José?" Sanchez said this matter-of-factly with no expression on her face, but her voice was strained.

"Do you have children, Sanchez? I would worry about my family if I were you."

Sanchez took the bait in spite of herself. "Oh, is that some kind of threat? I'm not afraid of you, José. You're just small fish."

The attorney broke in. "No one is threatening you, Detective. Not my client, nor any of his associates. Understood? Let's continue with the questions and keep personal grudges out of it, shall we?"

"OK. Let's talk about your purchase of a woman from the Westside gang. We know you took the woman from the Westside boss, Valdez. How did that happen?"

"I was not looking for a woman. He just came to me with a problem. He had this blonde woman who he wanted to sell or trade because he could no longer keep her. He was very weak. He said that his woman made him get rid of her. So I made a deal for her. I gave him two AK-47s with lots of ammo. I got a good deal."

"What did you do with her?"

"I kept her for a while and found out she loved heroin, a disturbing habit. I had sex with her many times. She was good in bed. She was a little smaller than you, Detective, but a lot of fun. She liked it rough. Do you like it rough, Sanchez? You look like the type." He leered at Sanchez across the table, scanning her body up and down.

Parlance broke in before Sanchez could tell Battelle where he could go. "Maybe we should take a break for a few minutes. Can we get more coffee?"

They broke up the meeting for ten minutes so they could go to the bathroom and stretch. They had been talking for three hours so far. Parlance walked down the hallway to make a call. When he came back, he looked grim and said he needed a few minutes in private with his client.

When they returned to the interrogation room, it was clear that something had changed. Battelle and his lawyer were both sour and looked as though they had changed their intention to cooperate. Parlance said, "We are not going to provide any more general information about cartel operations. My client has been advised to only talk about the few specific actions he has taken that are detailed in the specific plea bargain that he and the DA have agreed to. Is that clear?"

"Yes, I guess it is," Sanchez responded. "What happened to make you change your mind?"

"It's nothing. I have been in communication with my client's benefactor and was reminded of some provisions in the contract at hand. Now, where were we? We were discussing the specifics of the transaction involving a woman, I believe."

"OK. How long was the woman in your possession?"

"My client did not have anyone in his *possession*. He did, however, have a young lady at his home as a guest."

"My question was directed at your client, not you, Counselor. I repeat, José, how long did you have the woman at your home?"

"She was my guest for three weeks. She liked to have sex, so I helped her enjoy herself. She liked it rough, like I said. She liked to be fucked really hard and by lots of men. We tried to keep her satisfied." He glared at Sanchez. "I bet you like it hard too, don't you, Sanchez? Maybe when this is over we can have a party. Just you and me. What do you think?" Battelle looked directly at Sanchez's breasts and licked his lips. Then he moved his pelvis up and down in a suggestive manner. He grinned and stuck out his tongue like he was licking her body.

Sanchez was getting angry. "I would like to spend some time alone with you, José. I really would, but I wouldn't be the one being fucked! You asshole, you hurt her just for fun, didn't you? Made you feel like a big man."

"Yes, all the girls like me. They like a big cock inside them. How about you, Sanchez? I'd like to fuck you hard until you've had enough. And then some more, until I had enough. You understand me, *puta*?"

Sanchez leaned in and sneered at Battelle. "I understand you, José. I know about your problem. About how you can't get it up any more. And when you do, it's so small. Such a small dick, such a big mouth." She glared back at him. "And I heard you like it from the boys in prison. You'll have a lot of that when I'm through with you."

Battelle's eyes flashed with hatred, and he started rocking back and forth in his chair. He tried to stand up, but the leg chains held him down in a low crouch. He jerked up and down on them and gained a little height as he did so. Then his handcuffs pulled loose from the ring on the table, and he stood up. Only the chained leg irons held him back.

"I'll kill you, bitch!" he roared at Sanchez. "I'll make you hurt until you can't stand it no more!" Then he lunged across the table at her. His hands now loose, he reached for her throat and clamped them around her like an iron vice. His head butted into her face, causing her nose to gush blood.

Sanchez only had time to raise her hands and try to pry Battelle's talons from her throat. She clawed at his hands, digging her fingernails into his flesh. But the head butt had knocked her dizzy, and she had to focus all of her attention to fight back.

The attack unfolded as if it were a YouTube video. Bordou's first reaction was to punch Battelle in the side of his head with his fists. But Battelle didn't respond to the blows. He tried to pull one of Battelle's arms behind his back, but the man was built out of iron. And Bordou didn't have a weapon on him because they had left their sidearms outside the interrogation room. The guard who had been in the corner of the room hit the panic button, which alerted other guards in the area. Then he began to strike Battelle on the arms and shoulders with a heavy nightstick.

In a desperate attempt to free herself, Sanchez gripped Battelle's wrists and tried to twist the skin in a self-defense move she had learned early in her career. He did not respond to the tearing of his skin. She was getting weaker and weaker now because she couldn't breathe through his Herculean choke hold. Her vision began to fade as she stared into his hate-filled eyes, just inches from her own. She felt the blows that Bordou and the guard were delivering to Battelle shake through his body. But he would not let go.

Then she reached for the only weapon she had at her disposal. She felt for her notepad on the table and, next to it, her BIC pen was still within reach. She pulled her arm back, gripped the pen in her fist, and, with her last ounce of strength, rammed it into Battelle's right eye. It went in deep. He screamed as it sank into his eye and punctured his optic nerve. Blood and eye jelly splattered all over her face.

Finally, more guards arrived and pulled Battelle off the table, which released his iron grip from her throat. Four nightsticks pounded on his shoulders and head as he tried to shield them with his arms. Seeing that Sanchez had been pulled free, Bordou grabbed Parlance and dragged him whining and complaining out of the room so the lawyer wouldn't see what would happen to his client. Battelle had, after all, attacked one of the brotherhood of guards and cops who protected the city and one another, and there would be consequences. Bordou then ran back inside the room to get Sanchez.

Sanchez was curled up in a fetal ball on the floor, eyes closed, gasping for breath. Her face was a mass of blood and eye jelly. She was still breathing but only with great effort. He got her to sit up and tried to talk to her. She was scared out of her mind and reacted to his touch, striking him at first like he was trying to hurt her. Then she opened her eyes and saw it was him. She couldn't speak well but gasped a few words.

He pulled her to her feet and led her out of the room, away from the mayhem that was playing out there. He looked back and hoped the guards wouldn't kill Battelle.

In the hallway, Bordou sat Sanchez down on a chair and tried to stop her shaking. She was breathing better now. He wiped her face with Kleenex and told her she would be all right. He held her around the shoulders and told her it was over.

Then the EMTs arrived and took over. They got her on oxygen and examined her throat. Her neck was badly bruised but her windpipe had not collapsed. She would be OK.

After Battelle was subdued, and Sanchez calmed down, the two detectives decided to call it a day. Sanchez was still rattled and scared. She called Montero to join them for a beer at her place, telling him that a cool beer would soothe her throat.

Montero arrived at the apartment soon after they got there, and Bordou summarized the events that had taken place at the prison. "That son of a bitch was hard to put down. It was like he was on PCP or something. I went back in to make sure the guards didn't kill him, even though he deserved it. They beat him pretty bad, two broken arms, a broken shoulder, a cracked vertebra, and a concussion. They hauled him out of there in an ambulance. He won't be able to testify for a while after that."

They updated Montero with the new information they had obtained about the woman in Parker's trunk—that she was sold to Valdez and later to Battelle. She was, they believed, the very same Tracy Mickelson who had gone missing on the Tempe campus.

***

The next day, Bordou found out that during the short break in questioning, Parlance had made a phone call to Mexico. He must have gotten new marching orders from someone in the cartel. That would explain the sudden change in his client's cooperation with the police.

Battelle was admitted to a restricted wing of the hospital for treatment. When his health improved, he was to be transferred to solitary confinement at a state prison until the time of his trial, which would likely be delayed until he recovered. Sanchez went to see him at the hospital over the next few days and she noted that he wore a black eye patch to cover the vacant cavity in the right side of his head. He became more and more agitated each time she came to observe him, and he glared at Sanchez with real hatred whenever he saw her.

Chapter 19

May 8, 2014

Three days later, Montero and Sanchez got together for beers at Salvador's Grille after work. She was sporting a brightly colored scarf around her neck to cover the extensive bruising that had turned her neck various shades of black and blue. She wore blue jeans and a plaid short-sleeved Western-style shirt with snap buttons and had traded her work shoes for a pair of flip-flops.

She had just received the results from the fingerprint comparison between Parker and the dead woman in Puerto Vallarta. The department sleuths were 100 percent certain the dead woman was not Parker. She was now officially a Jane Doe.

"Well, Guillermo, I'm back on active duty. And the captain put me in charge of the new Sarah Parker case."

"Congratulations. You must be happy to be back in the game."

"Yeah, it feels good to get back in the saddle. I never thanked you for going down to Mexico when I couldn't, so thanks." They clicked bottles together. "Anyway, we're pretty sure that Sarah Parker killed Jane Doe to cover her tracks and exchange identities with her." Sanchez sampled the chips and salsa. "What's the latest from Officer Hermoso? Do they have any more to go on?"

"He said they've now declared the woman's death suspicious. The mayor doesn't want to call it a homicide because that would be bad for business. They've had some trouble with the drug gangs coming into the area, and that has raised the crime level lately. Any hint of an unexplained murder might keep tourists away."

"Did they ever find Parker or learn anything about who the unknown woman was?"

"No. They found absolutely no trace of Parker in any hotels. Hermoso said that the case has been largely dropped now because they have other headaches to worry about. It will probably never be solved. At some point, they'll have a funeral for the woman and bury her in the public part of the cemetery. You would think that someone would come forward to look for her."

Sanchez took another swig of beer. "Yeah, I've been thinking about that. With all the dysfunctional families these days, there are a lot of people who have no one to care whether they come home or not. Who knows what her situation was? You would think if she had children, though, someone would notice her disappearance."

"You'd think so. But it certainly made her a target of opportunity for someone who was looking to change their identity. If Parker was looking for someone to trade places with, she would've looked for just such a person: someone who lived alone with no close friends or family."

"She might've befriended her at a bar. It would've taken some planning, but she was apparently good at that."

Montero signaled the bartender for another Sol. "Even if they find her, the Phoenix DA is never going to prosecute her for anything related to Brown's disappearance. What could they possibly charge her with? Helping to set up a crime scene? It would look bad for the city and the state, and there are too many people whose careers would be damaged if the case went to trial. And the Mexicans don't have anything to go on either. They have their own political issues preventing them from acting too."

"But I think the Tracy Mickelson case might be her undoing. We have witnesses to testify she was involved and video putting her at the scene where Mickelson vanished. We have one witness to swear that she sold a woman to the gang—two if we can get Valdez, the Westside boss, to verify that he bought her and sold her to José Battelle. We have to lean on Battelle to tell us exactly where she went in Mexico, but I don't know if he'll ever talk now. His fear of the cartel is so strong I think he'd kill himself rather than snitch."

"You still don't have any hard evidence to prove Parker kidnapped her, do you?" Montero asked. "And the testimony of gangbangers is always suspect in court, especially if they cut a deal with the DA. How do you think Parker disabled the girl at the garage, and how did she keep her quiet all that time in the trunk?"

"I think she either used ether or hit her over the head. Lope said she had blood in her hair when they cleaned her up at the gang's hideout. He said she acted real punchy when they got her. Maybe she was shot up with ketamine or another tranquilizer. Or more ether, but that wears off pretty fast. So that probably wasn't it."

"How about a date rape drug? That has similar effects. I don't know much about it. Just an idea."

"Wait—what if there is still evidence in the car? If Parker drove her Honda and held Mickelson in it for a long time, maybe there's still some evidence in the trunk." Sanchez was excited. "Maybe something can still be detected."

"But you don't have the car."

"True, but maybe we can get it."

Sanchez punched a number that she had retrieved from her shoulder bag into her phone. She telephoned Emilia Flores at the Artistas Mexicanas to ask when Carlos Gonzales would next be visiting the city. She learned that he would be in Phoenix the very next day. That meant he would likely be driving Parker's old car. Sanchez decided that if she acted fast, she could get a warrant to impound the car and have her lab team go over it with a fine-tooth comb. Maybe they could turn up new evidence. She ended the call and ordered a round of margaritas.

Montero looked surprised. "So, what are the margaritas for?"

"Well, I think we should celebrate our success with the investigation. We wouldn't have even linked these two cases if you hadn't started looking for more unexplained disappearances, Montero. The link between them has tied Sarah Parker to Tracy Mickelson's kidnapping and sale to the Westside Glendale Lokos gang. And you did exemplary work in Mexico finding out about Brown and Parker. So here's to you, my investigative partner in crime. Or in crime solving, at least."

When the margaritas arrived, they held up their glasses and clinked them in a toast.

***

Sanchez obtained a search warrant for Gonzales's car, the Honda he had bought from Parker. The criminal investigation team set to work on it right away that afternoon based on the high priority she had given it. She had them focus first on the trunk, looking for any evidence of fluids from Mickelson that might remain discoverable. They had found nothing by the end of the day. The crime lab director told Sanchez that, after all, it had been a year since the kidnapping, and it was apparent that someone had cleaned the trunk's surfaces with strong cleaners and probably bleach. The team would resume their investigation the next day.

The forensic work continued for five days. The investigators found traces of blood on the car jack wrench, the type that had teeth on one end for gripping the jack more securely. The blood was lodged in the teeth of the wrench, which had otherwise been wiped down.

When the forensics team pulled apart the trunk, they found that a seam where two sheets of metal came together had retained traces of dried blood and another fluid, possibly urine. The lab crew worked hard to recover enough of a sample for DNA analysis, and everyone was pleased when the results came in, unadulterated and usable in a court of law. However, legal counsel warned that the chain of custody might be an issue. The trouble was they had no sample of Mickelson's DNA to compare the evidence against.

Sanchez was assigned the difficult task of calling the girl's parents in Minnesota to see if they had anything of hers that could be used definitively for a DNA test. The father told her no, regrettably, they did not have anything like that to make such a comparison. He was ready to end the call when his wife said just a minute. They did have a lock of her hair from her childhood, and they still had her baby teeth in a little glass case. Would that be helpful?

The new evidence arrived by FedEx the next day with signatures to verify chain of custody. Testing would take several days because the recovery of DNA from the samples would have to be done at the FBI lab in San Francisco. They just had to wait.

In the meantime, the lab team found something unexpected in the car—a set of fingerprints on the passenger side door that matched those of the Jane Doe in Puerto Vallarta. The car had been used to transport the woman there while she was alive. That presented a breakthrough in the Mexican murder case and finally directly tied Parker to Jane Doe before she had been killed. But had Parker killed her, or had she merely known her?

Throughout all of this, Sanchez was growing more and more impatient for results. She had elicited all the information from Batista, Lope and Battelle that she could. She had compiled it all in a report for her captain to review. She held meetings with the DA's office to discuss the evidence they had and to identify any deficiencies she needed to work on. In short, she was ready to finalize the report as soon as she received the results from the FBI lab and her lab people pulled it all together. The waiting was driving her crazy.

***

Sanchez got the results on May 14 when she was sitting at the Alamo Bar with Montero and Bordou, having an iced tea in the early desert heat. They were going over what they knew about Parker's whereabouts.

"We don't know what happened to the woman," Bordou said. "That's the problem. Even if we have a good case against Parker for kidnapping and human trafficking, we still don't have the woman herself to charge. So all this work may be for nothing. That's what has me pissed off." Bordou sipped his beer and looked at Montero to excuse his language. He did not know Montero for as long as Sanchez. She appeared to have a pass from the priest in the bad language department.

Montero ignored him and said, "There has to be some way to track down Parker under the name she assumed after she killed Jane Doe. Unless that was just a way for her to ditch her identity and assume another one altogether." Montero was thoughtful.

Sanchez said, "I talked to Officer Hermoso yesterday, and he said they'd whittled the list of outgoing airline passengers from PV down to twenty-six women matching her general description who flew out of town within three days of Jane washing up on the shore. They don't know where to go from there because they don't have security cameras in the airport except in the passenger arrivals area and the general waiting lounge. There are a lot of blind spots, so Parker could easily have ducked the cameras or worn a disguise." Sanchez felt like she was running out of options.

"Have you contacted Homeland Security about reviewing the photos taken of people arriving from Mexico on those days, the ones from PV?" Montero asked.

"They said we don't have enough to go on. They're short on resources as it is, so they don't want to spend time downloading data unless they have to or we give them a specific flight number. They argued that she might even not have flown from PV but could have taken a bus to Guadalajara or another airport and flown out from there. Or she could still be in Mexico. Too much uncertainty."

"We may never find her," Bordou lamented.

Sanchez's cell phone rang at that moment, and she checked the screen. Area code 415: San Francisco. "Hey, guys! I think it's the FBI lab."

She answered. "Hello, this is Sanchez. The results are on the way? Who are you sending them to? Milner in our lab? Excellent. Did you find a match? I know it's not final and that it jumps protocol, but did you find a match to Mickelson's DNA? . . . What? . . . *Holy shit* . . . *Really?* . . . I don't get it; who else? No match? How can that be? But you're sure of the sample then? OK, I'll alert our lab guys if you can't raise them. Hey, thanks for the call." Sanchez put the phone away with a puzzled look on her face.

"What is it?" Montero asked as he noticed the look. "What did they say?"

"They got good samples from the hair and teeth, so they have a DNA profile for Tracy Mickelson, no question. And they ran it against the blood samples from the car. The blood on the wrench is definitely hers. But they have questions about the blood sample collected from the trunk. The lab director didn't want to say what the problem was. He wants me to talk to our lab people about whether that sample could have been contaminated."

"Why?" Bordou asked.

"Because there are signatures from two different people in the sample. One appears to be from Mickelson. The other is unknown, which could screw the sample as evidence. Oh, damn it! That's all I need."

"But now we have evidence proving it was Mickelson in the car," Bordou said. "That's good news. We've proved Parker is guilty of kidnapping and trading her." He always looked on the bright side.

Sanchez stared at him as if he didn't get it. "Don't you see? If one sample is suspect, then the second sample will be viewed with suspicion too. A defense attorney will use it to raise doubt about the data. It could dump the whole case. I mean, how likely is it that we have two people's blood in the trunk of a car?"

"You're right. That wouldn't happen in a million years." Bordou's voice betrayed his disappointment.

Montero spun around on his bar stool and started to say something but then thought better of it and stopped with his mouth open. He shook his head and took a sip of beer.

Sanchez saw his expression. "What? What were you going to say, Guillermo? I hope it's positive because I can't hear any more bad news right now."

"What I thought—and this may be just crazy thinking—was that you could have two unique blood results if two people had been in the trunk, both bleeding. But that could only happen if Parker had done this before."

Chapter 20

May 15, 2014

The next day, Sanchez, Bordou, Captain Teller, and the entire forensic lab team held a meeting to discuss the results sent from the FBI lab in San Francisco. Teller was in a bad mood, and it showed on his face and in his demeanor. He was more intense than usual, sweat beading on his forehead below his receding hairline, so he held his handkerchief to dab away the moisture. His normally meticulous mustache and comb-over were askew, his clothes rumpled, something Sanchez had never observed before. She thought he must have had a rough night. She hadn't really thought about his home life before.

At first, he cut into the lab team and Sanchez for somehow screwing up the evidence. But as the meeting went on, he seemed to realize that it was possible no mistakes had been made. They conferenced in the FBI lab director to get his input on the matter, and he, in turn, put his chief investigator on the line to explain their findings.

Normally, results like these indicated some contamination of the sample or a procedural error. But after reviewing the work in their lab and the sampling documentation, both the FBI and the Phoenix scientists agreed there was only one explanation for the results: There were, in fact, two distinct blood signatures in the car trunk sample they had collected. Two individuals, both bleeding, had at different times occupied that cramped space.

After some discussion, the lab personnel decided it might be possible to follow two paths of investigation. The Phoenix PD would run a nationwide search of all appropriate databases to try to find a match for the other unknown person, given that they could safely conclude that Mickelson was the primary blood source. The FBI lab would now try to identify the age of the other blood sample, assuming it was from an earlier event. It would take time but still might be possible.

After the meeting, the captain asked Sanchez to step into his office. He sat down behind his desk with a fresh cup of coffee and had her pour herself a cup as well. He began by apologizing for blowing up at all of them in the meeting. Then he got down to business. "Sanchez, this case has taken a new direction and may turn out to be a major investigation. What I want to know is, can you handle it?"

Sanchez took his lack of confidence to be a slight, no matter how nicely it was intended. "Sir, I can handle it. And I'm probably the *only* person who has worked *all* the evidence and knows how it's related. If you try to replace me now, a lot will fall through the cracks."

Now that she had shown she knew what he was thinking and had called his bluff, he backed off. "OK, that's fine by me. You've got the lead, but I want to be involved, especially since this is going to turn political with the DA's office. We have to keep it tight in house for a while, at least until the questions about the other blood sample can be resolved."

"Understood."

He leaned back in his chair. "This is the kind of case that can make your career, Sanchez. Or break you if it goes wrong in any way. I know you're a good cop, if a little hotheaded, so you'll do fine on the casework. But I'm worried about the politics. So that's why I want you to keep me informed as you move ahead.

Especially if the DA's office starts asking questions. I expect them and the mayor's office to get nervous about this case. Possible serial crime, possibly murders. It could all blow up."

"I understand that it's a real can of worms, sir, but I can handle it. The technical stuff should not be a problem. I only wish we could ID the dead woman in Mexico and the woman whose blood was in the car. I'll try to avoid the politics, but if anything comes up, I'll alert you right away. Then I think we can resolve those issues as they come up."

Teller was relieved and bounded to his feet. "Good. Thank you, Detective. You've done some very good work on this case. Let's hope some pieces of the puzzle fall into place soon, huh?" He waved for her to leave the room, but she remained in her chair. She was not finished.

"Sir, there's one thing we should discuss right away."

"What's that?" Teller sat down again on the edge of his chair, as if he might not like what he was about to hear.

"There's the matter of Allister Brown's body. We now have proof that he died accidentally in Mexico. We have the coroner's report, which I had a friend of mine in the Phoenix coroner's office look over unofficially to keep it confidential. He confirmed that the coroner in Mexico followed standard procedures, and there is no reason to question his findings. The coroner collected fingerprints from the body and made copies of Brown's identification papers. He didn't collect any tissue samples for DNA analysis because it was believed to be an accidental death. I had our lab guys compare the fingerprints to those presumed to be Brown's from the supposed crime scene here in Phoenix. They're a match. So the Allister Brown found dead in Mexico is the same man who lived here and was supposedly murdered here last year. All of this information is strictly confidential now because it's part of the ongoing investigation of Parker. But it raises some issues."

"What issues did you have in mind, Sanchez?"

"Well, sir, it would be standard procedure to request to exhume the body to collect DNA samples for positive identification."

Teller jumped to his feet and shook his right fist in the air. "Are you crazy, Sanchez? That would reopen the whole Simpson case and stir up the DA all over again. That won't happen. And the coroner's report you have from Mexico was obtained unofficially, so it can't be made part of the record."

"But, you see, I already requested and received copies of those documents through normal channels too because I anticipated that there would be a problem. They're part of the file now."

"Oh shit!"

"But we don't have to exhume the body now to proceed with our investigation of Parker. You see, sir, as long as this is all related to Parker and she is the focus, there is no need to reopen the Simpson case. They follow parallel paths, and since our current investigation is still ongoing, we can keep the new information quiet for now."

"Oh, I see. Well, Sanchez, maybe you're better prepared to handle this case than I initially gave you credit for. You said 'issues,' as in more than one." He settled back in his chair, pulled it up to his desk, and made an open-handed gesture as if asking, "Now what?"

"There is a moral issue," Sanchez continued. "If we know where Allister Brown's body is buried, don't we have an obligation to notify the family? And if we do, it's possible *they* may want to exhume the body for a positive ID and bring it home for burial in California where his family lives. If they exhume the body and do the ID privately, it saves us the trouble."

Teller's eyes signaled the onset of panic. "But do we have to tell the family—or, at least, when do we have to tell them? If word gets out that he didn't die here in Phoenix, it would make the department look bad, not to mention the DA." He looked around like a trapped rat. "Holy shit, Sanchez! Just when I thought things were under control."

"Sorry, sir, but it has to come out sometime."

"The governor will want my ass for this. He signed off on the execution of an innocent man. What will we do?"

She waited expectantly, ready to provide her own solution to the problem. Teller began to pace back and forth behind his desk, head down, eyes focused on the floor, deep in thought. "OK. Keep this between us for now. Who else knows about Brown in Mexico?"

"Me; Bordou; Father Guillermo Montero—he's the one who actually discovered much of this info—some of our lab guys, but they don't know the whole story; and several police officers in Puerto Vallarta who are working their own case there for a possible murder related to Parker. I think that's it. They're all in-house people except Montero and the PV cops, but the PV police are under their own department rules and want to keep it quiet. Bad for business."

"How about this priest, Montero? Is he the crusading type? Will he want to take it to the press or something?" Teller's voice rose as, in his panic, he visualized the worst possible outcome: the mayor hanging him out to dry. "Oh Christ! He's not one of those anti-death-penalty people, is he?"

"No, no. He's not that type. In fact, he used to be with the El Paso PD. He's an ex-cop, so he knows how it works, and he's been an important resource on the case. He can help us do things unofficially."

Teller looked confused but somewhat relieved. "Let me

handle the question of notifying the parents. I'll talk to Legal about that." He held up his hand as if to ward off any more upsetting news. "Who have you been working with over at the DA's office on the Parker case?"

"Assistant DA Clara Alvera, sir. She only knows the facts surrounding the kidnapping and the Tempe case. She's been helpful too. But if this turns into a serial deal, then it may be kicked upstairs and out of her hands."

"Let's get to work, and let me know what you get from the lab boys."

Sanchez left the office as Teller reached for the phone. Her head was spinning. *Holy shit!* she thought. *This is going to get interesting, and not in a good way.*

***

The next day, Montero called Sanchez to talk. She told him that it would likely take six months or longer for the Sinaloa Cartel case to come to trial because the DA wanted to tie all of the cases together into one trial: the drug distribution, drug smuggling, gunrunning, and missing-persons/human trafficking charges. She thought it was too ambitious. If one case blew up, then all the others would too because they were dependent upon one another. But it would make a big splash in the papers. That was all the politicians seemed to care about.

Montero changed the subject to the lab results. "So, what happened with the more detailed DNA testing? That's what you wanted to talk about, right?"

"The results came in today. They show not two, but three blood signatures in the car. The blood on the wrench is only from Mickelson, so that's clean, solid evidence against Parker. The sample from the trunk has a clear signature of Mickelson, but there is an even stronger signature from another female, and that signature is three to five years old. The final sample contains evidence of a third person's blood, but it's a weak signature, also from three to five years ago, and possibly not useable in court."

"Wow! So Sarah Parker has a history of kidnapping, or worse. How long did she own the car?"

"Bought it new in 2006. Her parents gave it to her as a high school graduation present. She's been the only owner until she sold it to Mr. Gonzales."

"That links two of the samples back to her Berkeley days. Have you contacted Detective Carter since there may be some new evidence in his cases?"

"No, I can't. Not yet, anyway. That was one of the things I wanted to talk to you about. My hands are tied by some of the political constraints on the case. Teller says I can't let Carter know anything until it's cleared here first. It's partly to protect our case, but also because of the DA. The whole Simpson mess has everyone scared, and the captain is afraid of what the DA will do if any of this comes back on him."

Montero was intrigued. "Explain why the DA has everyone so nervous. Who is this guy?"

"He's John Davies, who has just won the special election for district attorney of Mariposa County, the biggest and most powerful county in the state. He has more power than most state officials. He's from an old political family, a long line of judges, senators, and even a governor. It's rumored that he's being groomed to run for the US Senate in two years. He's on a political fast track, so nothing can go wrong to upset that plan." Sanchez paused while she handed a file to another officer. "He's running on a tough-on-crime, pro-police platform, and all the police departments like the guy. It's nice to have someone who believes in what we do, right?"

"So *that's* why this is so touchy. Now I get it. But what you're doing doesn't affect him."

"His people are concerned that if it comes out that Brown didn't die as it was shown at trial, it would make him look bad. But I don't think it would be the end of the world for his career. Maybe a setback."

"What about Mickelson? Any idea where she went in Mexico? Do you even know a city where she might have gone?"

"José Battelle was pretty cagey about where she went. He said she was packed into a crate on a truck to Nogales and then Juárez, but he began to hedge when he thought he could get a better plea deal. Then he lawyered up with that shyster who works for the Sinaloa Cartel. He hasn't said anything more since my interview with him. Besides, he hates my guts, so he might not talk if he thinks that would screw up my investigation. I tried to get him to loosen up, but there's only so much I can do to pry it out of him. If the DA got more involved, then more juice could be applied to get him to talk. But that will take time."

Montero thought about this for a moment and then said, "If she's in Juárez, there may be hope of tracking her down, assuming she's still there in one of the brothels that Sinaloa runs. But again, with the drug overdoses, beatings, illness, and other things, the girls don't last long in those houses. If they put her out on the street, her chances are much worse."

"If we got confirmation of the town, could we find her? It would take cooperation with the police in Juárez, and probably the FBI would have to get involved. It would be an administrative nightmare." Sanchez felt it would become a lost cause in a bureaucratic interagency tangle.

"You wouldn't want the local *policia* involved. They work

with the gangs sometimes, and she'd just disappear, probably be killed. And the politics could get very messy. When I was on the PD in El Paso, we only had success if we worked with individual cops who worked with us unofficially. The Mexican government doesn't want to admit that women are kidnapped in the US and taken across the border, especially for prostitution. You would never get it to work."

"But how else can we find her, then? I can't go down there to look."

"There are ways. I may know someone who could help, if I can find him." Montero was silent for a moment. "See if you can get confirmation on the Juárez location. It's a big city, so a name for the bordello would help."

***

Two days later, Sanchez and Teller waited in a quiet conference room on the top floor of the county courthouse, standing by the floor-to-ceiling glass windows looking out over the center of the city of Phoenix. They didn't say anything, partly because they were mentally going over the presentations they would make in their meeting with District Attorney John Davies. They were also silent because they suspected someone might be listening to them on a microphone hidden in the room. Something about the marble walls and fancy curtains made them feel ill at ease.

The door opened, and Cory Bartlett, the DA's public relations advisor, rushed into the room and shook their hands.

"OK, Captain, Detective Sanchez. I told Mr. Davies your idea, and he liked it in general, but he wanted to see you and hear more about it directly from you. And he wanted your supervisor here to make sure it was legit from his point of view. So when we get in there, you have fifteen minutes to sell the deal. Understand?"

He led Sanchez and Teller into the DA's private meeting room located in a corner of the building, with big glass windows on two sides. Here, mahogany paneling replaced the marble walls of the conference room. John Davies and two other people were already waiting. One was his second in command, Jack Frisser, the chief assistant DA. The other was Assistant DA Clara Alvera, the point person on the Parker investigation for the DA. They all sat down.

This was the first time Sanchez had met or been in the same room with Davies. He looked like an alert, middle-aged man with a friendly enough face. But something about him seemed hard, maybe his gray eyes that didn't give anything away. He was one of those guys who had been around government for years and knew how to wield power, giving him a real presence. Sanchez noticed he was wearing a beautifully tailored silk suit.

Davies spoke first. "Thank you both for coming over today for this meeting. Captain Teller, Detective Sanchez, I hear you've been doing a great job over there in the Phoenix PD. I'm a little short on time today, so we can't really chat, but I hope that as this work progresses we have a chance to learn more about each other."

Bartlett leaned forward to whisper a few words to his boss.

"Thank you for meeting us today, sir," Teller replied.

"Let's begin, shall we? I heard your proposal and like the way you made sense out of our need to accomplish our goals without any unnecessary collateral damage. I understand that you want to encourage this gang member, Battelle, to reveal the location of the kidnapped girl. What is her name?" Bartlett leaned in again. "Oh yes. Ms. Mickelson. He indicated she was in Juárez, but you would like him to be more specific. If we can work him a better deal, then he might help you find her so she can be rescued, right? I like the idea of getting her back. It's a terrible thing, these kidnappings, and the case could draw attention to the lawless behavior of the Mexican gangs that operate here in our state. It wouldn't hurt the PD's reputation to solve such a case and rescue the victim. I'm onboard with this."

Sanchez took his pause as her cue to make her case. "Thank you, sir. The captain and I think it would also help us with our other objective: to coax Battelle into giving us more info on a major gunrunning operation he managed for the Sinaloa Cartel. It would be a real blow to the cartel if we can get him to talk—"

"And stopping the gunrunning is something the ranchers along the border and a lot of other constituents would really support," Bartlett interrupted. "It would buy us a lot of goodwill."

"Right! Right! Go on," Davies agreed emphatically.

Sanchez continued. "The rescue of the girl would draw attention to Sarah Parker, who we now believe was involved in at least two disappearances, possibly two murders. If we can help the Puerto Vallarta police with their case, I believe they will help us with the Parker case. But more important, sir, is the fact that Parker withheld the location and death of Allister Brown. If they had come forward, there would not have been a murder conviction for Mr. Simpson. She withheld vital evidence that would certainly have never placed the Phoenix PD or the DA's office in the position of convicting anyone of a capital crime. One might argue that they were accomplices in an effort to mislead the court."

"I see where you're going with this, Detective. It's possible that Parker was the ringleader in this effort to misdirect the court, helping to provide false evidence about Mr. Simpson's guilt. She could be held responsible for his conviction and the resulting sentence because she did not come forward. But why would she do that? It doesn't make a lot of sense." Davies turned to his advisor. "Bartlett?"

"Sir, I think, with some effort, we can spin that to our advantage," Bartlett said. "Especially if we can prove this woman was a serial killer. That fact alone will take attention off the Simpson affair. The media people have already forgotten about it, according to our survey."

Sanchez and Teller sat quietly, holding their breath, hoping for the DA's approval of their plan.

"Is that right?" Davies returned his attention to Sanchez. "Well, excellent work. OK, young lady, it sounds like we can live with the spotlight on Sarah Parker for a while. What else do we have?"

"Sir, in order to do much of this work, we'll need your office to help us interface with officials in Mexico. And there may be other needs that come up as we move forward. Captain Teller can address those issues better than I can."

Sanchez looked over at him. Teller now took over. "Yes, sir. There are several things we need to do in order to tie up the Parker crimes, especially the three unsolved missing-persons cases at Berkeley. We need to work with the Berkeley PD to clear those up. But there is an issue that is politically delicate, I believe. That is the question of when we can tell Allister Brown's parents that he's buried in a cemetery in Mexico. They should be informed."

"I see. We have to discuss how best to do that. I assume that sooner is better." Davies looked over at Bartlett for a suggestion but received none. "Bartlett and I will discuss that. It's a sensitive matter that needs to be handled carefully. Captain, I want to coordinate *that* with your department too." His comment clearly meant, *Don't do anything without my approval.*

The meeting broke up, and Sanchez went over to talk to

Alvera. Then the two cops drove back to the station.

"You handled that very well, Sanchez," Teller complimented her. "You managed to thread the needle between the issues and left the DA in a good position. I don't know if I could have thought of that compromise."

"Thank you, Captain. I just hope we can make it all happen."

Chapter 21

May 20, 2014

Y ou know how the Feds work, Sanchez. We do all the legwork, and then some FBI special agent takes credit for all of our good effort but blames us if the investigation goes to shit. That's why I don't want this to get out to them."

Detective Louis Carter had called Sanchez to discuss her new findings in the Parker case. He needed her help in tying the California cases to the work she had already done and was trying to talk her and Teller into working together without seeking input from the FBI. Carter had had a bad experience with them in the past and didn't want a repeat performance. Once the FBI got their hooks into a case, the local police lost all control.

"I think I can sell it to my captain on this end. He has no love for the Justice Department and their heavy-handed ways. We share credit on the California cases with you in the lead, correct?"

"Yeah, sure. And we already have the DNA samples on file for each of our three missing persons. But I'll have to verify that everything is kosher with the evidence chain of custody and lab procedures. OK?"

"Send me the DNA signatures for the three victims, and we'll do the digital match here. If we get a hit, I'll let you know right away. Then we'll know that we are barking up the right tree." She paused for a second. "I don't know why I used that corny saying. But you get what I mean."

"Yes." He chuckled. "I'll send that over today."

Sanchez went upstairs to inform Teller that he would have to talk to Carter's superior to keep it all official, even though she and Carter had already mapped out a strategy to investigate his unsolved missing-persons cases. It would all begin with the DNA comparisons. Then she had to hurry to a meeting with Alvera about the gunrunning case. Davies wanted to get the Bureau of Alcohol, Tobacco, Firearms and Explosives involved. But Sanchez and Alvera knew that was risky because ATF had a way of playing fast and loose with shared information. They often just wanted to do things their way and didn't concern themselves with their local partners. The Feds always thought they were better at their job than any local or state police. But lately, they were behaving more like team players since their huge failure in the Fast and Furious scandal.

She marched right into Alvera's office and dropped her files on the side table. "Hi, Clara. Sorry I'm late. I got hung up on the phone."

She took off her suit jacket and hung it on the back of her chair. She was wearing a new white blouse, her best dark skirt, and heels for the appointment. She had decided she needed to step up her appearance for meetings at the DA's office since she spent so much time with Alvera now. Somehow, Alvera was always dressed in elegant yet businesslike attire, with her model good looks, slender figure, and fabulous hair in a class of their own. Sanchez was aware of her own more casual style.

"Hey, Lori. You seem to be everywhere these days. I saw you at the preliminary hearing for José Battelle this week too. You must be burning at both ends."

"Who needs sleep, right? Say, have you heard any more about chasing down the Mickelson woman?"

"Well, as you know, Battelle verified that she went to a cartel brothel in Juárez. He gave us the name of the brothel, and we asked the Juárez police to check to see if she was there. They did, after stalling for three days, and said she was no longer there. Apparently, the gang moves the girls around between properties to keep the clientele happy with new meat. It's disgusting what they do." Alvera shook her head in anger. "But we aren't sure how interested the local cops are in finding the girl."

"I was afraid of this. By making it official, they may not want to find her. Too many vested interests. Even if some cops want to find her, others in the same department will tell the cartel, and they'll move her before the police show up. If they feel threatened, the cartel might move her to another city or, worse, just kill her. I wish we could just go in there ourselves and grab her. Then we could cut through all this bullshit."

"It would be nice, but there *are* little things called a border and national sovereignty that get in the way. I'm just afraid it's going to take a very long time to find her and then extricate her. . . if she's still alive."

"And Battelle? Where is he being held?"

"We have him in solitary confinement down at Florence. He should be safe there until the trial begins four or five months from now. We transport him up here for hearings."

"I was surprised he gave us as much info as he did. Is he feeding us false leads, do you think?"

"So far, his information checks out. Although until we move on the cartel's operations, we won't know if we've been had or not." Alvera looked at her watch and made a face. "OK. Got to run." She threw on her jacket, grabbed her leather briefcase, and rushed off to the courthouse, looking elegant the whole time.

Sanchez's phone dinged, indicating she had an email from

Carter. It read: *Here's the DNA data.*

She perked up and walked briskly—as briskly as she could in three-inch heels—back to her office to download the file attached to the email. She immediately forwarded it to her contact in the lab and called to tell him she was on her way downstairs.

Blake Jones, Phoenix PD's expert on classical jazz and all things forensic, greeted her when she pushed open the lab door. "That was record time, Sanchez. You must have called from the elevator."

"I never use the elevator. It's too slow. How does the data look?"

"I'm just loading it into the computer now. Let's see . . . everything looks cool, so let me change it into the right format for our fingerprint software. OK, looks good. Now, to compare against the main unknown DNA signature, Person A." He pressed a few keys and sat back for a few seconds, as if ready to carry on a conversation while the machine calculated a match. The computer screen instantly flashed *99% acceptable match.*

"Wow! That was fast," Sanchez said.

"Yeah, it looks good. One of your samples is a match for Lucy Johnson. I can't believe it. That was an old sample, and the software had no trouble matching peaks. It was a good sample, even after all this time." He began to save the results and print a hard copy to give the lab director for his report.

"Come on. You can work on your report later. Try the next unknown signature, Person B."

"OK, OK. I'll just save this and load that."

The machine worked for about two minutes while they stood by holding their breaths. Then the answer flashed on screen: *63% match, unacceptable.*

"Shoot. What does that mean?" Sanchez asked.

"It means that there are some similarities, but the comparison is weak. That happens if the sample is degraded or if there's a lot of noise in the sample for some reason. We may be able to enhance the quality of our sample or reduce the noise numerically. Let me work on it a while and see what I can do. I have to follow standard protocols for it to be valid in court."

Sanchez was becoming impatient. "OK, try the last signature. Let's see if we have a match on it."

Jones began the comparison of the third sample. The program ran for three minutes and then simply displayed *Fail* on the screen.

Sanchez said, "That's bad news."

Jones looked puzzled. "I'll need time to find out what went wrong," he commented. "Call me later."

"Yeah, see what you can do. Print the first comparison out for me, won't you?"

Sanchez went straight up to Teller's office and waited for his assistant to finish showing him some papers. When he waved her in, she slapped the printout on his desk with a triumphant smile on her face. "We got her. We got Parker in another kidnapping."

He looked at the results and smiled. "So you have evidence she had someone else in her trunk? Who was it?"

"It's Lucy Johnson, the first of the missing women in Berkeley. And Blake Jones thinks he can improve the quality on the second unknown, so we may have more on that in a day or two."

"Well, it looks like good work. This means that Parker was involved in at least one of those other cases in California too. Have you notified the people out there?"

"No, not yet. I wanted to show you the results first."

"Good. Send them the results. Remind me who you're working with out there."

"Carter, sir. He has been involved in all three of the missing-persons cases."

"Let me know what he has to say."

Sanchez returned to her desk and called Carter. He didn't respond to her news in quite the way she had expected him. The man was perplexed. After five years, he had thought the case was dead. "It's good news, I suppose. It might take a while for it to sink in, though. Let me think about what I have to do now. This means Lucy Johnson was transported somewhere either before she died or afterward. I don't suppose you have any idea how much blood was originally in the car, do you?"

"No, just the trace we found in the seam of the sheet metal. How much was found at the crime scene?"

"Not so much, but someone had cleaned the scene up. Hey, let me think about this and call you back with questions. There isn't any chance I can get you to fly out here, is there? It might be productive if we went through the cases together, with your knowledge of Parker's more recent activities."

"Yeah," Sanchez said. "That could be helpful for the development of our case too. Let me talk to my boss about it. I'll call you with an answer soon."

She put her phone away and leaned back in her chair at her desk, thinking about what she could learn if she went out to Berkeley. For a small additional investment of department resources, they could perhaps find out more about what had happened to the other women. That would support the Parker case because it would show a pattern of behavior needed to establish Parker as a serial criminal. In any case, she would wait to approach Teller until she heard back from Carter.

She called Montero to tell him the news. She mentioned she might need to travel to California to pursue the new leads.

He asked when. "I'll be out in San Francisco for two days next week for an ecumenical meeting and planned to stay for the weekend. If you do your work and time it right, we could see the sights on the weekend. What do you think?"

"Well, I don't know for sure that I'm going yet, but maybe it'll work out. I'll let you know."

***

May 22, 2014—Berkeley, California

Sanchez met Carter at his office at the Berkeley Police Department on the following Thursday morning. They had coffee and discussed her travel arrangements as he showed her around the station house. He was an average-looking man in his early sixties with graying hair and a weary smile. His mannerisms reminded her of her father, so she took to him right away. He wore a faded tweed jacket, which made him naturally fit the role of an experienced detective.

He had reserved a workroom with two large tables in it for them to use for the next few days while they reviewed the missing-persons cases. They started by going through his three cases in detail so Sanchez was up to date on all of them. She, in turn, explained everything she had turned up on Parker and the Mickelson case.

"So she could be implicated in three disappearances here and one in Tempe, as well as the murder of the woman in Puerto Vallarta," Sanchez said. "We think we have her tied to both the Mickelson case and the Johnson case through hard physical evidence. Our lab in Phoenix thinks the second blood signature can be resolved, but until it is, we can't assume she was involved in your other two cases, Jones and Serano."

Carter scratched his chin before he responded. "Yes. It's unfortunate that we've come up with a suspect so many years after the crimes took place. The odds of finding any relevant physical evidence now are almost nil."

"How about any bodies? Did you check for any possible Jane Does in any other precincts who might have matched the missing women?"

"I've done all that. No luck there. I went as far afield as LA, since that is a city where all sorts of unexplained bodies show up, the most in the state. During the period when these women disappeared, it was standard practice to save and analyze DNA from all unidentified bodies with the expectation that someday a match would be found. But no luck there either."

"Maybe we should look at it from Parker's point of view. If she kidnapped and murdered the women, how would she dispose of their bodies? I can't believe she knew gang members who could help her dispose of the corpses while she was in college. How did she handle them and finally get rid of them?"

"I tell you what: Let's visit each of the crime scenes, and maybe we'll see the difficulties she could encounter at each location. Maybe it will make us think of something we didn't find in the files."

Sanchez and Carter walked downstairs to the basement garage and placed three file boxes in the back seat of Carter's unmarked car. They drove off into midmorning traffic, stopping at a local deli to get sandwiches on the way.

The first crime scene was that of Johnson, the woman whom they could definitely tie to Parker. They were able to talk the building manager into letting them into the apartment that Johnson had occupied with a roommate in 2008. It was furnished with some of the same furniture that had been there when Johnson had rented it. It was currently vacant, so they felt fortunate that they could spend some time in the unit. The manager explained that it had been repainted and some minor remodeling had been done after Johnson had disappeared. He had not worked there then, so he could not provide any new insight into the investigation. He left them to do whatever they had to do.

The kitchen area was where the blood evidence had been found and where the perpetrator's cleanup activity had been greatest. The hypothesis at the time was that Johnson had been struck on the head or stabbed in the kitchen, causing blood to fall on the floor. The cleanup had focused almost entirely on that room. Now, of course, there was nothing for the two detectives to see. They went through the case files and old photos.

They went through the whole apartment to get the feel of the crime scene and later poked around in the kitchen. Then Carter's cell phone rang, and he stepped out to take the call. "It's about another case. I'll be a few minutes."

Meanwhile, Sanchez decided to reenact the events of that night and walk through them from the beginning. She stepped outside the apartment and looked down the hallway to imagine how she might carry out a kidnapping. First, she checked the approach to the door from the elevator, assuming that Johnson would have come up that way. If so, she had to walk about twenty feet to her door. Sanchez pulled her own keys out of her purse like Johnson would have done that night. When she got to the door, she looked around to see if an attacker could blindside her. No, the hallway was one of those long corridors where there was no place for someone to hide. She would not have been easily caught off guard.

Sanchez went inside the apartment and closed the door. What if Johnson had been attacked and pushed *inside* the door? That would have required the door to be unlocked. Then there could have been an altercation just inside the door, and if she had been hit, some blood might have fallen there. But the crime scene investigation did not find any blood or signs of a fight in that area.

The next option that ran through Sanchez's mind was that Johnson might have let the person into the apartment herself. With the door closed, she looked through the peephole to see what she would have seen that night. Maybe that was what had happened?

Sanchez closed her eyes and tried to visualize the scene. Maybe Johnson had come home and settled in. Then someone knocked on her door. She would have asked who it was, but you can never understand what people are saying through the door, so she would have had to look out the peephole. She had seen someone standing there. What had they wanted? Had it been a friend who had stopped by? Had it been a neighbor who had needed help in the middle of the night? Whoever it was, she had known them well enough to open the door and let them in.

But the signs of an altercation were in the kitchen, not by the door. Maybe. Sanchez tried to envision the scene. *If it were me, I would let the person in and stand and talk a bit. If it was someone I knew, I would probably lead them into the living room next. Maybe we would sit down, and then what? I would offer my guest a drink, probably beer. I would go into the kitchen to the refrigerator, right? I would have to turn my back on the guest to reach inside the fridge. That's when the attack would happen. With the first drink or the second, it wouldn't matter. The same opportunity would be there each time.*

The attack was bloody. We know that because the cleanup was centered in the kitchen. Yes, right in front of the fridge. It makes sense. But how was it done? Assuming it was premeditated, would the attacker have brought a knife or a club with him or her? A knife would be easy to conceal but a club, not so easy, especially if we sat down. A knife attack from the back would be tricky. There are no easy kills from behind unless you have had some training. Ribs get in the way. A club would be better, easy from behind. One good hit, and your target goes down. Then you keep hitting until the person is dead. No fighting back.

Sanchez came out of her imaginary reenactment. But which weapon was it? She looked around at the nearly empty apartment with only the basic furniture left. She sat on the sofa that remained in the living room. She could see into the kitchen from there. If she were the killer, what would she see? Would a weapon of opportunity present itself to her?

She decided to look at the crime scene photos to see what the apartment had looked like that night. She found six photos of the living room and eleven showing the kitchen from various angles. There was no door to the kitchen; it was an open space like in most small apartments. In the first photo, she noticed a small display table against the wall, just before the entry to the kitchen. There were several objects on the table all lined up. She looked closer and saw that they were trophies, like the ones given for track-and-field events. There were four of them in a row, but they were not evenly spaced. She looked at another photo, which covered the same area. They were definitely trophies of different sizes, but there was a gap in the lineup. Like one was missing. She checked the field notes and verified that the crime scene guys had inventoried them. High school trophies for basketball.

Sanchez went back to the living room and sat down on the sofa. *If I was going to take someone out, it would be easy to pick up one of the trophies and follow Lucy into the kitchen. A trophy would be heavy and solid. The ones in the photo had rectangular bases. That would make a hell of a dent. And it would probably be bloody.*

She got up again and went into the kitchen. Maybe Johnson had been hit with a trophy and there had been a lot of blood, so the attacker had to do a cleanup. He or she would have used whatever was there already. Nobody plans for blood—not the first time they kill someone, anyway. Sanchez referred to the file to read which areas in the kitchen had been cleaned. But the bathroom, entryway, and part of the living room also had been wiped down as if someone had been careful about leaving fingerprints. It all fit.

At that moment, Carter came back to the apartment and knocked on the door. Sanchez let him in and told him what she had discovered. He said he liked the way she had reconstructed the sequence of events. In fact, he had noticed the missing trophy at the time of his investigation and had similar ideas. So they felt they understood how it had happened, but then, how was the body disposed of?

They set about solving the problem of how the body of an average-size woman could have been moved from the apartment. If Parker was the only person involved, she would have had to drag it from the apartment to the staircase or the elevator. How would she have disguised it?

"She could just drag it rapidly to the stairwell. The disappearance occurred at night, so it's unlikely she would meet anyone on the stairs at a late hour. Let's see . . . Lucy was five feet six inches tall, of medium build, and weighed a hundred and thirty pounds. Not very heavy. A bit shorter than you, Sanchez. And you are about the same height as Parker. She was five feet nine inches and physically fit. So she should have been able to move a hundred-and-thirty-pound body like that. Don't you think?"

"Well, yes. I could do it, and I'm about the same size, but it's difficult to move a limp body. She probably couldn't lift it, but she could drag it, all right. So let's say she wraps the head so the body doesn't bleed while it's being dragged. She could go to the stairs easily."

Sanchez mimicked dragging a body to the stairwell door. She stood in the stairwell and looked down. "It's only three flights down to the garage level. Easy to do going down."

They walked down and stepped into the garage. "And she could pull her car up here to the door and muscle the body into her trunk," Sanchez said.

"So there's no magic required there. Now she gets in the car and drives off. What does she do with the body?"

To answer that, they checked the police case files and found out that both Johnson and Parker had worked for a while at a restaurant ten blocks away, although at different times. They drove there to look the scene over.

The restaurant sat on a corner lot with a parking area for eight cars in the rear. A large steel dumpster standing against the back wall of the building looked like a reasonable place to dispose of a body on the lot.

Carter referred to the file and said, "The police looked here after Lucy was reported missing. But that was seven days afterward. The dumpster may have already been emptied by that time. So it's possible Parker put the body in there, and it was taken away. It might have made it all the way to the landfill without anyone seeing it."

"Yeah, I suppose that would be an easy way to get rid of a body. But why here? If the body was discovered, it would tie her to the crime. What if Lucy wasn't dead? What would she do with a live person for a few days?"

"That's a whole different matter. Do you think she could have lifted a body up into this thing?" Carter indicated how tall the dumpster was with his hand.

"I think so. I could, but I work out. She was in good

condition then. But when did she work here? I thought she worked at a restaurant later on."

"Let's see . . ." Carter looked in his notes for a couple of minutes. "At the time Lucy disappeared, Parker didn't work here. That was earlier. So she must have known about this dumpster. But at that time, she was working at the summer camp, I think." He rifled through the pages of the report. "It isn't clear. She had started to work at the summer camp in late May, and Johnson disappeared in early June. So Parker would have been out of town much of the time. According to the file, she stated that she wasn't even in town when Lucy disappeared. She was at the camp near Lake Tahoe. And Peter Simpson was away on a field trip that week. No one else knew anything about the disappearance, no other friends or neighbors. They just thought Lucy went away for a few days. Her roommate came back after the weekend, and she was gone. After four days, she called the police."

"So she disappeared on the weekend?" Sanchez asked.

"Yeah, on Saturday, as near as they could tell. It wouldn't be unusual for her to go out and meet someone. Bring him home and then find out that the Mr. Right she picked up at a bar was really Mr. Wrong. So, at first, the police figured she was just shacked up somewhere. They weren't concerned right away."

"Did you say, 'Shacked up'? I haven't heard that in a while."

"Well, sorry. That's what we used to call it in my day." Carter chuckled and looked at his watch. "Look, it's getting late already. If you need to check into your hotel, I can run you by there. Did you get a room at the Oxford near the station?"

"Yes, I did. I guess it *is* a bit late to continue to the other crime scenes. Do you have to get home to the family?"

"Well, yes. But I told my wife I might run late because you were coming out to help with these cases. So I was going to suggest that you check in, we go to the second scene, and then get dinner at a nice Italian place I know. I can head home after that. What do you say?"

"Sounds good to me. Let's go."

Carter drove Sanchez to the Oxford Hotel, where she checked in while he waited in the car. They then drove over to the apartment house where Naomi Jones had lived when she had been dating Brown. They knocked on the door of the apartment she had occupied and found a young woman—obviously a college student—at home. They showed her their credentials, and she let them in. She acted extremely nervous when she heard why they were there.

"You mean a girl disappeared right from this apartment with no clue? No way. How come no one told me? Is it safe to be here now? What happened to the girl? Does anyone know?"

Sanchez tried to explain that it was an old, unsolved case and she should not be alarmed, but the damage had been done. The young woman began to freak out, which brought her roommate out of an earbud-induced state of consciousness in the bedroom. They worked each other into a panic and asked what they should do. Maybe one of the other renters had done something, kidnapped the girl or something. Maybe the guy was still in the building. They thought of one guy down the hall who seemed kind of creepy. Was it him?

Carter left the apartment after trying to reassure the women. He decided he wouldn't ever tell any other girls that they lived in an apartment where someone had gone missing. He and Sanchez checked the staircase and parking lot in the back of the building. The layout was similar to the scene where Johnson had lived. They found nothing new.

At dinner, Carter told Sanchez the story of his life, which he thought had been interesting so far. He had been in the army and got into police work after he had returned from a year in Vietnam. He had taken to the work and had enjoyed walking the beat in Berkeley most of the time. He had seen a lot of petty crime, drunkenness charges, and lost dogs. Everything seemed so real to him after the war and his experiences overseas. But Berkeley had had its share of antiwar protests and riots. He had worked his way up to detective the old-fashioned way, one year and position at a time. He liked the job. He had a wife and two kids and was happily married. Sanchez thought it all sounded pretty good.

After dinner, Carter dropped Sanchez back at her hotel, and they arranged for an early start in the morning. She went to her room and called Montero, who was across the bay in San Francisco attending his meetings. He didn't answer, so she left a message.

She decided it was time to take a hot bath and wash off the travel grime acquired from the long day. She submerged herself in a deep, hot bubble bath and relaxed. She pulled her hair up and flipped it over the back of the tub, settling down in the water.

She tried to relax, but her mind kept working through the crime scenes she had seen today. She wondered why more young women weren't assaulted each day in cities like Berkeley and Oakland. Her experience while living in LA had been a little grim at times, having been bothered occasionally by weirdos and aggressive men. But she had learned how to be on alert and defend herself. Young college women were just so vulnerable.

She tried to push these concerns out of her mind and think happy thoughts. The bath felt fabulous. It had been a long day, and she needed to relax. Her thoughts drifted away from the missing women to what it would cost to get a massage and maintain this warm, soothing sensation.

***

The next day, Carter and Sanchez visited the last crime scene on their list. It was the restaurant where Tina Serano had worked in 2011. They went to the back parking area to see where she had been abducted. There, they were surprised to see that several halogen lights and a pair of surveillance cameras now covered the whole lot. They met the restaurant manager and sat down with him at one of the tables near the front of his establishment.

"After Tina disappeared, we decided we should upgrade the lighting to protect our employees and customers," the manager said. "We had a few cases of car vandalism before that too, so it seemed like the right thing to do. Then, a year later, one of our girls said a transient tried to grab her on her way to her car one night, so we added the cameras. Just having them there with big signs saying that the parking lot was under surveillance made a difference. We set it up live so we could watch the lot on monitors inside. It made everyone feel a lot safer."

Carter led the questioning. "So it was not very well lit at the time Tina was there. Didn't an employee see her with someone that night?"

"Yeah, that's right. She left right after another waitress, named Dottie, who saw her talking to someone in the lot. A woman. The girl told the police that when they came around. It should be in your report."

"I don't see it," Carter said, thumbing through the file. "Did Tina have any problems with anyone at the time that you can remember? Anyone bothering her?"

"Boy, it's been a long while now. I think there was an ex-boyfriend at one point just before she disappeared. I don't recall anymore." The manager scratched his head. "You should talk to Dottie. She hung around with Tina some then." He looked toward the back of the restaurant. "I think she just came in for the early shift. Let me get her for you."

The manager walked away for a few minutes and returned with two cups of fresh coffee, which he offered to the detectives. "Here you go. We always like to serve cops, so come in for dinner sometime or lunch, you know. I made the coffee black 'cause I don't know how you like it. There's some creamer and Sweet'N Low over there." He checked the creamer and loudly called out, "Hey, Dottie, bring some cream up here with you when you come." Then he told Carter and Sanchez, "She'll be here in a minute to talk to you. Just take a seat. I have to see a man about the dairy delivery." He excused himself and walked to the back of the restaurant.

"Hi, here's the cream. Who wants some?" Dottie asked. "The manager said you had questions about the night Tina disappeared. What's happening? Are you still looking for her?"

"We have some new leads that we want to check out," Carter said. "You left the restaurant just before Tina the night she disappeared. Is that correct?"

"Yeah, yeah. I had closed out and was sitting in my car listening to one of my favorite tunes on the radio. Then she came out to her car and someone walked up and started talking to her as she left the restaurant. The song finished, and I drove home. I didn't see anything more."

"Who was it that talked to her? Could you see?"

"No, it was dark. I just saw the shadows by the back door. But it seemed normal. I only saw them for a minute. I was late to get to my boyfriend's place, so I didn't stick around."

"Did Tina have any trouble with anyone that night or in her personal life? The manager just said she might have had trouble with an ex or something."

"Well, she did dump Johnny a while before that, and he was mad at her. But the police said he was working in Oakland that night. Right? He called me and was mad because I told the cops about him bein' Tina's ex."

Sanchez dug in the file. "Yeah, it says he was working at a print shop all night. People there verified his alibi. He was ruled out of any connection to Tina's disappearance. It says here that you said Tina had no problems with anyone that night. Just as you say now."

Carter asked, "So did she have a new squeeze after this Johnny guy?"

"Squeeze? Oh, I never heard that before." Dottie laughed. "No, as far as I know, she didn't have anyone in particular she was seeing. But she was checking it out, you know. She flirted with some of the customers, maybe too much sometimes. The boss told her to cool it. He was worried if she dated a regular and broke up, he wouldn't see the guy again. A little flirting is part of the job, but no dating. That's his rule."

"So she got along well with the customers and staff. No arguments with anyone, right?"

"Well, not on the night she disappeared. She got into it with a woman the night before that."

"What do you mean?"

Dottie looked around to see where her boss was. "I didn't want to get Tina in trouble, but I think she might have been seeing someone. The night before, I saw her back by the bathrooms with this woman, and they were talking in whispers. But *loud*. They were arguing about a guy, I guess, one of the regulars. The woman came in sometimes with a cute guy and sometimes with other people. I don't know her name because they were always Tina's customers."

"But you didn't tell anyone about this before. Why not? I don't see any mention of it in the file under your comments."

"I didn't want to get Tina in trouble." Dottie repeated it as if they should understand. Then she lowered her voice. "OK, she told me there *was* a guy, but she wouldn't say any more. I didn't know what happened, so I didn't say anything."

Sanchez cut in. "Wait! What did this woman look like? Did she have dark hair, about five feet nine?"

"Yeah, maybe. It was a while ago. She was all right, I guess. Oh, she and some friends came in one night to celebrate because they had just graduated from college. They had a big meal and lots of wine. Tina served them and even had a drink with them later."

Sanchez dug in her shoulder bag and brought out a photograph. "Here's a photo of someone who used to come here. Do you recognize her?" She handed Dottie the photo of Parker.

"Oh shit! That's her. That's the woman who was arguing with Tina." Dottie's eyes went wide in recognition.

"Are you sure? It's been a while." Sanchez fished out another photo, this time of Brown. "How about this guy?"

"He looks like one of the guys who came in a lot. Yeah, he was with the girl in the photo sometimes. They looked really happy. But he flirted a lot and was a good tipper. You always remember the good tippers."

"How about this one?" Sanchez held up a photo of Simpson.

"Maybe. He might have been the guy who came with them once in a while. I'm not sure. Who are these people? Do you think they had anything to do with Tina?"

"We don't know. But you've been very helpful. Can you give

Detective Sanchez your contact information so we can get a hold of you again later if we need to? I'm going to talk to your manager again." Carter got up with the photos in hand and left Sanchez to finish the discussion while he tracked down the manager.

Sanchez and Carter left the restaurant at noon when the place began to get busy. They stopped at the sandwich shop near the station to discuss the new information. It seemed to Sanchez that Carter was acting strangely. He appeared to be running a number of things through in his mind. She asked him what he was thinking.

"I'm angry because we should have had this evidence before. I didn't personally interview the employees at the restaurant. I arrived after the preliminary investigation had begun. I was only brought into it when it became apparent it was a case that was similar to the other two missing-persons cases. The fact that Parker had words with Tina may not seem like a big deal, but it might have given her motive to harm Tina. I'm surprised no one brought it up."

"This confirms that Parker was the jealous type," Sanchez said. "She may have done things to keep other women away from her Brown. But Lucy Johnson disappeared earlier, when she was dating Peter Simpson. Maybe she kidnapped her for the same reasons?"

"We may never know why she did what she did. But it *does* look like there's a pattern. Certain women who were interested in her lovers were made to disappear, as you said earlier. The fact that those women have not been heard from again suggests that they were killed. The exception is your girl, Mickelson, whom Parker traded to a gang. I've never run into anything like this in my nearly four decades of police work. You have pieced together the keys to the puzzle."

"That may be, but it's still a puzzle. Without any bodies, it can't really go anywhere. We have to find them."

"I agree, but where are they?" Carter finished his sandwich.

"Right now, all we have is a hypothesis that she dumped the bodies in a dumpster. There are a million ways she could have disposed of them, but none of them have turned up. Many times people think they can just tie a rock to them and drop them into San Francisco Bay, but they always show up after a while. At least, unless they are very careful."

"Did you talk to people at all the places where Parker worked? Now that we can focus on her, maybe something will turn up, even though it's been a long time."

"As I recall, she worked at a number of jobs around the city. The only place that looked like a regular job was the summer job up by Lake Tahoe. I never talked to anyone there. Maybe that was an oversight on my part. But there was no reason to suspect her."

"We could arrange to go up there tomorrow to ask what they know. Let's go back to the office and make some calls. Could you get away tomorrow to drive up there? We could make a quick trip of it while I'm still in town." Sanchez felt optimistic.

"I can't go. I have to be in LA tomorrow for a family get-together. It's been planned for months. But you could go if I called ahead. Maybe I can find someone in the department who can go with you on short notice."

"Wait, I may know someone who could go for a drive tomorrow. My friend Father Montero and I were planning to get together in San Francisco to see the sights, but a drive might work instead. I'll have to call and see. He's very familiar with the case and worked out most of the Mexico connection himself. Let's get started on phone calls before people leave work."

Something told Sanchez that the case was about to break.

Chapter 22

May 24, 2014—Lake Tahoe, California

The drive up to Lake Tahoe took longer than Sanchez had thought it would because of heavy weekend traffic. She and Montero had set off at seven o'clock Saturday morning from Berkeley, where Montero had picked her up in a rental car. They had headed up I-80 in a sea of weekender cars and had made it to Truckee by noon. They had grabbed food at a Burger King and headed south on State Highway 89 to Meeks Bay on the west shore of Lake Tahoe.

Sanchez's thoughts drifted back to a happy camping trip her family had made to Tahoe many years earlier. It was still the breathtaking countryside she remembered. The weather was beautiful, and the lake was as pristine as could be in the midday sunshine.

Sanchez drove the last hour from Truckee, along the dusty road that turned off from the highway near Meeks Bay and meandered to the rambling Enchanted Children's Camp, their final destination. She pulled up in the parking lot at the side of the main administration building. She and Montero got out of the car and stretched in the warm sun. Then they marched up the steps of the building and into the reception area. Montero rang the countertop bell, announcing their arrival.

As they waited for someone to respond, Sanchez commented, "I hope Mrs. Jergens is here. She was the one I talked to yesterday and said she was going to be here in the morning. I hope we didn't miss her. She worked here when Parker did."

A clatter of firewood hitting the floor accompanied the arrival of Emily Jergens, the assistant camp manager, in the reception area. She was a slightly plump woman with wire-rim glasses and a helpful smile. "Hello, hello. How was your drive? You have certainly driven a long way to see us at the camp."

"Hi, I'm Detective Sanchez. I talked to you on the phone yesterday along with Detective Carter from the Berkeley Police Department. I'm actually with the Phoenix police, but we are working a case together. And yes, it was a long drive today."

"Yes, I remember, Detective. I am glad you made it. What can I help you with?"

"And this is Father Guillermo Montero, also from Phoenix. We've been working on a missing-persons case that goes back to the time when Sarah Parker worked here in the summers 2008 through 2011."

"I remember Sarah. She was quite an enthusiastic person. She taught reading skills and also gardening. In fact, she volunteered to teach gardening because she loved it herself so much. She was here for four summers, as you know."

"Yes, and she knew at least two women from Berkeley who went missing during that period. I wondered if you have records of what days she worked and if she had any visitors."

"I may still have our employee pay records for those years. They would have the days and hours she worked in them. But she volunteered extra time at the camp too." Jergens adjusted her glasses. "You see, we take in new children on Sunday afternoons, and they leave us on Saturday mornings. So our staff usually has Saturday off, from noon until Sunday noon or later. That way everyone has a little break each week. But a few of the student teachers stayed overnight on Saturday instead of going home or elsewhere. So the camp was usually pretty empty on Saturday night, except for a few stragglers, like Sarah. She stayed over sometimes."

"What did she do during the extra time?" Sanchez asked. "Prepare for classes? Study?"

"No, not Sarah. She usually worked in her gardens. Just loved her flowers. You see, we teach the children about growing vegetables so they know where healthy food comes from. But we don't plant flowers except for landscaping." Jergens folded her hands on the counter as she spoke. "Sarah started to do more planting when she came here, mostly flower beds on the weekends. I guess she had more time then."

"That's interesting. Can you show us around the camp a little?" Sanchez asked. "How big is this place?"

Jergens led them out into the side yard. "We own thirty acres next to Forest Service land so we can provide plenty of opportunities for the children to go hiking and horseback riding there. We also have access through the neighbor's property down to the lakeshore where we teach canoeing and swimming. Mostly, we just try to get the children interested in the outdoors and let them have fun in nature. It really helps many who are only used to living in the city." She stopped and made a sweeping gesture with her arm. "You can see the whole camp from here, so there isn't much need to walk around unless you want to. We teach the classroom subjects in the two classroom buildings there." Jergens pointed to two metal-roofed structures. "We hold rainy-day activities in there too."

"Can you show us the gardens where Sarah worked?" Montero asked.

"Sure. You no doubt already noticed the daffodil and tulip beds in front and some other flowers scattered in several small beds around the administration building and dormitories. And, of course, we have Sarah's favorite, her rose garden just to the side here." Jergens smiled and waved her hand at four small rose beds that arced around the side of the buildings. "She even bought the roses herself at first and spent her free time planting them. Everything had to be *just so* for her. The right soil, lime, water, and sunlight. She wanted those beds to be just for roses."

"They are lovely. It must have taken a lot of work to get them started," Sanchez commented.

"Yes, well, she didn't do it all at once. She did a little each year. She sort of left her mark on our little camp in that way. Anyway, I'll run into the records room and see what I can find for you. Why don't you walk around and get to know the place in the meantime?" With that, Jergens hustled off into the administration building.

Sanchez and Montero walked around the perimeter of the property and down to the lake. "Boy, I would have loved spending summer vacations up here when I was a kid," Montero said as he looked out over the lake. "It would be nice to canoe out there right now, wouldn't it?"

"Yeah, it would. But right now, we need to hurry because Mrs. Jergens will want to leave soon. Where should we look if Sarah was going to dispose of a body here? It looks hard to do because the camp is bordered on three sides by private property. Do you think she would bury a body up in the forest?" Sanchez thought out loud.

They walked back toward the administration building. Montero quietly took in the scene and pondered. "I don't know. It looks like it would be hard for her to dispose of a body here. There are a lot of people around during the week, so I don't see her doing anything then. It would have had to be on the weekends when there were fewer people. She might have been able to move a body then without being seen, but where would she have put it?"

"Before we came up here, I suspected the vegetable garden. The soil would have already been worked over, so it would be easy digging. And people were accustomed to seeing her working in the garden, so it wouldn't draw suspicion if she spent extra time there. But it looks like these vegetable beds are planted over and over each year. They wouldn't make a good place to bury a body. Someone else might dig them up and find something."

"Let's say she did bury a body or two here. How deep a hole would we be talking about? She needs to go down about three feet to get below the vegetable planting depth, right? Someone might easily dig more than a foot. It's probably the same for any garden." Montero looked up to see Jergens leave the office building. "Oh, here comes Mrs. Jergens." He walked to meet her as she hurried toward them.

"I'm sorry. We don't have those records here anymore. Apparently, the manager took them home because they were so old. He can look for them later today for you. Can he call you when he finds them? I gave him your number."

"OK, sure," Sanchez said. "We can arrange that. We were looking at the garden beds and wondered how you tend to them each year. Do the children dig them up and loosen the soil before you plant your vegetables?"

"No. We plant about a quarter of an acre of vegetables. We hire a farmer to come and plow the beds each spring. Then the children just have to plant the seedlings."

"Oh, so you don't have any digging equipment here, then?"

"Well, we have one of those little digger machines . . . what do they call it . . . a Bobcat? We use it to grade the roads and clean up the horse manure in the barn. It's easy to use. Even I can drive it."

"Did Sarah ever drive it? You know, to move dirt piles around and stuff?" Montero asked.

"Yes, I think she did. Sometimes we had extra dirt to spread out on the roads and gardens. She liked to work some of the horse manure into the gardens to fertilize the vegetables."

Sanchez was curious. "Did she use the Bobcat to dig out the flower beds? Or the rose beds?"

"Maybe. I didn't see her put those in, so I don't know. I know she said the beds had to be deep because of the gravel layer we have under the topsoil. She wanted to get deep enough that the roses would be able to spread their roots. And she had bags of extra-rich soil to put down as she planted her roses."

"One last thing, Mrs. Jergens. Did Sarah get along well with the children?" Sanchez inquired.

"Yes, yes, she loved the children."

"We heard there was an argument once that might have gotten her fired."

Jergens winced at the mention of the incident. "I don't like to talk about that. She was a very nice young lady, and she got along well with everybody. But one day, she shouted at two children who were trying to plant potatoes in one of her rose beds. She got angry and told them to stay away from her roses—even swore at them. One of the boys she yelled at told his parents, and they made a big fuss. That was what got her in trouble with the manager. Apparently, it wasn't the only time she had sworn, and that helped cook her goose. But she was a very nice person." Jergens seemed disappointed that the subject had arisen. Then she perked up again. "Anyway, I have to run now, but you can stay as long as you want to. When you leave, will you close and latch the gate down by the highway? Call me if there's anything else you need. And call the manager for those records later, OK? I wrote his number down for you here." She handed Sanchez a yellow Post-it note and bustled over to her Ford Focus. She sped away on the gravel entry road.

Montero watched her leave and then turned to Sanchez. "Let's look in the barn. We haven't been there yet. There may be some tools stored in there."

"What are you thinking? Is it what I'm thinking? About those rose beds?"

"Great minds think alike, Sanchez."

They walked over to the barn and found a lean-to attached to it that contained gardening supplies and tools. The Bobcat was parked there also. Montero sorted through various garden tools and pulled out a shovel and a long thin steel fence post. "I think this might be useful for probing the soil." He held up a small temporary rod used for electric fences, sharpened on one end so that it was easy to push into the ground. "Let's get back to the rose beds."

They walked to the oldest rose bed and looked to see if there were any people around. Sanchez grabbed the steel rod and began to poke it into the ground. She could force it in about a foot and a half or so, but it wouldn't go any deeper. Then Montero tried and pushed the rod down another six to ten inches with his added weight. He probed for anything solid under the surface every six inches or so in a grid pattern near the center of the bed. Nothing.

After fifteen minutes, they moved to the next rose bed and resumed probing. At first, Montero pushed the rod into the ground several times with no result. Then he felt something odd at a depth of about two feet that was soft and springy. He tried again three inches away and hit something hard at a depth of about eighteen inches. He hit something again next to that spot. He probed in a systematic grid pattern, sometimes hitting something hard, then something soft, and all at about a depth of twenty-four inches.

"Are you ready to do a little digging?" he asked.

"Without a search warrant? I don't know."

"Let me do the digging, and you keep your hands clean. I'm an innocent civilian. Maybe you should walk over there and not see this. I can call you if I find anything."

"Just dig, will you? We need to get this over with," Sanchez said impatiently.

Montero put some muscle into it and quickly excavated a small hole in the rose bed with the shovel. Soon, he encountered the zone of soft, springy material. At first, he thought they had just hit some roots from the rose bushes, and there were plenty of those there. But when he pulled up a spade full of soil containing a smattering of cloth and other debris, Sanchez reached down and pulled out a piece of burlap that had probably been wrapped around the plant roots. Next to it she found a piece of shiny cloth with a printed pattern on it. She looked up at Montero. "This may be something."

He pulled the shovel all the way out of the hole and turned it over by the side of the rose bed. Something one inch long and black was sticking out from the side of a clod of dirt. Sanchez poked at it, and it came loose. It looked like a small piece of bone.

"Shit, Guillermo, it looks like a finger bone. Why is it black like that?"

He picked it up and examined it closely. "This is a human finger bone that's not very old. It still has some flesh on it, I think.

Look here—you can see the rounding of the bone at the top of the joint."

Sanchez looked carefully and agreed. Suddenly, she felt queasy and even a little green around the gills. "Excuse me." She stepped away and breathed deeply, fighting the need to vomit. After a minute, she returned to the rose beds.

"I thought you would have seen this sort of thing a million times by now."

"I just wasn't ready for it like this. It just got to me, OK?" Sanchez looked up at him.

"Yeah, OK. We'll put it back in the hole for now." He carefully replaced the bone in the hole he had dug.

"We got us a crime scene, don't we? Well, I'll be damned!"

"But do we have probable cause to be here?" Montero was concerned.

"You mean for a warrant? Yes, we had reason to suspect that Parker had disposed of bodies here. First of all, we knew that the missing girls all disappeared on Friday or Saturday nights. Her obsession with the rose beds is quite suspicious. Now, as to why we dug into one is harder to explain, except that we wanted to know how deep the beds were. Were they deep enough for burial of a body? And the answer is yes."

"And Mrs. Jergens left us on our own to carry out our investigation. So anything we might stumble on outside of the buildings is openly discoverable, isn't it?"

"I think so. Let's call Carter and tell him what we suspect before we go any further."

They contacted Carter on his cell phone and went over the details of what they had discovered so far. He felt that their actions were reasonable and suggested they look over Parker's time sheets before they decided whether they had grounds to obtain a warrant or not.

Sanchez called the camp manager and learned that he did indeed have employee records for the years 2008–2011 at home. They drove over to his house and looked at the time records for the pertinent dates. They found that the camp had also kept an entry log for its employees, created when they keyed in the access code for the front gate. The manager also had located receipts showing he had reimbursed Sarah for rose bed supplies on three weekends.

A pattern began to emerge. Parker had driven up to the camp late on the Saturday night in 2008 when Johnson had disappeared. She had been found digging the first of the rose beds on the following Sunday morning. Nearly a year later, Parker had again logged in at the front gate one Saturday night. It was the same night of Jones's disappearance. The second rose bed had appeared early the next morning before anyone arrived for work at the camp. Then, two years later, in 2011, Serano disappeared one day after she had an argument with Parker. Another rose bed appeared the next day. The timing of the beds' construction exactly matched the dates of the disappearances.

However, Montero thought, there was one problem. They had three missing women and four rose beds. Why?

Based on the new evidence, Carter, as lead investigator, made a Saturday late-afternoon telephone call to the sheriff of El Dorado County in Placerville, California, more than an hour away from Lake Tahoe. The territory southwest of Lake Tahoe was within his jurisdiction, making it his crime scene. The sheriff decided to send a deputy from the South Lake Tahoe station to the Enchanted Children's Camp.

The deputy met with Sanchez, Montero, and the camp manager to evaluate what they had found. Everyone agreed that their findings had merit. The camp manager was afraid that if there were dead bodies buried on camp property, he and his staff would be designated suspects, which would ruin both him and the entire camp operation. The deputy voiced concern that if word of an investigation of a serial killer got out, even if it wasn't true, it would scare the hell out of all the tourists during the high tourist season.

Although it was getting late, the team of investigators decided it would be best to obtain a search warrant from the El Dorado County judge that very day so that they could confirm what was really buried under those roses. The sheriff made it happen by supplying the necessary information and submitting his official statement as quickly as possible. He then drove at breakneck speed up Highway 50 to Lake Tahoe in his squad car, reaching the camp with warrant in hand.

Meanwhile, Carter was already on his way from the rather dull family reunion in LA to Truckee by air. He rented a car and joined Sanchez and Montero at the site that evening. They all spent Saturday night in South Lake Tahoe, exhausted after a long day.

The next morning, the El Dorado County forensics team took over the site and began a preliminary investigation focused on the oldest of the rose beds. They dug with hand implements to do as little damage as possible to any evidence they uncovered. It took fewer than thirty minutes to verify that human remains lay beneath the first rose bed. At that point, they declared the entire camp a crime scene.

The camp manager went about notifying eighty sets of parents that the camp would be closed for a few days due to unexpected conditions. There were many disappointed children and families, many of them who were already en route to the camp or already at the gate.

By late Sunday afternoon, the full complement of crime scene investigators were on site. They brought ground-penetrating radar with them, equipment that could slide over the ground and detect objects buried up to six feet underground. They cut down all of the rose bushes, scanned the rose beds with the radar unit, and found evidence of four badly decomposed bodies under the four beds. Each site was indexed and a team assigned to investigate them one by one. Additional resources were obtained from the Berkeley Police Department and the California Bureau of Investigation. By Monday, the site was swarming with investigators.

Sanchez and Montero met for a late lunch with the county sheriff and Carter at the Derby Café in South Lake Tahoe on Monday. They had been at the camp all morning, had many questions to answer, and even more details of the crime scene to work out. The sheriff began the conversation.

"We have four bodies so far, and I've decided to use the ground-penetrating radar unit to scan the entire property in case there are any more surprises for us out there. I hope to God there aren't any." He directed his attention to Carter. "Geez, this is already turning into a nightmare for the county and the locals. I have the Chamber of Commerce on my back about what this is going to do to business and summer vacation rentals. That's why I want to do as quick and thorough a job of screening the site as possible. I also want to release some information to the media to put an end to any speculation about what happened here. I need your input before the press gets ahead of the story."

Carter diplomatically responded, "Listen, Sheriff, I understand where you're coming from. We all want to get the preliminary work done in as fast and accurate a manner as possible. That's why

I wanted to make this a joint effort between my department and yours. We can share resources and call in as many people as we need. But this is a big story, and there's no way to hide that from the press and TV crews. The twenty-four-hour news cycle is a real bitch to deal with. Those reporters all want to get the story first and will run with anything they hope is even remotely true. I've told my people that I'll cut their tongues out if they say anything about the investigation to anyone outside of our department. I assume you've done the same with yours."

"Yes, I made it pretty clear last night. But we also have the civilians at the camp and even here in town to worry about. In a case like this, rumors will always get started, and they're the hardest things to deal with. If you deny them, the press will believe it's proof of a cover-up. You know how they work. So we have to be sure our people don't talk about it at dinner or out at the bar, or it will come back at us."

Sanchez looked at the sheriff and asked, "What can we do to help? Your people have the ground operation well in hand, I'd say. But if you need more troops, I might be able to get you some lab help or even technicians through my department. Though I suspect that we can best help with background on Parker."

"I appreciate your offer. I think we have all the investigators we can manage right now. But I would appreciate any help you can give us to understand this Parker woman and why she would do these heinous things. And, according to what you and Carter say, we have one more victim in the ground than you expected to find. Any idea who it is?"

"No," Carter responded. "That's something we need to quickly find out. We don't know of any other women who went missing in Berkeley in the summer of 2010 when that rose bed was planted."

"I have a deputy checking that right now. I recall a young

woman who worked in South Lake Tahoe disappeared around then. We should know by this evening. The camp manager is going through his reimbursement records again to tell us when the fourth rose bed was planted. Now he's scared that by paying for the roses he may be liable for something. He's going to talk to a lawyer today, who may very well advise him to shut down any help to us. That would be a real setback. I think he wants to help but is scared to death."

Montero had talked to the manager about his records and didn't see him as any kind of accomplice. "He doesn't seem like the type to help a serial killer. Can you just have your DA cut him a deal right away so he feels he can cooperate?"

"Yeah, I agree," Sanchez said. "I don't think anyone at the camp knew what was happening. Parker was a meticulous planner. From what we know about her activities in Phoenix, it's clear she was a lone operator unafraid to take big risks."

"Sanchez, what do you think her motive was?"

"Well, Sheriff, she was extremely jealous of anyone she thought was making moves on her boyfriend or lover. She followed the same pattern each time. She apparently killed Lucy Johnson when she was dating Peter Simpson to get her out of the picture. Then she killed Naomi Jones to get her away from Allister Brown so she could date him herself. She removed Tina Serano for just flirting with Brown, but it may have been more than just flirting. Maybe the fourth victim also crossed Parker in some way."

Carter added, "I have someone checking that already. We don't know yet. If we can find out the exact date she was buried, that would help a lot to narrow down the time frame."

Their lunch came, and they had to stop talking in front of the waitress, who was lingering near the table. The sheriff told her that was all and stared at her until she moved away.

"I wonder where in the world Parker went," Sanchez lamented. "We lost track of her in Mexico, and we don't have a good means of tracing where she went now that we know she has changed her identity. Guillermo and I have been trying to find her for weeks. She needs to be brought down. Who knows what else she's done that we haven't discovered yet? Or what she's about to do."

Chapter 23

May 27, 2014—Phoenix, Arizona

Montero and Sanchez had only been back in Phoenix for two days and were sitting in Montero's den when they got a lead about Mickelson from a source that Montero had in El Paso. He had contacted an "old friend" there, simply named Rascal, whom he had worked with in the past. He had asked Rascal to find out what he could about her location in Juárez, if she was still there, and call back when he had something. The call came in, and Montero stepped out onto the patio to talk. When he came back inside the house, he had an odd look on his face. He was both pleased and sad at the same time. Sanchez suspected why he had that look.

"Was he able to locate Mickelson?"

"It's good news and bad news. The good news is they found her after checking sixteen brothels. She's been moved around because the cartel has figured out we're looking for her. The bad news is she's not well. She has some respiratory problem that has lingered for some time. Rascal's people weren't able to talk to her directly, but talked to another girl who works in the same brothel. They couldn't do more than scope out the place. Her working name is Cheri."

"How creative." Sanchez sighed. "So she *is* there. Well, what do we do now?"

"My friend says he thinks he can get her out under the right conditions."

"What conditions?"

"Good luck and twenty-five thousand cash."

"Holy shit! Your friend is a mercenary?"

"Sort of, but not really. He does need to pay a number of people on a mission of this type. And he should be paid something for his risk. He's more of a recovery specialist than anything else. And believe me, twenty-five thousand is very generous on his part. If he or his men get caught, they'll die a grim death."

"Then what's in it for him?"

"Because it's a mission for him in more than one way. He's made it his cause to rescue people from difficult situations and only works on recoveries in the El Paso-Juárez area. He used to work a larger territory but lost some good people doing it. So he scaled back."

"Was he Special Forces or something?"

"Or something. My deal with him is to say nothing. It's safer that way."

"Wow. Real need-to-know, huh?"

"That's how it is. What we need to figure out now is, will the Phoenix PD come up with that kind of cash for an illegal international operation that they can't control?"

"Don't hold your breath. The department won't do it, and I doubt the DA has that kind of leeway. I suppose we could ask Mickelson's parents for the money."

"It may take them time to do it, but they are our best bet. Parents usually pay in a situation like this. It keeps the deal private. Do we broker the deal through the DA or off the record?"

"You got me there, Guillermo. Let me call Clara at the DA's office off the record and see what she says to a hypothetical situation. Maybe there's a way."

Sanchez called Alvera's cell. "Hi, Clara. It's Lori Sanchez . . .

Hi . . . Fine. How about you? . . . Yeah, it was real crazy up at Tahoe . . . It was a real shock, yeah . . . Hey, I need to ask you something off the record. Your phone isn't recorded, is it? . . . Good." She listened to Alvera for a minute. "No. I have *not* committed any major crimes lately." She laughed. "Here it is: Suppose it was possible for someone to hire someone to go into Mexico to recover someone who shouldn't be there. Is that anything that your office would want to know about?"

Sanchez listened and talked to Alvera for several minutes. Then she finished the call and looked pensive. After a moment, she told Montero the upshot of the conversation.

"She said the DA's office would not want to know about such an operation because it breaks several laws in both countries. But if it were to occur in someone else's jurisdiction, they would be powerless to intervene. They could not know anything about it ahead of time and could not be involved in authorizing or supporting it, but they understand that such things happen. She's sending me the Mickelson family contact information so I can call and console the family. Isn't that some classic legal spin? I'm amazed."

"And if you tell them about this, you'll get in trouble if anything goes wrong. It so happens that I'm an experienced grief counselor," Montero said. "Why don't you contact the family and tell them that I will be calling to give them the latest information about their daughter? The greatest way to relieve their grief is to offer them hope of a solution. Don't you agree?"

Sanchez made the initial call to Mickelson's parents. They remembered her from their previous conversation and were relieved to learn there was news about their daughter. She explained that there was a private contractor available who could possibly rescue their daughter. He was completely independent of the police department.

"I don't want you here when I call Rascal," Montero told Sanchez. "It could implicate you too easily."

Montero called the Mickelson home after Sanchez drove away. The family was very happy to hear that their daughter had been located. He gave them the barest amount of information about the mysterious rescue/recovery expert and the capabilities of his team. They had never heard of such operators but were glad to know that people did this sort of work. How else could families cope with this kind of situation? Montero tried to explain the risks.

"Listen, there is no guarantee the operation will work. She may be moved before the team can rescue her. In that case, they will try to find her again. They usually start by bribing one or two people to let her escape, and the team then picks her up and brings her to the border. But if there's a problem—there may be an altercation—it's always possible that she could get hurt during the escape. But the odds of that are low. Do you understand? That's the setup. I want you to think about it and talk about it only between yourselves. No one else, understand? No police or FBI. I'll call you back at this number in two hours to see where you stand."

Montero finished the call. What he was doing was technically illegal. And yet, he was merely informing the family of an illegal arrangement, not making the deal per se. He had done this before and had a clear conscience.

He called the Mickelsons back in two hours. They had decided they would do it. They could cash in two certificates of deposit in the morning and have the money ready by midafternoon. They could wire the money to any account he gave them. Montero told them that he would not be handling the money transaction.

Someone else would now contact them with information on how to move the money in several transfers of less than four thousand dollars each over several days so as not to arouse suspicion. If there was a problem, they could call Montero back, but not unless it was significant. Everything was agreed to.

***

Sanchez kept busy working on the Parker case for the next few days. She was coordinating with Carter in Berkeley about the missing women. *Murdered women*, she corrected herself. *How could all of this come about because of jealousy?* It was a powerful emotion and an even more powerful motive in crimes of passion. She had heard this over and over at the police academy; she just had not seen it in such raw form until now.

The fieldwork at Tahoe was now essentially finished. The crime scene investigators had scanned the entire grounds of the camp and found no more human remains. The locals were all relieved that the revelations had stopped and life could return to normal. The four bodies were brought to the forensic laboratory in Sacramento, California, where intraregional investigations were conducted. The workup on the bodies indicated that they all had died of blunt-force trauma to the head. Three of the victims were identified as the ones from Berkeley—Johnson, Jones, and Serano.

The remaining victim was thought to be a woman who had worked at a bar in South Lake Tahoe during the summer of 2010. It turned out she had disappeared two days before the third rose bed had been installed on the camp's property. She had been a seasonal employee, had only lived in the area for a couple of months, and had been seen with a man who had worked at the camp that summer. She had disappeared one night after her shift had ended at the bar, and her fellow employees had thought nothing of it. They had thought she just had skipped town for unknown reasons. A link between her and Parker had yet to be established outside of her being buried at the camp. The authorities had no idea who the young woman's family was. Someone was out there without a daughter and would likely never know what had happened to her.

Sanchez knew that if Mickelson was rescued from Juárez, she could interview her about her abductors in Phoenix and Mexico. Information that Parker had sold her to the Westside Glendale Lokos Gang would provide the necessary proof for filing kidnapping charges against Parker. Mickelson's testimony could also help twist José Battelle's tail so they could extract more information out of him. It was an inefficient and convoluted way to get criminals to talk, but it worked most of the time if they were completely cornered.

Her concern today was arranging to interview Mickelson in El Paso, if and when Rascal rescued her. She did not want to know the schedule for the rescue. Deniability. She kept reminding herself of that, sincerely hoping it would be a successful operation. She could not talk to Montero about it either, which worried her a lot. He had said they should not talk about it for her own good. But he also thought it best for them not to socialize until after it happened, just for appearances' sake.

Chapter 24

June 9, 2014—Juárez, Mexico

The dark, bearded man called Rascal walked a short distance up the narrow, crowded street and bought a taco and a Dos Equis beer at the street-side stand. That gave him an excuse to lounge at the small taqueria's shelflike table while he ate. He had been on this street before and had met a couple of men who frequented the same eatery. One ran the bicycle shop on the corner. The other worked for a hardware shop on the same street. He kidded around with them in Spanish while he kept an eye on the doorway to El Paraiso, the brothel down the street on the opposite side. A tall heavy-set man stood there with a gun bulging from under his shirt, tucked in at the back of his pants.

Two Americans walked up to the brothel and talked to the man who stood guard there. He asked them some questions and then quickly frisked them before allowing them to enter the establishment. The two men were very drunk and did not care about being frisked. They kept on making jokes and slapping each other on the back. One nearly fell down from so much laughter. The guard smiled and made a joke about how stupid they were to get so drunk, but they didn't really understand what he said anyway. They went inside.

A few other people came and went from the brothel as Rascal ate his taco. It was quite late, and the street was becoming less crowded as vendors decided to call it a day and pack up their wares. The prospect of selling tourist items had come and gone long ago by this time of night on most days of the week.

Rascal checked his Timex watch and finished his beer. He said *buenas noches* to the others at the table and walked down the street to the brothel. He stopped to talk to the guard whom he had met a few days earlier while visiting for his own entertainment. In fact, he had recently been to this particular brothel twice. One of those times he had slipped the guard a few pesos to let him bring in his own bottle of tequila, which he did again tonight. He held out his shoulder bag to let the man feel inside for anything unusually illicit. His payment for the favor tonight was a bottle of good Herradura tequila for the guard to keep. They patted each other on the back, and Rascal went inside and upstairs to the salon where he would meet his date for the night, or at least for the next hour.

The guard grew tired of standing in the doorway and decided that he could stand a swig of the fine tequila that his new friend had given him. He cracked open the bottle cap and savored a long drink of the smooth liquor. He was impressed with the quality and looked at the label to discover that it was the best grade of the product. He took another slug and recapped the bottle. He settled on the stair just inside the doorway and felt comfortable. He waited there, on guard as usual.

Rascal walked into the salon where the madam of the establishment, known as Kitty to Americans and Juanita to well-heeled Mexican customers, was waiting. He greeted her as if he were drunk, which most customers were when they came here. Kitty walked him around to see all the girls, and he pointed to the one who seemed to be hiding from sight, coughing and looking ill. No one wanted to screw a sick woman, and Kitty let the girl know she had better shape up.

The girl moved forward and pushed up against him, her

blouse open so he could see her fine breasts. Soon, they went up more stairs to her room.

When they entered, she motioned him to the bed, but Rascal didn't appear to understand. She spoke to him in Spanish, but again, there was no response. Then she spoke in English as she slinked over to him in her scanty top and shiny panties and put her arms around his neck, drawing her lips close to his. "Hi, I'm Cheri. We're going to have such a good time. I'll do whatever you want. I'm here to make you feel special."

"Hi, Cheri. You look lovely tonight. Just give me a minute, will you?"

He was friendly but seemed unsure about what to do, so she rubbed her breasts against him to get him in the mood.

"Ready when you are," was all he said, and she thought he was talking to her. He reached into his shoulder bag and brought out a roll of duct tape. He held a finger up to his mouth. "Shh! I won't hurt you."

Rascal saw Cheri's alarm bells go off right away, no doubt because other men had told her the same thing before they taped her mouth shut and began to treat her like an animal. She opened her mouth to scream as the tape was secured in place. *The first and most common response to being rescued without warning.* Then Rascal threw her on the bed face down and taped her hands behind her back. She was sobbing quietly when he sat her up on the edge of the bed.

"Sorry, Tracy," he said. "But I can't take a chance you'll scream. We're here to get you out and back to the States. Your parents hired me. Be quiet and let me carry you out of here."

Her eyes went big as saucers, and she fainted. *The second most common reaction to being rescued without warning.* Even though she was unconscious, Rascal gave her a shot of sedative to keep her out for a couple of hours.

Rascal cracked the door of the room open to see if his other men, the Americans who had entered the brothel earlier, were in position. He called them Two and Three for security reasons.

Two was in position in the hallway and said, "Let's go, follow me. Three's on our six."

Rascal passed out the guns he had in his bag of tricks and left an extra bottle of tequila in Mickelson's bedroom as payment to the guard outside. He picked Mickelson up and threw her over his shoulder. Then the three men—Two in the lead, Rascal in the middle, and Three bringing up the rear— quietly walked down the stairs. The girls in the parlor barely noticed what was happening until Kitty rushed out from behind her desk to stop them. Two put his finger to his mouth and whispered, "Shh!" He also waved a gun in her direction, so she stopped and let them pass.

A guard rushed into the salon from the adjoining hallway just as they started down the lower staircase and began to pull his revolver from his belt. Two shot him in the chest three times with a Taser. The three men continued down the staircase to the front door. They passed the door guard, who sat sleeping on the stair, feeling the effects of the doctored liquor he had sampled. Rascal's men stood in the doorway for a second until a black van pulled up in front, and they climbed through the sliding side door. The door closed, and the van pulled away.

They drove ten blocks to a side street, where they exited the vehicle. Mickelson was placed in a wooden crate on the back of a flatbed Chevy truck, and the top of the crate was nailed shut. The crate was labeled *Turbo lateral base, Hecho en Mexico*, with a customs seal affixed to it. The truck immediately pulled away and headed for the Ysleta Bridge on Zaragoza Street and the border patrol station on the north end of Juárez. Two and Three left in a separate car and followed the truck at a distance. Rascal paid the driver well for the use of his van and his help. He stepped into the darkness as the van drove off.

Rascal walked to a car parked on an adjacent street and drove toward the border crossing six miles away. Within the hour, the truck and the two cars had crossed into Texas at El Paso. Rascal breathed a sigh of relief as he pulled away from the check station. He drove to the warehouse his crew used for operations and pulled the car inside. He parked and walked over to the truck. The others had already removed Mickelson from the crate and placed her in a small office, blindfolded, but with the tape over her mouth removed.

She shifted position in the chair when she heard the door to the office open.

"Who are you? What do you want from me?"

"I am the man who got you out of Mexico. You're in El Paso now," Rascal declared as he cut away the rest of her restraints and took off the blindfold. He wrapped a blanket around her. "In a few minutes, I'm taking you to a clinic where a doctor will check you out. Wait here."

Rascal paid off Two and Three, and they left after they stowed away their gear in a storeroom. Rascal reentered the office and led Mickelson to the car. He drove a few miles along city streets and then merged onto a state highway for several minutes.

Mickelson was shivering and showing early signs of withdrawal from drugs. She looked out the window as they drove, her mind trying to take in the fact that she was back in the United States. "It's so unreal. I can't remember the last time I was free." She began to cry softly.

"Look, Tracy, you're going to be all right, OK? The sudden change must be a shock. We had to tie you up and tape your mouth so you wouldn't freak out when we needed you to be quiet. I'm sorry we had to do that. I know it was scary for you. But now you're here in El Paso, safe and sound."

"I don't know what to say. It was so awful there. I thought I would die." She burst into tears again, then started to cough uncontrollably.

"Here's what we are going to do now: I'm taking you to a clinic where a doctor friend of mine is going to examine you. He'll run a number of tests to make sure you're OK and get you started on treatment for the heroin you're hooked on. Probably methadone or whatever is the new replacement drug. How long have you had that cough? It sounds pretty bad."

"It feels like forever. I just cough and cough and can't stop."

"He will document bruises and that sort of thing too. You'll have to stay overnight. That's normal. We'll have someone there to protect you the whole time, so you will be safe. No one except my people know you are here, no one in the cartel. The doctor will help you get some fresh clothes after that."

"How long will I be at the clinic? When can I go home?" Mickelson asked meekly.

"Listen, you've been through a lot. I know it's difficult. You're going to need a few days to get used to the fact that you're free. There's a policewoman from the Phoenix police who will be coming to take your statement when the doctor says it's OK. We don't want to rush you. It's just something the police have to do. When that's done, a counselor will help you work through what happened to you. It's just a start. The doctor will explain."

"When will I see my parents?"

"You can see them as early as tomorrow. They are standing by to fly down here when you are ready. I have helped people before. Sometimes a woman who has lived through what you have needs a day or two to prepare before she faces her loved ones again. You see, it may be hard to explain to them what happened to you. They may have a hard time understanding. You have to decide how much you'll tell them, at least at first. Do you understand?"

"I never thought of it that way. My dad is very religious. Yes, he might have a hard time with it. Oh shit! What will I say?"

"The counselor is very good at this sort of thing, so talk to her. And my friend who will be guarding you can help too."

"I couldn't talk to a man about what happened."

"She's not a man. Her name is Mara, and she's done this before. You'll like her, you'll see."

They pulled up to the back door of a white building surrounded by grassy lawns, where a very fit-looking woman wearing black slacks and a white utility shirt was standing next to a wheelchair. She wore practical black sneakers and a welcoming smile.

Rascal parked the car and walked over to introduce Mickelson to Mara. They transferred Mickelson into the wheelchair just before she suffered a long bout of coughing. When she had caught her breath, she turned to Rascal and asked, "*She* is my security?"

"Don't let her good looks fool you. I've been in combat with her. She's very good at this. I'll say goodbye now. I hope you get well soon."

"You aren't coming in?"

"No. It's better that no one sees me now. You're in good hands." He shook her hand and got in the car. Mickelson waved as he drove away.

Chapter 25

June 14, 2014—Phoenix, Arizona

The call came in as Sanchez and Montero were walking into the Don Quixote Bar and Grill on Eleventh Street. Sanchez answered her cell. She listened for a few seconds, ended the call, and then looked at Montero. "We have to go. Do you mind a short ride-along before lunch?"

"No. What's happened?"

"I'm not sure. Bordou called and asked if I had heard anything about the prisoner transfer this morning. He said the guards didn't call in when they were supposed to. When the station radioed them, they said things were fine. He wanted to know if I was close to the county jail and could drop by to confirm that the convoy arrived all right."

Sanchez and Montero got in her Ford Interceptor, and she gunned the engine. She had asked the boys at the garage to add a little horsepower after they had fixed the radiator and other damage she had sustained while running down Battelle at the McDonald's a few weeks ago. They had hooked up a supercharger and a new computer chip to give her more response when she needed it. Now she revved the engine a few times so Montero could appreciate the sound of all four hundred and sixty-two horses under the hood. They smiled at each other. *Real nice.*

She started driving toward the jail. "You know, answering my phone is getting to be a workplace hazard. Things are really busy with the gunrunning trial. Bordou said that the prisoner transfer team was bringing José downtown today for a court hearing tomorrow. It should go smoothly enough since they scheduled it today and not in the morning."

They were cruising west down Van Buren, watching traffic and looking ahead for the turn to the Maricopa County Fourth Avenue Jail on Fourth and Madison. As they approached First Avenue, they encountered a convoy of two unmarked cars, one leading and one following an armored truck with county plates but no other markings. It turned from First Avenue onto Van Buren just ahead of them. Sanchez fell in line behind the other vehicles as they made their way toward the jail. "If they go the usual way, they'll turn down Fourth Avenue and swing around behind the building to unload."

Montero was a little keyed up. Prison transfers were always tricky. And transferring gang members was even trickier because the gang would do whatever it took to pull one of their own out of the justice system. Police either had to go heavy on support troops or go light like this transfer and hope to keep the route and timing secret.

The convoy turned onto Fourth, going south toward the jail. Only a few more blocks to go. By now, everyone in the convoy was probably getting antsy to get the transfer over with and hopefully move on to more interesting duties.

The convoy stopped at the light at Washington Street next to the courthouse and waited for the light to change. It took a long time. Sanchez didn't like the way they were all just sitting still like this. The hair on the back of her neck began to rise as she sensed something bad was about to happen.

Suddenly, a garbage truck came reeling out of nowhere from the left and slammed into the lead car in the convoy, pushing it to the curb. A second truck, a Home Depot delivery truck, raced up from behind Sanchez's car, swerving to crash into the tail car just two car lengths in front of Sanchez and Montero. A man jumped down from each of the trucks, holding an AK-47 assault rifle, and sprayed the cars with automatic weapons fire. The cops inside didn't stand a chance as they struggled to get out of their cars.

Sanchez leaped out the driver's side door in the blink of an eye. She pulled out her Glock and yelled at the gunman near her to drop his weapon. He spun around and sprayed her car with several rounds before she fired two slugs into his chest.

The drivers of the trucks were already out of their vehicles and on the ground with compact submachine guns. She didn't see the driver of the Home Depot truck until she ran past the front of his vehicle and he surprised her. She quickly backed up behind the front of the truck as he came around the left front fender. That's when she shot him. He went down yelling noisily. She intended to sprint over to help the officers in the police tail car but was cut off by the screech of tires as two black Cadillac Escalade SUVs roared up the street and slid to a halt just past the delivery truck that Sanchez had used for cover.

Montero had ducked down in his seat when the first bullets had hit the police car in front of them. He saw Sanchez rush forward to engage the attackers, who he assumed must be part of the Sinaloa Cartel. They certainly had the weapons for the job. He reached over to the driver's side of Sanchez's car and pulled the trunk release latch. Then he scuttled to the rear of the car and flipped up the carpet that covered Sanchez's "backup plans." *This little lady travels heavy*, he thought. The trunk was filled with black weapons. He reached in for a shotgun and her police-modified AR-15 with its loaded magazines in a sling bag. He slung the shotgun's ammo belt over his shoulder.

Twelve men got out of the SUVs, all heavily armed. They sprayed the armored truck with lead and used a bullhorn to demand that the cops inside open the door and let the prisoners out. When there was no response, one of the attackers hefted an RPG rocket launcher on his shoulder and fired at the truck. A huge explosion shook the street and crumpled the left side of the vehicle.

In a few moments, the back door of the truck opened up, and three prisoners jumped down onto the street. One of them was Battelle, a black patch over one eye. One of the attackers ran over and handed him and the other escapees weapons. Battelle immediately hobbled in his leg irons to the open door of the transfer vehicle and fired several rounds, killing the cops inside. One of his fellow escapees climbed in to get the key to their handcuffs and leg irons. Soon, they were all free.

Sanchez backed herself up to the Home Depot truck for cover and took on one of the men firing from the closest SUV. She saw one of his companions from the SUV run to her left to outflank her by coming around the back of the truck. Then a third man approached from the front. She was pinned down and would soon have to fight front and back at the same time. The men in front made their move, and she knew she couldn't look back for an instant. One man peeked around the fender at her, and she managed to shoot him in the head. But the other came on just as she had to drop a magazine and reload. Then she heard the boom of a shotgun behind her, but she still couldn't turn to look. She had to take down the guy in front of her. He got a few rounds off, but they went wide. Suddenly, he gurgled up some blood and looked very surprised as he fell to the ground.

She spun around with her weapon raised for a fight behind her when she saw Montero standing at the rear of the truck, loaded

down with black weapons, a smoking shotgun in his hand. *Holy shit!*
That was close.

Montero handed her the AR, and she racked a round into
the chamber. She came around the front of the truck and laid
into the nearest SUV like an avenging angel. Montero moved to
the rear of the truck to back her up and fired the shotgun to keep
any other gunmen from suddenly appearing. Between the two of
them, they took out the guys on the right side of the closest
SUV. The remaining attackers from that vehicle climbed into
their vehicle, anxious to flee the scene. Then the driver of the
SUV hit reverse, and the overpowered vehicle flew backward in a
cloud of smoke, tires spinning wildly. Sanchez stepped forward
to pump more gunfire into the driver's side as the SUV made a
hurried Y-turn, but the driver aimed right for her, and she had to
jump aside to avoid being hit. Montero ducked behind the Home
Depot delivery truck to avoid the fusillade of bullets coming
from the speeding vehicle as it roared up Fourth Avenue.

By that time, two squad cars had arrived from the
courthouse a block away, and the security guards from the
adjacent municipal building had come out to aid their fellow
officers. One squad car rammed the fleeing SUV, disabling it half
a block away, and the security guards pinned the occupants down
with their own gunfire.

The second SUV was another matter. Its crew had loaded up,
and the car had roared off in the opposite direction in a cloud of
smoke. *Smoke grenades. Great idea,* Sanchez thought. *Shit. Where is he?*

Battelle was gone.

She looked everywhere. He wasn't there. He had gotten away.

Then she heard the second Escalade screech around the
corner and slide to a halt next to a Chevy Tahoe out on
Washington Street. There! She saw Battelle on the street, pulling

a refined-looking woman out of her white Tahoe SUV and throwing her on the pavement. The other two escapees pulled another woman from the passenger side, and they all jumped in. Battelle got behind the wheel and punched it. The bulky vehicle apparently had the turbo package because it lurched out of the lane and accelerated, flying down Washington Street. The heavily armed second black Escalade fell in behind and acted as a rear guard as they escaped.

"Guillermo! He's getting away! Get to the car."

They both ran back to Sanchez's car and tumbled in. She started the big engine. "Better buckle up. This won't be easy."

Sanchez burned rubber as she backed away from the delivery truck. She threw the supercharged Interceptor into drive and peeled out after the attackers. The car slid on all four wheels through the turn as she roared onto Washington Street in hot pursuit. Drivers of two squad cars saw where she was going and fell in behind, sirens blaring.

Sanchez buckled up and put her flashing light cone up on the roof. She couldn't let Battelle get away. *I can't let him escape. I can't let Tracy Mickelson down*, she thought. She floored the gas pedal, and the speedometer reached seventy in no time. They raced down the street searching for the fleeing vehicles. Where were they?

Montero spotted them as they approached the intersection at Seventh Avenue West. "Slow down! They're turning onto Seventh Avenue southbound. You'll miss the turn!"

Sanchez hit the brakes and cut the wheel to the left. They skidded to slow down, and she punched it again to complete the turn with the wheels mostly on the ground. As they sped off to the south, they could see the black and white SUVs ahead.

They briefly lost sight of their target as Sanchez crossed the railroad tracks near Jackson Street. A squad car now caught up with them and took over the lead. "That's Johnson! What does he have in that thing?"

Johnson raced south right behind the black SUV with Sanchez close behind.

"They're turning left onto the freeway!" Montero exclaimed. "There! They're going east. Johnson's right on them now."

Sanchez braked to make the same turn, but a semitrailer rig had stopped to let the racing cars go through, blocking the on-ramp. Another car blocked the approach from the south. The only remaining way to get onto the ramp was over an earthen mound left from recent construction.

"Hang on. I'm going for it!" Sanchez gunned the engine and spun the car around to cross a construction zone where dirt was pushed up in a broad pile along the entry ramp. Without hesitating, she roared up the slope at an angle, arcing up and around the semi. She brought the car back down hard on the ramp and raced onto the freeway.

The whole time she was driving, the police radio was alive with chatter about the attack and the ensuing chase. Montero took the radio microphone. "We're on I-17 headed east. It looks like they're going to get on the I-10 freeway, probably going south."

"Who's this?" the dispatcher asked.

"Father Montero. I'm in hot pursuit with Sanchez. Stand by."

He handed the mike to Sanchez as she passed several cars at seventy miles per hour and gained speed. "Dispatch, Montero speaks for me. I'm busy chasing those escaped assholes. Over."

"Copy that, Sanchez. Good luck!"

On the freeway, Sanchez pushed her car to the limit. She was doing over a hundred as they shot past trucks and cars that had pulled over to let the car chase pass them. Johnson's car was right on the black SUV's tail. Gunfire was hitting his car, shattered glass was flying everywhere, but he kept up the chase. They merged onto the southbound I-10 freeway at high speed.

Sanchez made one more desperate effort to close the distance between the Interceptor and the SUVs and caught a break when the attackers came up on a car that would not move out of the left lane for them. They slowed considerably as they tried to go around, finally succeeding to pass on the outside. Johnson punched through the same gap in traffic. Sanchez was right behind.

Then a shot blew out Johnson's windshield, and he lost control. He spun out, rolled, and slid upside down along the roadway. His car came to a stop next to the median and caught fire.

Sanchez saw the crash but continued to drive through the careening debris in hot pursuit. They were now only a few car lengths behind the black SUV.

In an instant, Sanchez hatched a plan. "Take the wheel. Now! Take the wheel." She unbuckled her seatbelt.

He was surprised but caught up in the moment, with adrenaline pumping through him like many times before. He nodded because he knew what she had in mind. He slid in under her and put his foot on the gas while she slipped her foot out. Then he took the wheel and squeezed into the driver's seat. He buckled in as she climbed into the back seat where they had thrown the hardware. They had lost some speed and had to catch up again.

He had not driven a raging car this fast in many years, and it felt good. He pushed down hard on the accelerator and watched the needle on the dash climb to a hundred and thirty in no time. The car felt light on its wheels, a sign they were on the edge of control. They closed in on the SUV.

Montero raced up to the back left quarter panel of the black Escalade and got ready for a nudge. Then as the escapees began to shoot at the windshield, Sanchez leaned out the right side window with the AR-15 and blew the glass out of the SUV's rear window. At the same time, while they were ducking, Montero rubbed bumpers with the Escalade and executed a spinout maneuver, causing the SUV driver to lose control. The vehicle began to swerve, and the driver couldn't correct enough, oversteering a little each time the car swung further and further out of control. When it was clear what would happen next, Montero gunned the engine and passed on the left as the Escalade swerved to the side and rolled over. It flipped along the roadway ten times by the time it stopped, landed upside down, and slid on its roof. Most of the bodies inside were expelled.

Montero was way ahead of the Escalade by then and closing in on the white Tahoe SUV with Battelle inside. It swerved into traffic merging from the Hohokam Expressway, squeezed between two lanes of traffic, and maintained speed. Montero did the same and made up the distance between them. Two men in the back seat were shooting at them out of the rear window. He swerved to avoid getting hit as they closed in; it was becoming nearly impossible.

Sanchez set to work trying to pick off the two men in the Tahoe. She could see Battelle at the wheel, looking over his shoulder once in a while to see where they were. He locked his one good eye with Sanchez for a split second and increased speed.

Montero came up on the Tahoe's rear bumper to try the same maneuver that had taken out the other SUV. But it was too dangerous with the two men shooting at them, so he backed off a little. Sanchez kept firing, and one of her shots hit Battelle in the neck. He jerked in response, and in so doing, turned the steering wheel toward the centerline barrier. In an instant, the white Tahoe slammed into the barrier at an angle, climbed it, and went airborne over the median into oncoming traffic. A semitrailer truck hauling gasoline in the opposite lane collided head on with the Tahoe, and both vehicles disappeared into a fireball as the Tahoe's gas tank ruptured. The damaged semi swerved and rolled, and its gasoline load burst into flames. The whole freeway was on fire.

Montero hit the brakes, skidding wildly, and brought the car to a halt next to the median, tires smoking and engine overheating in the hot afternoon air. He and Sanchez looked back at the huge fireball and then at each other. *That could have been us!* They got out of the car, carefully checking to make sure that the hail of bullets had not hit them.

They surveyed the scene. All traffic on the I-10 freeway had come to a complete stop in both directions. The Tahoe was completely destroyed, smashed beyond recognition on impact and now on fire. There were no survivors. Battelle was dead. *Shit!* Sanchez thought, *there went our key witness and maybe much of our case. What do I tell the captain? What do I tell Tracy Mickelson?*

Within minutes, squad cars pulled up on both sides of the freeway and set up a perimeter to hold people back. There was no way they were going to get traffic started anytime soon. An officer came over to see if Sanchez and Montero were OK. He said that Johnson had miraculously survived his crash and added that two of the attackers in the black Escalade had also survived. They were the two buckled in with seatbelts on. *Too bad*, Sanchez thought.

The fire roared up into the sky, accompanied by the sound of secondary explosions as different compartments within the semi's huge cargo tank burst into flames. A tall column of black smoke rose into the clear blue sky of an otherwise perfect day.

Chapter 26

June 16, 2014

Sanchez and Montero spent the next two days in a preliminary hearing, justifying their judgment and use of force in the pursuit of the attackers on the police convoy. Sanchez told the brass the whole story, leaving nothing out about how the event had unfolded. She had killed at least three gunmen with her handgun at the original scene of the attack. Then she had shot one more dead with her AR-15—a bit unusual and not recommended in urban environments, but within limits for its use. Several other officers verified her actions, even commended them. The first three kills were ruled to be self-defense. The fourth was found acceptable in defense of fellow officers in the line of duty.

Her pursuit of the attackers was considered what any good cop would do, even though her driving was a little wild. The circumstances were considered appropriate, given all the factors involved. However, turning the driving of a police vehicle over to a civilian midway through a high-speed chase, even one with police training, was considered risky at best.

The review board argued for and against reprimanding her and finally decided that under the circumstances it would not be politically advantageous to officially do so. Sanchez's response of "Should I have let Montero do the shooting instead?" stopped that line of questioning. The priest had been a cop after all, and the members of the investigating committee all hoped that they could respond in the same way to help a fellow officer if a similar situation ever happened to them. Although there would be no official reprimand, Teller told her she would have to go on paid leave while they quietly reviewed their decisions. The shootings on the freeway in pursuit of armed and dangerous felons were justified in the interest of public safety. Sanchez was credited for killing one of the gunmen in the black SUV before it crashed. The rest died from injuries received during the high-speed crash, as did the three escapees in the wreck of the Tahoe.

Montero's shooting of a man with Sanchez's shotgun was ruled to be self-defense. His madcap driving was called heroic in support of an officer in hot pursuit. He was not charged with anything but was warned to stay out of police business. Several officers thanked him for helping out in the emergency.

As expected, the two survivors from the Escalade crash turned out to be members of the Sinaloa Cartel. One of them, Diego Garcia, was a close associate of Battelle and managed most of the gunrunning business for the gang in the Phoenix area. Over the next few days, he was quite cooperative during questioning, and Alvera cut him a deal to avoid the death penalty. He agreed to give up the cartel's entire gun operation on this side of the border in exchange for protection while in prison.

Sanchez participated in Alvera's interrogation of Garcia and took the opportunity to ask him about the cartel's other activities. "Are you the man who transported Tracy Mickelson to Mexico last year?"

"The little blonde woman with nice tits? No, I don't know what you're talking about."

"Can you tell us how you got her?"

"If I *had* a woman, *maybe* someone José gave me to use and then to take to the border, I would give her to Pepe in Nogales. You know, for the whorehouse there. That could happen."

"And you don't know where she went after that?"

"No."

After the interview with Garcia, Sanchez and Alvera discussed his other statements and came to the same conclusion: Their case against the Sinaloa Cartel was still strong, perhaps stronger now that they had a more cooperative witness in Garcia, who had agreed to give up more information than Battelle had. And he was the man who had transported Mickelson, so they could show a convincing link between her kidnapping and the Sinaloa Cartel.

***

Sanchez, Bordou, and Maria Sandoval went out for a steak dinner after work one night a week after the escape attempt to celebrate how well things had turned out for the case.

Montero was missing from their little party. He had dropped out of sight after he had finished answering questions at the station. He had gone back to his office to think and come to terms with the day's events. He had killed a man, not something a priest was supposed to do. It made him wonder if he was justified or whether he should have just watched the shootout. No, he knew that if he had stayed out of it, Sanchez would be lying in the morgue, so he had had to act. What he had done was morally correct, but it still bothered him that maybe he had compromised his vows to the church. He would have to talk to someone in the church about this. It might lead to some questions about his involvement with the police department, which he had been warned about before.

***

The next evening, Montero and Sanchez met for a beer at their new favorite watering hole, the Cactus Lounge in Scottsdale. They settled into a booth and ordered two Dos Equis beers with chips and salsa. They wanted to get back to some sort of normal routine after the last week of grizzly events. It was their first real opportunity to reflect together on what had happened.

Sanchez planned to attend the funeral service for the policemen killed in the shootout at the Fourth Avenue Jail and then take the week off to spend time with her parents. The service was scheduled for the following Saturday, and hundreds of police officers from all over the state and other departments were expected to attend. She would also receive a commendation at a news conference.

"Guillermo, I haven't had a chance to tell you before now, but thank you for saving my ass back there on Fourth Avenue. If you hadn't taken that guy out, I'd be dead meat. I really appreciate it. You make a good partner. I know I can trust you." She gave him a thoughtful look.

"Well, I did what I had to do. I didn't really think about it, you know? It was like it just happened. That's what you do when you're under fire. You help your buddy out. You should know that I've got your back. I just feel a little confused about killing that man . . . . I'm a priest, after all. I'm supposed to protect life, not take it."

"Hey, *I'm* the one you protected, right? *I'm* here because you did the right thing. Now don't get all philosophical or religious on me. You protected life. You shouldn't have any doubt about that." She took his hand in hers. "You saved my life. You understand? *My life.* I owe you big time, Guillermo, and I'll always be in your debt. I'll always have your back too. You can count on it." She smiled and let go of his hand.

Montero nodded his head in silence.

Then Sanchez chuckled and added, "And in your honor, tonight, the drinks are on me. Ha, ha! Caught you off guard, didn't I?" She threw up her arms and waved the bartender over to order a round of margaritas.

"Sanchez, you're really bad sometimes. Here I am spilling my guts out to you, my inner feelings, and you treat your life like a coupon. *Here. Free drinks.*" Montero looked down and covered his face with his hands for a moment. He was shaken to the core by the recent events. Then he looked up at Sanchez. "I know I did right by you, but did I do right by God? I have to work that out. But not here tonight. We should celebrate that the case was not messed up without José, that awful piece of . . . well, you know what he was."

"And celebrate we shall. A toast to the case and the many things that are falling into place. Oh, and a toast to your friend Rascal. I heard that Tracy Mickelson met with her parents today, and it was all good. Her mother understands, and her father wants to. They are going to take her home to Minnesota tomorrow and will get her counseling there. She's been through a lifetime of hell. I hope she makes it through everything and can lead a normal life."

"Yes, she deserves it, if anyone does."

"And I heard from Carter. They have a definite ID on the fourth body: Kimberly Grosner, from the Midwest somewhere. They still don't have enough information to find her parents, but it's a start. So we now have Sarah Parker tied to six kidnappings or assaults and five murders."

"I bet she was involved in the death of that poor girl in San Francisco, Mexico, too. That case smells too much like her motive and MO."

"You're right. I didn't count that one because we don't have a hard link to her there yet. Have you talked to Officer Hermoso lately?"

"No. I should call him to see if he's narrowed down the list of flights departing Puerto Vallarta any further." Montero made a face and grunted. "Where in hell is that Parker woman anyway? You have all this evidence against her, and we still don't know where she is."

"We'll find her someday. Maybe we'll get some help from the Feds. I hear the FBI horned their way into the Berkeley cases now that all the real work is done. They'll no doubt put a special agent in charge and take credit for all the work that Carter did. You know, the usual bullshit! Those guys should work cases as hard as they puff themselves up for the camera."

"Hey, hey." Montero waved his finger at Sanchez as if scolding her. "Don't dump on our fellow officers, even if they steal the credit much of the time. They have some real resources. You should find a way to get them to check all those flights out. They've got the juice to make Homeland jump on it."

"Yeah, great idea. I need to develop a strategy to get them to do it. But I have to present it as something *they* want to do, not give the reason why, or they won't want to do it."

"Now you're being mean." Montero sipped his margarita.

"No, I'm not. Every time the department has shared info with the FBI, they either take credit for it, or they refuse to cooperate."

"Hey, most of the agents I worked with were OK guys, but you have to realize that they live in a political pool, and their bosses are real asses sometimes. They all want to get promoted to a Washington posting and hit the big time."

"And I thought *I* was judgmental." Sanchez raised her bottle and pointed it at him.

"No, really. We should think of a way to get them to follow up on where Parker went. I bet we can come up with an angle to get it done. Let's think about how to do that. What do we need to do?"

"Maybe we should just ask?"

"Are you kidding?" Montero did a double take. "When did you fall out of the turnip patch?"

"Now you lost me. Turnips? Really?"

"No, wait. You're right, ask them. But not us. Maybe an up-and-coming DA could get some action."

"Wow! How many drinks have you had already?"

***

"I don't believe it, do you? In just a day?" Montero asked Sanchez on the following day at the Cactus Lounge.

"It's incredible, isn't it?"

"How'd he get it done so fast?"

"Alvera said the deputy director of the FBI went to grade school with District Attorney John Davies. Must be friends or something."

"Or something. Anyway, here's what they got from the Homeland people."

They both pored over a ten-page report about the flights in and out of Puerto Vallarta over a two-week period, looking for anyone who might match Parker. There was a lot of data, much more than they had expected to get. "Did you know that Homeland could do this stuff, Sanchez?"

"No way."

"It's like they have homing beacons on people. How'd they get all this information?"

Sanchez explained, "Clara said they coordinated with the NSA for cell phone chatter at the same time. That gave them ID info to correlate with other databases. I don't think I'll use my phone so much anymore."

"No way."

"As far as the NSA can tell, all but three women on this list called or texted someone just before they boarded their plane."

"What does that tell us?" Montero looked sideways at Sanchez while trying to get the bartender's attention at the same time.

"Well, we wouldn't expect Parker to be calling anyone, would we? She probably didn't have anyone to call to let them know she was coming home. Whoever the woman was she stole her identity from lived alone. At least, that's the assumption we've been making, right?"

"So if she traveled during this two-week period, she would most likely be one of the three women who did not reach out to anyone to tell them that she was coming home. Isn't that right?"

"Yeah. *If* she flew in those two weeks," Sanchez responded. "Remember, she's a desperately cagey person. Maybe she had no reason to leave Mexico right away. If she was cunning, she might have changed IDs again before she left."

"Oh sure. I never thought of that. She is clever and would know that we would check the records around that period. Geez! What if she never left? Maybe she's still in PV."

"Well, we still have to look for someone who arrived in Mexico before Jane Doe was found and see if she left the city by plane."

"Right. Now, let's see. We have a couple more women who meet *that* criterion. The first is fifty-five years old, way too old to be Parker. Next is an African American woman from Georgia. Probably not her. Then we have a Ms. Jordan, age thirty-seven, from Chicago, an advertising clerk. Maybe? I don't know . . . . Then a Mrs. Powell, age thirty-three, divorced, a music teacher. I'm not sure . . . And finally, a Ms. Butler, single, a sales agent at a candy store. No age given, from Boston. I'm not sure how to weed them down to the right one, Sanchez."

"We need more info. When did these people leave PV? Or did they leave from a nearby city like Guadalajara?"

"In that case, we need to come up with more criteria for the

FBI to follow up on. Let's make a list, and you can give it to Clara tomorrow, OK?'

"I'll have to be specific about the request. We can't do this too many times."

***

They got more information from the FBI to work with and narrowed the list down to two women who Parker might have stolen identities from, both living in Chicago. Hillary Jordan was an advertising clerk who went on a one-week holiday and never returned home. Her ticket had expired because she didn't call to change her return flight. Sanchez and Montero weren't sure from her photograph if she could be the Jane Doe in the Puerto Vallarta morgue. They decided to send her photo and vital statistics to Hermoso for his evaluation.

The second woman on their list was a woman named Susan Lipinhall, a schoolteacher from Chicago who had flown out of Guadalajara eight days after the dead woman had turned up in Puerto Vallarta. They examined her airport surveillance photograph and concluded she was a possible match for Parker—she had the same height, hair and eye color, and general look. She was definitely not Jane Doe. They decided they should send her information to Hermoso too.

The next day, Sanchez turned over the names of the two women to Teller, and he notified the FBI to follow up.

***

Sanchez had to postpone her vacation trip to the West Coast and Lake Tahoe with her parents because she was getting increased pressure from the department to wrap up the drug and gunrunning case after the shooting. For the next few days, she worked hard to tie up loose ends, working with Alvera to strengthen their evidence and arguments. It was all coming together well now—with information from Mickelson, Lope, and Garcia—to close the loop on Mickelson's kidnapping. Sanchez felt confident that Garcia's testimony would seal the gaps on the gun case, bringing at least seven Westside gang members and Sinaloa gangsters to justice.

Montero came through with a special arrangement for Carlos Batista to be accepted at a ranch for juvenile boys near Santa Fe, New Mexico, after he testified at trial. Batista was recovering nicely from his wounds in an outpatient facility and was excited about the ranch opportunity. He had always wanted to ride horses.

Davies was extremely pleased with the way everything was turning out. The return of Brown's body to his parents had gone smoothly. He was so impressed with Sanchez's work, as supported by Alvera, that he recommended her for a special award five weeks later, which Teller arranged. Teller was happy because the whole Simpson case had not resurfaced and blown up in his face as he had feared it might. He even eased up on yelling at Sanchez for a few weeks.

Chapter 27

July 7, 2014

Two weeks later, Sanchez and Montero found themselves waiting to eat dinner at Salvador's Grille. They had passed their findings along to the proper authorities through Alvera.

As expected, the FBI took the lead investigating the two women from Chicago and staked out their apartments. After five days, federal agents knocked on the door of Jordan's apartment and found no one home. They asked the building superintendent to open the place up for them and found everything one might expect in the apartment of someone who had gone on vacation and never come back. A neighbor was looking after her fish and was concerned that she had failed to return as planned. The FBI obtained a search warrant and collected samples of hair from the apartment for analysis. The samples matched those collected from Jane Doe in Puerto Vallarta. At last, they had an ID for the poor woman, *la mujer de hielo*. But it appeared that no one other than the neighbor had been in Jordan's apartment since she had left for Mexico.

FBI agents then went to the second apartment, that of Lipinhall. Again, they found no one at home. But a neighbor who lived in the apartment next door swore he had seen Lipinhall there since she had returned from her Mexico trip. He didn't know her very well because he had only moved into his apartment a few weeks before she had left for vacation, but he had talked to her a few times in the hallway before and after the trip. He said he had noticed how much tanner she was when she had returned and had chalked it up to two weeks in the sun.

"So the guy didn't really know Susan except for a few minutes of chat in the hall. He wouldn't have noticed if Parker took her place or not." Sanchez was summarizing the report she had just read at the office.

"But someone was there in the apartment for a few days and then disappeared."

"Yeah, the FBI investigators think that Parker came in to assume Lipinhall's identity and maybe used it for a while. She took some clothes and things from the apartment to develop her cover and stayed there maybe four days."

"And the only person to notice was this guy next door?" Montero asked.

"Yes. It sounds weird, doesn't it? I guess nowadays people can live in a city and not really know many people at all. That's true for me too, I suppose. I know people from work and people I meet through work, like you and a few others. But I don't know my neighbors except to say hi in the driveway. It's a strange way to live our lives, isn't it?"

"I suppose," Montero said. "But what else did they find? Any proof that it really was Parker there?"

"Well, yes and no. The FBI went over the place with a fine-tooth comb. They found evidence of Lipinhall—hair, fingerprints, et cetera—in a few places like closets, the kitchen, and the bedroom, but no evidence of Parker. You know why? Wait for it."

"Why?"

"Because the common-use areas were wiped clean. Someone used cleaners and Clorox to wipe down everything. Now does that sound like something we've seen before? I call it the Parker signature. They found one hair that was not Lipinhall's, so it might be Parker's. That's all."

"Wow! She was thorough."

"And get this: they realized they don't have any DNA for Parker, at least DNA they can prove is really hers. Detective Carter has been trying to tie down some loose ends, and he checked all State of California records for the woman. She first appears in the public record when she entered university. Her school records show her coming from the town of Tulare and graduating from Tulare Western High School. But the school has no record of her being there. No grades, no attendance, nothing. No picture in the yearbook. He checked the other schools in the city and found the same thing: no Parker. There was no Parker family in Tulare when she supposedly went to school there. The state has no birth record for a Sarah Parker either. Carter has no idea who she is or where she came from."

Montero shook his head. "Weirder and weirder. So all we have to ID her with is two photos and fingerprints from years ago."

"That's it. Anyway, getting back to Chicago. Lipinhall had a large balance in her bank and investment accounts. She apparently inherited a large sum of money when her parents died. The accounts were all drained while Parker was there."

"She picked her victim with some care then?"

Sanchez read ahead in the report. "The last thing the FBI found out was that the woman known as Lipinhall packed a bag and ran into the same neighbor three weeks ago when he last saw her. She told him she was going on vacation. He asked where. And she wouldn't say."

"Where did she go?"

"The FBI used the date of his conversation to check flights out of Chicago that day. A Susan Lipinhall took a flight to

London that morning. They lost all track of her once the plane landed at Heathrow Airport. They are working with London police, but it looks like a complete dead end."

Montero said, "It sounds like Parker was bold enough to do whatever it took to protect herself and her relationships. And now we know she took the identity of another woman, this Susan Lipinhall in Puerto Vallarta, to throw us off track. There must be another body in Puerto Vallarta for the police to find. And we almost missed it. She's certainly diabolical."

"And so the story ends, for now, at least. I guess we'll never know who she is or where she went. Now that she's in Europe, she'll be hard to track because it's like the States over there now. You know, open borders. And if we *do* find her, most of the EU countries won't extradite if the criminal is wanted for a death penalty case like this." Sanchez signaled the bartender for another round of margaritas. When the drinks arrived, she said, "You know, Guillermo. We make a pretty good team, you and I. Don't you think?"

Montero sat up and looked at his enthusiastic friend. "You're right. We *are* a good team. But right now, I'm thinking about Salvador's roast chicken. I'm hungry. Let's eat."

Montero led the way over to a booth where they could order their dinner, then continued. "OK. But you have to admit that now we know who committed the murders. Even though we don't know where Parker is."

"And now we don't even know *who* she really is."

"Pretty strange, isn't it?" Montero looked around for their waitress and caught her eye. Then he changed the subject. "You know, I'm having some friends over for dinner on Saturday night. Would you like to come? You know a few of them already, but there will be a couple of characters there whom I'd like you to meet. It should be fun."

Sanchez smiled at him with a look that suggested she had a secret. "Gee, Guillermo. I'd really like to come, but I have plans already."

"You have plans for a Saturday night? Not work? This is new. It wouldn't have anything to do with an Officer Smith from ASU, would it? I know you two got together for coffee last week." Montero gave Sanchez a mischievous, inquiring glance that he reserved for special situations.

Sanchez couldn't help but laugh and said, "OK, so you found me out." She straightened up and flipped her hair back with one hand. "You're right. I have a date with Tom Smith Saturday night. It should be fun." She blushed a little. It had been a while since she had gone out on a real date.

"Really? A date? I'm happy for you, Lori. I was beginning to worry about you." Montero chuckled to himself. "You could bring him to my house for dinner."

"Now, don't give me a hard time about it, OK? It's just a first date. He's a nice guy. And interesting too." She waved the waitress over, then added, "Maybe I *will* ask if he would like to go to your place for dinner." She winked at Montero.

They ordered dinner and celebrated the successful conclusion of Sanchez's investigation into kidnapping, gunrunning, and gang drug sales. The trial was scheduled to begin in three months, and they both felt it would be successful. The only loose end was Parker, at large in Europe somewhere. They ate wonderful roast chicken with their margaritas.

Chapter 28

July 10, 2015—Chandler, Arizona

One year later, Montero scrolled through his emails in the coffee shop of the Barnes & Noble bookstore in Chandler, Arizona. He was meeting a friend who was running a little late. After a while, he grew tired of waiting and decided to browse through the newly released books to pass the time. He picked through the main table of choices and then moved to the area where local-interest books were displayed.

Then he saw it on the top shelf among the books listed as National Best Sellers: a novel titled *The Perfect Crime* written by Peter Simpson. He picked it up in disbelief. It had been published in London and New York. He flipped to the copyright page and read: "Copyright Sarah Lipinhall, Lipinhall Literary Agency, Andorra la Vella, Andorra.

"Holy shit!" Montero said out loud, and people nearby glared at him.

He pulled out his phone and accessed the internet. He looked up the list of countries that had no extradition treaties with the US. Andorra was near the top of the list. *Of course*, he thought, *Andorra, home of paella, no extradition, and no income tax.*

Then he called Sanchez. When she picked up, he simply said, "Guess what? Peter Simpson finally got his novel published."

Coming Soon!

Desert Sanctuary

By Fred G. Baker

Detective Lori Sanchez finds herself accused of a fatal shooting in this high-energy novel about police corruption and drug gangs. As Father Guillermo Montero helps her track down the real killer, they uncover a major drug trafficking operation right under the noses of the political elite of Phoenix.

About the Author

Fred G. Baker is a hydrologist, historian, and writer living in Colorado. He is the author of *Growing Up Wisconsin: Remembrances from the American Midwest, The Life and Times of Con James Baker of Des Moines, Chicago and Wisconsin*, and *The Light from a Thousand Campfires: Improving Your Hiking, Backpacking and Camping Skills* (with Hannah Pavlik). He is currently working on a sequel to *An Imperfect Crime*, The Modern Pirate Series of digital shorts, a collection of short stories, and an adventure thriller, *Zona*, set in Siberia.

Request for Reviews

Thank you for reading my book. If you enjoyed it, please write a review on www.amazon.com. Reviews are important to help authors get the word out about their books. I would appreciate your taking the time to write one.

To find my other books on Amazon and Kindle Books, just type in my name to see other titles that may be of interest to you. You can also check out my website at www.othervoicespress.com.

Made in the USA
Monee, IL
16 September 2022

14143064R00156